Johnny Mack is author of the thriller *The Pinned Butterfly* (2023), published by Hypnotic Highway.

DARK EMPATH

A Thriller by Johnny Mack

Published by Hypnotic Highway

Phnom Penh, Cambodia

Charlie Leung met her at a hostess bar on Street 104. Her name was Kesor, and she was the only woman working in the bar that night who spoke English.

Instead of taking her to his room after he paid the bar fine, Charlie brought her to the FiveFive Rooftop Restaurant with a view of the Tonle Sap River and the Royal Palace, of temples and casinos. The darker the sky, the more luminous the city below.

Charlie ordered wine from the server. Château d'Yquem. 1997. Six hundred and fifty dollars for the bottle.

"You stay here?" Kesor asked.

Charlie nodded. The restaurant sat on the roof of a five-star hotel. He'd checked into his room earlier that day after a short flight from Hong Kong, his home.

Kesor was probably used to spending nights in temporary housing rented by liver-spotted sexpats, a single room with a hot plate and a narrow bed, the walls stained from leaking roofs and retribution. Phnom Penh was a city with countless old scores that got settled in such places.

The server arrived with the wine, uncorked it, and poured a taste for Charlie. Charlie motioned for her to keep pouring.

For their meal, Charlie ordered Norwegian Salmon Teryaki, Seared Hakkaido Scallops, Black Pepper Lamb Chops, Angus Tenderloin Skewers, and Grilled Tajima Striploin, but when the food arrived he couldn't eat any of it. The sight of it all made him queasy.

"Why?" Kesor asked, looking concerned.

Charlie said nothing. The truth was that he was nervous. He knew what he wanted, but the gulf between desire and execution was as vast and murky as the river below. Only after Kesor was done eating did he explain his reasons for hiring her.

As Charlie talked, Kesor wiped her eyes with the side of her arm, clearing away tears.

"No," she said, turning down his request.

"Please," Charlie said. And then, again, but with more desperation: "*Please.*"

Kesor shook her head, defiant.

He pulled out his wallet and removed one thousand U.S. dollars.

"This is for tonight," he said. "This is for having dinner with me. Tomorrow? If you do everything I've asked? I'll pay you *twenty thousand* dollars."

She didn't say yes, but she didn't say no, either.

"Why?" she asked.

"No questions," Charlie said.

Before he could secure an answer from her, four servers approached their table singing "Happy Birthday." A young woman carried a slice of chocolate cake with a tall lit candle while another held a flare that burned bright.

They set the cake down in front of Kesor. Two tables away, a man and woman watched with intense curiosity. Mid-song, the staff seemed to realize their error. The cake belonged to the other couple. The singing, however, continued, and Kesor blew out the candle.

After the staff made their swift exit, Kesor said, "Okay. I'll do it."

The next morning Charlie Leung walked from his hotel to a nearby temple. A monk glanced up from his iPhone, assessed Charlie, and then looked back down, scrolling with his finger.

Charlie took off his shoes at the temple's entrance, entered, bowed to the imposing Buddha before him, lowered himself to his knees, and prayed, but he felt empty inside, his silent chant hollow, so he cut short his prayer and stepped back outside, put his shoes back on, and gave the monk a hundred dollar bill in U.S. currency, crisp the way the Khmers liked it. They were suspicious of folded or soiled bills, often holding them up to the light, searching for creases and rips.

Charlie noticed that the monk had a pack of cigarettes semi-hidden by his robe. Charlie motioned to the pack of Cambo, and the monk begrudgingly offered him one. Lately, there had been a rash of crimes committed by monks – crystal meth distribution, rape, murder.

Was this monk a good man or a bad one?

Honestly, Charlie would have had more in common with the latter than the former.

"Thank you," Charlie said, leaning in close for the light. The monk used a disposable lighter, the kind Charlie once used, before the money came pouring in. He now had a collection of over two thousand Zippos, many of them having belonged to U.S. servicemen in Vietnam. His most valuable was solid gold and worth twenty-five thousand dollars.

Though Charlie had given up cigarettes twenty years ago, his lungs welcomed the smoke the way the body craves a vitamin it needs to survive. Why had he deprived himself of this pleasure? What good had it done him?

Charlie pulled out another hundred and gave it to the monk. "For the cigarette," he said.

That evening, Kesor arrived at Charlie Leung's hotel suite as he had instructed her to do. He poured two glasses of champagne, handed her one, and said, "Happy birthday."

"Why did they think it was my birthday?" Kesor asked.

Charlie shrugged. "Mistakes were made. A miscommunication."

Since Charlie hadn't eaten in over twenty-four hours, the champagne packed a punch. He didn't want to be drunk – he wanted to be present for what was about to happen – but he needed to take the edge off.

Kesor wore a black cotton dress. It was tasteful, sexy even, but not elegant. Her heels were scuffed. Her sadness was infectious; he felt it in his bones. He wanted her to be happy. She was about to make twenty thousand dollars, after all. What kind of world would it be if money no longer made people happy?

"Is it time?" she asked.

"Almost," he said.

"Where's the money?"

"I explained to the man at the front desk that a young woman will ask him to call me. If I answer, you won't get the money. But if I don't…" He took a deep breath. "If I don't, he'll hand you an envelope with the money." He forced a smile. "The bills look brand-new."

She nodded and sipped more champagne.

The four-poster bed was equipped with restraints, one for each post.

Charlie Leung lay naked on his back, wrists and ankles restrained, the rope stretching him so that he could easily be quartered. He watched as Kesor lifted her dress up and over her head. She removed her bra. She removed her underwear. Only her shoes remained. It was how he had imagined her – or a version of her – three days ago when he had booked the ticket to Cambodia.

He could see all her scars. He could tell she was a mother. She was older than he had guessed yesterday when she was still clothed and heavily made up, their dinner lit by the moon and a couple of 20-watt bi-pin bulbs strategically placed in the latticework overhead.

"You're beautiful," he said.

It was true – she *was* beautiful – but these were the words he had told her he would say. They were her cue to begin.

Kesor crawled on top of Charlie and pressed herself against him. She reached between her legs, took hold of him, and put him inside her. Slowly, she lowered her hips until he was all the way in, and then she rose until he was almost entirely exposed again. And then back down. As she continued this motion, she reached under the covers and removed a roll of duct tape. She tore off a strip and placed it over Charlie's mouth then tore off two more strips for reinforcement, placing them vertically on either end of the strip already across his mouth.

Charlie could still breathe but only through his nose now. He started feeling lightheaded, though.

Kesor removed a silicone earplug from under the covers, tore it into two pieces, and inserted one piece into Charlie's right nostril.

Charlie tried relaxing, accepting what he himself had put in motion, but panic was setting in. He wanted more time, but it was too late.

Kesor inserted the remaining silicone ball into Charlie's left nostril. Her eyes were wet as she stared down at him. She took no pleasure in what she was doing.

Charlie could still suck in a bit of air…but not enough.

Kesor removed the pillow from behind Charlie's head and placed it over his face.

He started to thrash. As Kesor pressed down, she sped up her motions with her hips, as Charlie had requested her to do. He had wanted to mitigate the fear, he had wanted to leave this world with some lingering pleasure, but he was too focused now on his own terror.

In less than a minute, he lost consciousness.

Though an accurate time would never be determined by the Ministry of Health's medical examiner, Charlie Leung died at exactly 10:33 p.m. in Phnom Penh, Cambodia.

He was not alone. Across Southeast Asia, wealthy men were taking their own lives.

The day before Charlie's death, a man named Trung Nguyen had jumped off the patio of his fifteenth-floor condominium building in Ho Chi Minh City, Vietnam.

Juan Ramos of Makati, Philippines, walked into the middle of Ayala Avenue and shot himself in the head.

In Chiang Mai, Thailand, Phailin Chaichana sprinkled arsenic into his jasmine tea, sat in a flower garden in his own backyard, and sipped the tea until he felt the first symptoms that would eventually lead to his death.

By the end of the weekend, all told, a dozen men had taken their lives. None of them knew each other, but they had killed themselves for the same reason.

In the lobby of the hotel in Phnom Penh, Kesor asked the concierge to call Charlie's room. Her hands were shaking as the phone rang and rang. It was an old phone with a cord and buttons, and she could hear the ringing from where she stood.

The concierge returned the receiver, reached into a drawer, and removed an envelope.

"This is for you," he said in Khmer, bowing as he handed it to her.

Kesor took the envelope and stepped outside. Another man who worked at the hotel held the door open for her. It was 10:45 p.m. and 35.5 Celsius. Hot and stifling. Kesor tried not to draw attention to herself as she walked away from the hotel, but after turning the corner, she slipped off her high heels, picked them up by the straps, and ran barefoot as fast as she could. Her only witness was a monk enjoying a cigarette, two crisp hundred dollar bills in his possession, a weak man haunted by vices and longing, blowing seemingly endless smoke rings into a warm and moonless Phnom Penh night.

PART ONE

Chapter 1

Shane Doyle sat in a canoe for only the second time in his life – an odd fact for a fifty-five-year-old man who'd spent thirty-seven years of his life in southern Louisiana. The only other time was with his late wife, in this very lake, but he didn't want to think about that today.

There was too much unpredictability outdoors. Today was no different. From his canoe, Shane could see two alligators. The largest rested on a log, side-eyeing him as he twisted the cap off a bottle of Abita Amber. The other, also on a log, didn't appear to give a shit one way or the other.

The sun was another issue. Shane was Irish, fair-skinned, and prone to skin cancer. Only a month ago he'd had to have a pea-sized tumor removed from his temple, leaving a longer scar than he'd anticipated. Fortunately, it was only basal cell carcinoma. The good cancer, he was told. The wound, still raw and pink, throbbed now from the punishing Louisiana sun.

The only upside to Lake Martin: there were no mosquitos. Dragonflies appeared like miniature drones all around his canoe, mechanically dipping and bobbing before soaring away. Shane had read that one dragonfly alone could eat hundreds of mosquitos in a single afternoon. In an earlier life, he had helped people with compulsive behavior. But what if the body could accommodate the compulsiveness? What if compulsion gave a person unparalleled strength?

Shane was no longer in the helping business. He was in the advertising and marketing game now. In the canoe next to him sat Phil Corbett, his business partner.

Having lunch today in canoes had been Corbett's idea. Whenever their business reached a new milestone, Corbett memorialized it by doing something special. In more ways than Shane could count, Phil Corbett had saved Shane's life. The least Shane could do was indulge the guy.

"Is this it?" Shane asked.

"What?" Corbett asked.

"Your secret place," Shane said. "You're always late after lunch on Wednesdays."

"In France," Corbett said, "they take two-hour lunch breaks. Brazil has two-hour lunch breaks. Hell, even China has a two-hour lunch break. China, for God's sake!"

Corbett was the same age as Shane, but unlike Shane, whose default facial expression was that of a man wearing damp underwear, Corbett was quick to smile. When they first met, Shane had assumed Corbett's abiding happiness was part of his salesman shtick, but he came to realize that the optimism was genuine, the smiling sincere.

Shane nodded toward a gator. "I used to think they'd chase you on land," he said. "Turns out, they're more likely to kill you in water. Roll you under and drown you."

Corbett's eyes lit up. "You think I brought you here to kill you?" he asked.

"I rule nothing out. But not by alligator. Skin cancer, I'm guesing. You're playing the long game." Shane imagined the grief his dermatologist would give him if she saw him without the ridiculous UV hat she had wanted him to buy. "Did you know alligators can live up to fifty years? That one right there? Alive during disco!"

"Ever heard of the Greenland Shark?" Corbett asked. "They live at least two hundred and fifty years. Maybe as long as five hundred."

"You're full of shit," Shane said.

"Don't believe me? Go to the Norwegian Sea and check it out for yourself."

Corbett was always spitting obscure facts whereas Shane mostly kept what he knew to himself. If he wanted, Shane could have shot back trivia about the Atchafalaya Basin; about crabbing, frogging, and trapping; about the turtle industry, the alligator industry, the bee industry, and the moss industry. Back when Shane was a therapist, most of his patients were Cajun, and he'd listened to countless family tales. He had become an anthropologist of the swamp even though he was neither Cajun nor an outdoorsman. Hell, he wasn't even from Louisiana. He was from a Chicago suburb. He'd come down to LSU for college and never left.

"All right, asshole. You and your Greenland shark win," Shane said. "So what's the good news?"

"Slow down. Take a breath. Enjoy your beer first." Corbett chugged half of his Abita in one try, gulping in his surroundings after he lowered the bottle.

Shane admired Corbett's ability to look like he belonged wherever he was. He wasn't Cajun either, but he had assimilated well. Right now, with Spanish moss draped behind him and the sun beating down on him, he looked like he'd spent his entire life riding fan boats. Shane paddled away from Corbett so that he could park under the shade of a live oak. The sun was killing him. Literally.

"I'm meeting that film crew after lunch," Shane said after Corbett paddled over and joined him, their canoes touching.

"In Abbeville, right?" Corbett said.

"What do you know about them?" Shane asked.

Corbett shrugged. "I saw their reel. They do good stuff. I figure we'd save a shit-ton in the long run if we have a permanent production team. I don't like relying on freelancers. There's no loyalty." Corbett grinned. "You ready for all this?"

"For what?"

"How fast we're expanding."

"We just need to be prepared," Shane said. "Take on only what we can handle."

"If you like the team in Abbeville, make them a full-time offer."

"Really? You don't want to meet them?"

Corbett shook his head. "I trust you."

Shane nodded. "Okay."

After a long pause, Corbett said, "So, listen. Do you have a passport?"

Shane nodded. He'd gotten his first passport only a few years ago when he was thinking about finding another country with a lower cost of living – a backup plan.

"What's your dream vacation?" Corbett asked.

After what had happened at the end of his last job, the idea of a vacation, let alone a dream vacation, had become as unlikely as a trip to Mars.

"I don't know," Shane said. "The Norwegian Sea? I hear there's a five-hundred-year-old shark up there I should see."

"Wrong answer," Corbett said. "You're going to the Philippines. Tomorrow."

"*Tomorrow?* What the fuck! What do you mean *tomorrow?*"

"I've been talking to a pharmaceutical company over there. They're huge. They want to expand." He reached over and rocked Shane's canoe. "This could be big."

"You should go. Not me. Why didn't you tell me about this a month ago?"

"I didn't want to say anything until I knew it wasn't bullshit. And guess what. It's not."

Shane sighed, loudly, for Corbett's benefit.

"You've never seen a therapist, have you?"

"No. Why?"

"Because if you had, you'd know how fucked up this is."

"Since when is it fucked up to embrace an opportunity?"

"For starters, I don't know shit about pharmaceuticals." Shane hardly knew anything about the oil business, either. The only reason they had so many oil accounts was because he'd lived in Lafayette for thirty years and almost everyone he'd met when he was a licensed therapist worked in oil, from engineers to roughnecks.

Corbett said, "I booked an extra week so you can do some sightseeing. Go to an island. Eat a pig. Do whatever the hell people do when they go to the Philippines."

Shane considered this information. He couldn't imagine another job where a partner would insist that he take extra time off, let alone in another country. So why was he so resistant to the idea?

Corbett pushed on with the sales pitch: "If Manila doesn't float your boat, catch a cheap flight to Honk Kong. Or Vietnam. That's the great thing about that part of the world. Flights cost pennies compared to here. Fifty bucks gets you to another country."

"You spend a lot of time there? Southeast Asia?"

Corbett shook his head. "Just once. Long time ago. My backpacker days." His grin suggested more than backpacking. Girls? Drugs? Corbett's past was a mystery. "But I know people who live there now," he said. "You can retire like a king on two grand a month."

"Damn." Shane had never told Corbett about his own half-baked plan to leave the country. That was before he and Corbett went into business together. That was before his fortunes had changed for the better, thanks entirely to Corbett.

Corbett said, "I've got the pharmacy's portfolio back at the office. The flight's a motherfucker – thirty-six hours – so you'll have plenty of time to look it all over. No sweat." Corbett lifted his paddle out of the water and nudged Shane with it. Above them an owl watched, like an old security guard – judgmental but too tired to do anything about it. "Without me, you'd be an old man working at Burger King."

He pushed Shane again with the paddle. This time, an alligator looked up.

"Regional manager of Chipotle," Shane said. "At the very least."

When Corbett laughed, the owl took flight, and the alligator slid off the log and into the water, disappearing.

"Fair enough," Corbett said.

Chapter 2

Abbeville was a thirty-minute drive. On his way there, Shane called his pet sitter and asked if she could pick up his house key after dinner. He needed to clean his kitchen and pack a suitcase. He probably needed to do some laundry before he packed.

Shane appreciated that Corbett was making things happen for their company, *good things*, but last-minute plans of this magnitude would be the death of him.

In Abbeville, Shane zipped into the parking lot of an abandoned strip mall. There were fewer than a dozen cars spread out across the spider-webbed asphalt, and at least three of those cars looked abandoned.

Shane walked up to the empty store front, double-checked the address, then placed his cupped hands against the window and stared inside.

Sure enough, two men stood near the back of the all-but-empty room. When they saw Shane, one of them held up a finger while the other jogged to the door to unlock it.

"Thought I had the wrong address," Shane said when the door opened.

The young man, who looked Vietnamese, laughed too hard. He was good-natured but awkward, his personality fueled by nervous energy. "No, no, please, you're in the right place. Please, please, come in! Come in!"

He motioned Shane inside and locked the door behind them but not before surveying the parking lot, as though making the sure the coast was clear.

The other man was also Vietnamese. He was the hipper of the two – bleached hair, nails painted black, a Tom Ford t-shirt hugging his thin torso.

For a city of only 12,000, there was a disproportionately large Vietnamese population in Abbeville. When Saigon fell to the North Vietnamese, refugees poured into Louisiana. The landscape was not unfamiliar. The refugees landed jobs in the fishing and shrimping industries, same as the jobs they had back home. There were rice fields and rice milling companies here, too. Plenty of work shucking oysters.

But these two guys were obviously not refugees. Sons of refugees? Grandsons? Maybe. They looked barely out of high school, though Shane knew they had both recently graduated from UT-Austin; they'd both won awards for their filmmaking.

At the back of the cavernous space, a camera and lights were set up for filming. Also: an office desk and chair with a blue screen behind it. The furniture was high-end, in sharp contrast to the gutted room with its sticky cobwebs and graffiti spray-painted walls.

"This your office?" Shane asked.

The man who had let him in laughed. He let the question go unanswered.

"Glad you could finally make it," the bleached blond said. He checked his Swatch, aggrieved. He said, "Okay, we don't have much time left, so we should probably get going. We'll be lucky if have time for more than one take."

"One take?" Shane asked. "I'm sorry…what are you talking about?"

Both men stared at Shane as though he were a snake who'd slithered in from the cold.

"For the commercial?"

"What commercial?" Shane asked. "I'm here from Corbett and Doyle." When neither man reacted, Shane said, "The ad agency?"

"Pretty sure that's…tomorrow?" the awkward man said. He checked his phone. "Yeah, that's tomorrow. Same time, though."

"Shit," Shane said. "Really?" He checked his own phone. According to his schedule, he was here on the correct date, but there was no use arguing over it. "Well, hell," Shane said. "I'm flying to the Philippines tomorrow." He looked up. "I'm Shane, by the way. I'm the Doyle in Corbett and Doyle."

"Tam," the awkward man said, offering his hand. A limp fish.

"Kenny," the other man said. He was taller, more brooding, less ingratiating than his friend. He didn't offer his hand.

"We're supposed to shoot this commercial," Tam said, "but the actor is a no-show."

"Abbeville thespians," Kenny said, rolling his eyes. The irony wasn't lost on Shane.

"And you thought I was him?" Shane asked.

Tam offered a weak smile. Kenny offered nothing. He was like a Vietnamese Buster Keaton. The Great Stone Face.

In truth, Shane had a deep interest in acting. When he was fourteen he read Stanislavski's *Building a Character*, studied all the method actors, watched countless interviews with actors on PBS talking about their craft. He starred in twelve high school productions, but in college, unable to land even a minor role, he let it slip away, earning a BA in Psychology instead and then a master's degree in Social Work. But he still had the itch.

"Well?" Shane said.

"Well what?" Kenny said.

"*I* could do it," Shane said, smiling.

"Do what?" Kenny asked. "The *commercial?*"

Tam stepped closer to Kenny. "Really? You would?"

"What's it for?" Shane asked. "The commercial?"

"Local carpet store," Tam said. He looked hopefully back at Kenny.

Kenny shrugged. "Sounds peachy. But look, we have to return the U-Haul parked out back by five or else we start losing money on this whole deal." He motioned to the desk and chair, the rolls of carpet that Shane only now noticed. It had all been rented for the commercial.

"What size suit jacket do you wear?" Tam asked, smiling.

"I don't know. 44?"

Tam looked inside the suit jacket and grinned. He removed the suit jacket from the hanger and said, "44!"

"It's fucking Kismet," Kenny said, unimpressed, but Tam was beside himself.

Shane liked how flexible these guys were. It showed their ability to work under pressure. He knew Corbett would love this story. He already imagined telling him: *And when I offered to be their actor, they jumped at it. This is how we'll save the day, they thought.*

Shane slipped into the suit jacket. It fit perfectly.

Tam handed him a script. Shane looked it over. It was horrible.

"Did you write this?" Shane asked.

Kenny laughed derisively. "God, no. This is a work-for-hire gig. They tell us what they want, we hold our noses and do it."

"It's not *that* bad," Tam said, laughing nervously. He had the good sense not to insult a client in front of a potential future employer.

Kenny, the auteur, snorted. There was something admirable about his unwillingness to bullshit. It showed integrity.

"And the blue screen?" Shane asked.

"In post," Kenny said, "we'll make it look like you're sitting in an office. When we shoot you walking, we'll make it look like you're in a warehouse full of carpet."

Shane flipped through the script. "It's kind of long, don't you think?"

Kenny said, "They gave us eight minutes of content for a thirty-second spot. We'll shoot the entire script, and then by some miracle…" – he snapped his fingers – "…they'll get thirty seconds of something better than what they gave us."

"That's where AI comes in," Tam said.

"You use AI?" Shane asked.

Kenny looked perturbed by the admission. He probably didn't want Shane thinking he used shortcuts.

Kenny said, "Here, let's get you behind that desk. Let's start with…?" He cut his eyes toward Tam.

Tam, reading from the script, said, "*Here at Carpet Emporium, the buck stops with me.*"

Shane laughed. "How much am I going to regret this?"

Kenny shrugged. He said, "Think of the perks."

"What perks?"

"Carpet commercial groupies."

Shane laughed and took a seat behind the desk. "If you think this'll get me laid, you're an optimist." He ran a hand across the desk's hand-carved edges. Christ, he wouldn't have minded a desk like this for his own office. Where did they rent something this nice in Abbeville?

Tam pulled a comb from his shirt pocket. "Do you mind?" he asked and began combing Shane's hair.

"Here at Carpet Emporium," Shane said under his breath, "the buck stops with me." He looked over some of his other lines. *New carpet is a good investment that'll increase the value of your home…better than crypto! You're in for savings galore! Stop by our showroom and look over our portfolio. Our CEO is just one phone call away. My word is my bond.*

The script may have been shit, but Shane still wanted to do a good job.

Shane had transferred his knowledge of method acting to his career as a therapist. Both talents required burrowing into another's unconscious mind. It wasn't until you crawled inside another man's head that his actions began to make sense. The long script, for instance. It spoke of desperation. The CEO wanted everyone to know his story. To trust him. To give his business a shot. What had sounded corny only moments ago now seemed like a matter of life and death.

Kenny said, "Ready?"

Shane nodded.

Tam said, "Carpet Emporium. Scene one, take one." He walked in front of the camera and, using only his hands, imitated a clapboard cracking together.

As soon as Tam moved away, Shane stared directly into the camera. He dug in. He became another person. He said, "Here at Carpet Emporium, the buck stops with me."

"Damn," Kenny said. "That was actually good, my dude."

"Really?" Shane asked. "You want another take?"

"Another take? You think we're shooting *Seven Samurai?*" Kenny looked down at this Swatch and said, "Better hustle. We've got a shitload more to do."

Tam giggled nervously, probably afraid Kenny's coarseness would lose them the job.

Shane rubbed his damp palms onto his pants and said, "Ready when you are."

Chapter 3

On his way back to Lafayette, Shane called Corbett.

"Well?" Corbett said.

"I hired them."

"That's awesome. One less thing to worry about."

"And I'm in a commercial."

"You're *what?* What do you mean? What commercial?"

"Their actor didn't show up, so I stood in."

"Really? That's…weird. They put you in a commercial?"

"It's just a local spot for a carpet company."

"So our clients…they'll think you sell carpet on the side?"

Shane was silent. He hadn't thought through how it might affect their business. He suddenly felt the old familiar sense of fucking up. It was a feeling he'd had unremittingly back in grade school whenever he showed up to the wrong classroom or failed to bring the right school supplies. His teachers, many of whom were Korean War veterans, were never happy with him.

Corbett said, "I'm just shitting you. I didn't know you had any acting chops. Or did I?"

Relieved, Shane took a deep breath. He wished he wasn't so sensitive.

"It's just a silly commercial," Shane said. He suddenly didn't want to talk about it.

Corbett, already moving on, said, "Listen, I swung by your house and stuck the pharm portfolio in your mailbox. Saved you a trip to the office."

"You're a prince," Shane said.

"Hear me out. You should get on OKCupid tonight and change your location to Manila. Fifty Filipinas will be waiting for you at the luggage carousel."

"OKCupid? What year is this?"

"Fine. Use Tinder when you get there. Or Grindr. Whatever floats your boat."

"Right. Hey listen, I need to go. I'm almost home."

"Just do it, you piece of shit," he said. "You can say you're an actor."

"Tinder. Okay. Got it." Shane hung up and set down his phone.

A gust of wind hit the car, and a homeless man's trench coat flapped in front of him. Shane hit the coat but not the man wearing it.

"Fuck!"

In his rearview mirror, Shane saw the man flipping him off. He was bent forward, nearly overtaken by the coat. He was pushing a shopping cart – something else Shane had failed to see, hidden by the camouflaged man.

"Jesus Christ," Shane said. His heart was pounding. Berating himself for not paying better attention, he wondered what else he hadn't seen. The world was full of landmines, and a person's fate could change in the time it took to set down a cellphone, glance in the rearview mirror, or take too deep a breath.

Chapter 4

Shane snatched the portfolio from his mailbox and then hustled inside to start cleaning before his cat sitter Alyssa showed up for the spare key. He had only twenty minutes.

"Shit!"

Even a cursory cleaning job would take days, possibly weeks. His dishes alone had piled in the sink until he'd run out of Fiestaware. He hadn't seen a clean fork in days. An open bag of sugar fraternized on the countertop with a cylinder of Clorox and a handle of dish detergent.

The house was beyond hope.

Shane remembered the disarray of his father's house during his last years. Shane was rightfully horrified by the mess, but whenever he offered to clean it his father took offense and told him to leave him the hell alone. After his father died, Shane wanted to set the house on fire to avoid dealing with it. In the end, he hired a company to sort through the important documents and photographs, of which there ended up being not enough to fill a banker's box. How could a half-filled box have been the sum total of his father's life?

Unlike his father, who had spent his retirement watching game shows and infomercials, Shane worked sixty hours a week, sometimes eighty, leaving little time or energy to clean the dishes or vacuum. Shane *wanted* to keep his house clean.

Fortunately, there was no one to whom he had to explain himself – except the cat sitter.

Alyssa was an MA student in Philosophy, which meant she likely wanted to be a professor. What else did one do with a degree so intangible?

Before he could start loading the dishwasher, the doorbell rang. *Goddamn it!*

As soon as Shane opened the door, he said, "There's something I need to tell you before you step inside."

He explained the situation to her, emphasizing his embarrassment.

Alyssa acted like it was no big deal, but Shane feared, perhaps irrationally, that she would make a TikTok video of his house that would go viral.

"I'll pay you double if you could do the dishes," he said, offering a bribe.

Alyssa said, "Sure. But you don't have to pay me that much."

"I'm paying for your silence," he said. He smiled. "Trip was short notice. As in I just found out today. I barely have time to pack."

"Where's Larry?"

"On the couch."

Alyssa called out, "Larry! Guess who's here!"

Larry was his twelve-year-old mixed-breed with long black fur. The old guy was starting to show signs of arthritis, and his eyes were no longer the bright, clear orbs they'd been in his youth – but he was as affable as any house pet he'd ever had. Everyone loved Larry.

Shane watched as Alyssa lifted Larry and held him against her. She cradled the cat like a baby and rocked him. Larry purred. It reminded him of the times his wife had held Larry in the same position and said, "Look, it's our baby. Doesn't he look just like you?"

Shane had tried putting the past behind him and. Like a soldier who'd miraculously survived the worst battle of a war, he trudged on. But there were moments, such as now, when the good times sneaked up on him, buckling his knees.

"I'll leave a check on the kitchen table," Shane said with his back to her. He composed himself, turned around, and handed her the spare key. "My phone number probably won't work there, so hit me up on Messenger if you run into any problems."

Alyssa set Larry down and took the key.

"I'm sure everything will be fine," she said.

"Me too," Shane said. "But just in case."

"Of course."

Chapter 5

It was 4:00 a.m. Shane stood outside his house, waiting for an Uber.

Fucking Corbett. Why did he book such an early flight?

Shane's initial encounter with Corbett had happened in a nasty little bar called Romano's Cellar. The Cellar hadn't been renovated in decades, the bartenders not infrequently had their own run-ins with the law, and there was an ever-present puddle of piss in front of the only toilet in the men's room. Its only appeal was that it attracted a healthy cross-section of Lafayette, both white- and blue-collar, from twenty-one year olds to upper-seventies. Every race, creed, and sexual orientation ended up there. Nearby was a school for the blind, and on any given evening half the customers were sight-impaired.

On the night Corbett appeared for the first time, two blind men had started fighting over a romantic entanglement. When the man who always sat at the bar's corner snapped open his walking stick, Corbett quickly hustled over to the stool on the other side of Shane.

"This was *not* what I expected when I left my house tonight," Corbett said.

Shane smiled. "Just another night at Romano's."

"It's always like this?"

"More often than you'd think." After the bartender separated the pugilists, Shane turned to Corbett and said, "Name's Shane. Let me get your next one. What're you drinking?"

"If you're buying, vodka martini."

"Who are you? Jay Gatsby? Would you like some deviled eggs, too? Jesus. Does this look like a martini bar?" Shane was a little drunker than he realized, and he was having to yell over the music to be heard, but his mood was buoyed by the smiling man next to him. Corbett, Shane would come to learn, had that effect on people.

"All right, all right. Vodka tonic then," Corbett said.

"That's more like it."

An hour later, they were astonished to learn that they liked damned near the same things.

"Favorite Stooge?" Shane asked.

"Shemp," Corbett said.

"Same. Shemp was underrated. Okay. Favorite member of Led Zeppelin."

"John Paul Jones."

"Bingo. He's the secret sauce."

Corbett said, "The man could play the fuck out of the Mellotron."

"Truth."

Corbett raised his hand for a high-five.

Shane had hoped no one was listening to their conversation. They were starting to sound like two men on a first date. And just as giddy.

"So, what do you do?" Corbett asked, changing the subject. The music had been turned down a few notches, and they could finally talk without screaming at each other.

"Used to be a therapist," Shane said. "Thirty years."

"Damn."

"Let's just say I had a mid-life crisis." Shane didn't want to elaborate. "And you? What's your game?"

"Advertising." He laughed. "Ad man. I started a small company. I farm out a lot of the projects. Newspaper ads. A few commercials. Billboards. Business campaigns for this or that." He narrowed his eyes at Shane. His smiled faded. Was he going to punch Shane? He said, "You should be my partner."

"I'm straight," Shane said.

"Business partner, asshole."

Shane snorted. "I'm flattered. But I don't know jack-shit about advertising."

"You were a therapist. You must have a good bead on what makes people tick, right? A hell of a lot more than some twenty-one-year old with a useless degree in advertising."

"You're drunker than me," Shane said.

Corbett smiled. "Probably. But I'm also serious. Look, we can be equal partners. Co-CEO."

Was he serious?

Shane was warming to the idea: two people with no experience running an advertising firm. Hell, it wasn't like this was New York or Chicago. They wouldn't be competing against Ogilvy or Leo Burnett.

"Do you have an office?" he asked.

Corbett nodded. "In the Oil Center. Just signed the lease today."

Even if the guy was screwing with him, Shane had nothing to lose. Literally. He'd lost everything a year ago – his job, his savings, his house. He had nothing left except the payout from his wife's life insurance policy, and that was quickly dwindling.

"What time do you want me to come by?" Shane asked.

"Is eight AM too early?" Corbett asked.

"Yes."

"Make it noon then."

"I can probably do noon," Shane said.

One year later and they had hammered down several accounts, mostly in the oil sector, many of their clients within walking distance from their office. They'd hired an office manager and a tech support person. They had just signed two national accounts. Lafayette wasn't New Orleans or Houston, but there was a strong oil and natural gas presence in the area, along with health care, aerospace, and banking. Shane had replenished his savings account – not as much as he'd once had, but if things kept going in the direction they appeared to be heading, he'd have more money than he'd ever dreamed of having.

Quit bitching about everything, he told himself now. You're a lucky son of a bitch. Lucky to be alive.

When the Uber finally pulled up to his curb, Shane waited for the driver to pop open the trunk so that he could stuff his luggage inside.

"Early flight," the driver said when Shane slid in.

"It is," Shane said. "But I can't complain."

The driver grunted and said nothing more, signifying that he could complain but wasn't going to.

Chapter 6

The flight was Lafayette to Houston, Houston to Honolulu, Honolulu to Guam, and Guam to Manila. At a certain point during the Houston to Honolulu flight, Shane wanted to open the hatch and jump out. The trip had become a fever-dream as he dozed off and on for hours, sometimes for only seconds, as an elderly woman on the third leg of the flight fell asleep against him, as children cried as though forced to stand before a firing squad, as meals were served at unusual times and everyone woke up to dutifully eat whatever had been set before them.

During each layover, Shane ran from gate to gate, sometimes as his name rang out over the intercom system: *...paging Shane Doyle, paging Shane Doyle, this is your last chance to board Flight 3636...*

On the final leg, from Guam to Manila, Shane sat next to an American – an ex-cop who had retired to Dumaguete, Philippines. He was returning from Cleveland, where he had gone to settle his financial affairs. His name was Luke Bradfield. Even at sixty-five-years old, the man had a handshake like a vice grip.

"What's your line of work?" Luke asked.

"Advertising and P.R.," Shane said. "I was a therapist for thirty years, though."

"Is that so? I'd imagine that's a job with a high rate of burnout, listening to other people's bullshit all day."

Shane agreed, though that wasn't why he left. He'd loved his job. It was a profession that had given his life meaning.

Luke said, "So tell me about the ad game. What do you do? Commercials?"

"A little bit of everything. It's a small shop, but we're growing faster than we can keep up with. Mostly oil companies. That's our bread and butter. We do a lot of package projects where we frame the company a certain way for stockholders, potential investors, whoever. That's the P.R. side of things."

"How'd you get into this?"

"Met a guy in a bar," Shane said. "The next day, we were equal partners." Shane smiled and shook his head to bring home the absurdity of it.

"No previous experience?"

"Nope. None."

"And business is good, you said?"

"Booming. It's crazy." He told Luke about this trip, how they were trying to go international.

"Why would a pharmaceutical company in Manila hire an advertising company in Louisiana? No offense."

"Your guess is as good as mine. I guess I'll find out soon. Speaking of burnout rates. What about being a cop? Seems like you stuck with it longer than most."

Luke shrugged. "Once you've been a cop, everything else is tedium. I wasn't going to be a security guard at the mall."

"So you moved to the Philippines instead."

"My wife died two years ago," he said.

"I'm sorry."

"You married?" Luke asked.

"I was married for twenty years. And then she got colon cancer. Died four months later. One day we were living our lives. Five months later, I'm a widower."

Luke said, "My wife had stage-four breast cancer. Seven months from the diagnosis until she died."

Luke shook his head in solidarity.

"You ever think of getting married again?" Luke asked.

Sure, Shane had thought of it. But would he? Probably not.

"A few years ago," Shane said, "I burned everything to the ground. Given what I know about myself now, I don't think it would be prudent." The disaster Shane had brought to his life had been only two years ago, but it seemed like thirty now.

"It's good to know our shortcomings," Luke said.

Shane noticed Luke's intense stare. A cop's stare. "I'm sorry," Shane said. "I'm probably talking too much. Punchy from the flight. Did you always want to be a cop?"

"Always. And you? Did you always want to be a therapist?"

"No," Shane said. "I wanted to be an actor."

"An actor!"

"Yeah. Actually, I filmed my first commercial yesterday." Shane explained the circumstances. Had it really been only yesterday he'd stood in the warehouse with Tam and Kenny?

"A carpet commercial?"

"Carpet Emporium!" Shane grinned, as though he were the pitchman.

"Do things like this always happen to you?" Luke asked.

"Like what?"

"You meet a man in a bar and go into business with him the next day. Two years ago you burn down everything in your life, and now you're CEO of a successful company about which, by your own admission, you know nothing. You show up to interview a couple of guys and end up in a commercial. From where I sit, you're living a charmed life."

Was he? A charmed life?

"And now," Luke continued, "you're flying to the Philippines to meet a company about business…even though you're a small outfit in southern Louisiana. I hate to break it to you, but most people aren't this lucky."

Shane had always considered himself uniquely unlucky. It was funny how another person looking at the exact same set of facts could come to a completely different conclusion.

"What about you?" Shane asked. "Ever getting married again?"

"Actually," Luke said. "I have a girlfriend here. She's thirty years younger than me. Do you believe that!"

"Damn. And you think *I'm* living a charmed life!"

"Fair enough." Luke laughed. "You could say I got lucky this once. Divorce isn't legal in the Philippines, so it's hard to find someone over thirty who isn't married and doesn't have kids. Even if they're separated, you can't be shacking up with someone else. Don't get me wrong. People do it all the time, but… I'm too old for something that complicated. Also, it's my cop brain. I'm always looking out for ways I might get killed. I didn't make it this far only to die because of an angry ex-husband in the Philippines."

"I hear you."

Luke removed a pen from his shirt pocket and wrote his information on a napkin. "This here's my WhatsApp, this is my email, and this is my local number in Dumaguete." He handed over the napkin. "If you ever come back here, you should look me up. I'll buy you a beer."

Shane took the napkin, folded it, and tucked it into his own shirt pocket.

"Will do," he said.

He handed Luke a business card.

Luke studied it. "*Shane Doyle.*" He looked up from the card. "Well, that explains it. Luck of the Irish."

"I suppose so," Shane said.

Chapter 7

Fifty-three floors high, Shane soaked in the city below from his hotel room. Manila looked like any number of cities back home, with its Starbucks and shopping malls and KFCs. Surely the entire city wasn't all shiny high-rises and condos, green spaces and wide crosswalks. Hell, it even had its own Fifth Avenue. If you fly over 8,000 miles, shouldn't the city at least look different than Dallas, Kansas City, or Omaha?

Shane plopped down on a sofa that was harder than it looked. He checked Messenger.

Alyssa had sent him two photos: one of a clean sink and one of Larry.

Shane wrote back: You're the best!

Corbett had written: Are you there yet? Any questions before the big meeting?

Shane wrote: Just checked into my room. No questions. I'm jetlegged AF. Hope I can get some sleep before tomorrow.

He took a photo of the view from his window and sent it to Corbett.

He added: For all you know, I'm in Orlando.

And those were his only two messages – one from his business partner and one from his cat sitter. Pathetic, if he thought about it too long.

Despite flipping Corbett shit, Shane did in fact have an old OkCupid account on his phone, so he fired it up and changed his location to Manila. He spent only a few minutes swiping before heading to the bathroom to brush his teeth. He checked the scar on his temple from where he'd had the basal cell carcinoma removed. It was pink, still prominent. At least it was in the best possible location he could have hoped for. He looked like he'd taken a bottle upside the head and lived to tell the tale. He looked badass.

By the time he returned to the couch and checked OkCupid, he had a dozen matches, several introductions, and even a few Super Likes. Corbett wasn't lying about women waiting for him at the luggage carousel.

But when he looked closer, he saw that many of the women who had matched with him had conspicuously similar profiles:

I'm a simple lady who loves to be with a simple guy…

I'm a simple woman who live a simple life here in Philippines…

I am simple woman, funny sometimes…

I'm a simple lady…I love cooking, dancing.

I'm simple. I love to sing in karaoke.

I'm just a simple woman trying to find a good boyfriend that will be my husband soon.

Were all the profiles fake? Probably.

And then there were the women who fell squarely in the category that Luke the Cop had warned about: *I'm mother of a boy & a girl…I'm mother of four children…I'm looking for someone who will treat my children as their own.*

Shane shut the app. The sun had set, and Shane hadn't slept in over thirty hours. Instead of trying to sleep, he decided to go out. He was exhausted but wired. Too much caffeine, too little sleep.

While it was true that this part of Manila – BGC – could have been any number of indistinguishable cities in the West, one thing set it apart from back home: there were people everywhere. Back in Lafayette, you'd be hard-pressed to find anything open after 8 p.m. The pandemic had changed the rules. America had become a country of post-apocalyptic ghost towns. But not here. Businesses were open and thriving. Kids were out playing. Street vendors cooked their food with gusto. The skyscrapers were decoratively lit up, giving Shane the sensation that he was in a movie. His own hallucinatory jet lag added to this feeling. There was life happening here – and in abundance.

Walking through Uptown Parade, one of BGC's mall, Shane could just as easily have been shopping at an upscale mall in Los Angeles. Where should he go? Randy's donuts? Wow Cow Hot Pot? Nono's?

Against his better judgment, given his need for sleep, he opted for an iced café latte at Doppio. He sat at the U-shaped counter and ordered.

"I'll take a muffin, too," he said and pointed to the one he wanted.

The woman taking his order was young and pretty. He thought, *I'm simple. I love to sing in karaoke.* He smiled at the ludicrous repetition of the catfishers.

"Thank you," he said when his order arrived.

He had been so deep in his own sleep-deprived reverie, thinking how his coffee was the greatest coffee he'd ever tasted, that he hadn't noticed when someone sat down three seats away. He was startled to see her there the next time he looked her way. Furthermore, he was startled to see that she had been crying.

"Hey, is everything okay?" he asked. He leaned against one of the seats between them. "Are you all right?"

The woman looked up at Shane. She was in her forties. Not that Shane was any expert in guessing where people were from, but she didn't look like she was from the Philippines.

"I lost my passport," she said.

"Oh no," he said.

"I spent the last hour retracing my steps," she said.

"When's the last time you saw it?"

"This morning."

"Are you staying at a hotel? Have you asked someone at the front desk? I'm sorry…you've probably done all of this. I'm just thinking out loud."

She nodded. "No one's turned one in."

"When are you heading home?"

"Sunday."

Sunday was three days away.

"Where's home?"

"Vietnam," she said. "Saigon."

He was right; she *wasn't* from there.

"There's still time," he said. "Someone once told me that if you lose something, you should look under things. Most lost things aren't lost. They're just hiding."

She tried to smile, but there was nothing hopeful about it.

"I'm Shane, by the way. If there's anything I can do to help."

"My name is Hanh," she said.

When the server came over to take her order, Hanh said, "May I have a glass of water?"

Her English was impeccable.

"Bottle?" the server asked.

"No, tap?" She turned to Shane and said, "My money was with my passport. Credit cards, too."

"Oh here," Shane said, "please, let me pay for your drink. Order what you want."

"No. It's okay."

Shane had read on the airplane that it was common in Southeast Asia to offer something three times because it was impolite to accept the first two times.

"I insist," Shane said. "I'd like to pay for your drink. It would be my honor."

"I couldn't let you," Hanh said.

"But I would really love to. It would make me happy," Shane said.

"Thank you," Hanh said, and she turned to the server and ordered a milk tea and a slice of chocolate decadent cake. She looked back over at Shane, lowered her head in gratitude, and said, "Thank you so much."

"Of course!" Shane said.

"American?" Hanh asked.

"Yes."

"Where?"

"Louisiana."

Hanh said, "I went to school in America."

This explained her fluency in English.

"Where?"

"Stanford."

Damn. Shane was out of his league. LSU was a fine school, but it was no Stanford.

"For graduate school," she said, "I went to University of Chicago."

What little confidence Shane possessed began to wither. "What did you study?" he asked.

"In grad school? Computational Neuroscience."

He smiled weakly. "I'm not even sure what that is."

He expected her to offer up a graduate bulletin description of the program, but she just smiled. When her milk tea and muffin arrived, she thanked him again.

Shane felt a sudden wave of exhaustion come over him, the kind of fatigue that made him question whether he could even make it back to the Grand Hyatt.

"I better go. Jet lag is taking its toll on me. But let me give you my info in case you need help. Happy to help you follow any leads."

"You're so kind," she said.

Shane shook his head, fending off the compliment.

He wrote his WhatsApp number on the back of his business card.

"CEO," she said when she read the card. "I'm duly impressed."

He shrugged off the compliment. "It's a small advertising firm in Louisiana," he said. "Nothing special."

"Thank you again," she said, lifting her tea into the air and then sucking on the straw.

Chapter 8

Back at his hotel, Shane fell asleep on the couch while scrolling through his phone, floating through the room's white noise.

The hotel phone rang – a dagger through his heart.

"What the fuck."

He made his way to the bed and answered the phone.

"Shane? You alive?"

"Corbett? What time is it there?"

"I don't know. Six, I think?"

"In the morning?"

"No. Evening. You're fourteen hours ahead."

Still sleepy, Shane said, "I live in the future."

"What's it like?" Corbett asked. "The future?"

"Oh, you know. Hover cars and space suits."

There was silence. Shane started to doze. When the phone's receiver slipped from his shoulder, he repositioned it and said, "What's up?"

"You ever think about getting remarried?" Corbett asked.

"Hey man," Shane said, "I've got a meeting in a few hours. I still need some sleep."

"This is important," Corbett said. "I need to know."

Shane sighed. This was a subject he avoided.

"No," he said. "I don't."

"Why not?"

"After my wife died," Shane said, "I just…I don't know. I don't want to go through that again. It killed something inside me."

Corbett didn't say anything.

"What about you?" Shane said. "You never married. Why?"

"Just waiting."

"For what? You're getting a little long in the tooth, old man."

"I'm still hopeful," Corbett said. "I still see a wife in my future. A wife and two children." He laughed through his nose. "Boys," he said.

"That's where you and me are different, Corb. I'm not hopeful. Don't get me wrong. I'm grateful I'm still here. I'm grateful I'm still alive. But I'm not hopeful."

"That's what I was afraid of," Corbett said.

"Afraid? Why?"

"I worry about you, buddy. You're like a brother to me."

"Really?" Shane felt unexpectedly moved by the sentiment. But he didn't want Corbett to know the extent of his emotions. So he took a deep breath and said, "I'm glad you feel that way. But I really need to sleep now."

"Yeah-yeah."

"No, really. This is a big deal. You said it yourself."

Corbett said, "Don't put a lot of pressure on yourself. If it doesn't work out, it wasn't meant to be. What I want more than anything…"

Another pause.

"Yeah?"

"I just want you to have a good time on this trip," Corbett said. "You deserve it."

"I'll try."

The line went dead.

It wasn't like Corbett to confide in Shane. It spooked him. Early on in his therapy practice, Shane had a client who finally, after months of appointments, opened up to him; the next week, the client hung himself.

Don't hang yourself, Corbett, Shane thought as he slid back to sleep.

Chapter 9

Shane didn't wake up again until an hour before the meeting. It took a good five minutes to orient himself. Where was he? Was it day or night? What time was the meeting? The room was utterly unfamiliar. The pillow under his head wasn't his pillow. When the reality of the situation finally came to him, he panicked.

"Oh shit," he said. "Fuck! Fuck!"

After a quick shower, Shane took a Jeepney to the company. He didn't have time to wait for a Grab, their version of Uber, and he didn't see any taxis that didn't already have someone inside them. The Jeepney was a garish jeep taxi. *Chitty Chitty Bang Bang* meets *Pimp My Ride*. It was easy to board, but it proved a fatal decision for Shane as it stopped every few minutes to drop off or pick up passengers.

Shane's shirt was suctioned to his body as sweat dripped continuously down his face. *Please, hurry*, he thought futilely. *Please! Please!* The thought of flying eight thousand miles and then missing his meeting made him want to vomit.

When he saw that everyone on the jeepney was looking at him, he realized that he hadn't paid. He had read that you had to hand the money to the person next to you, and that they in turn passed it up to the front. He didn't have any small bills, so he handed over the smallest that he could find. As he waited for his change, he checked his phone's map and realized that the jeepney was heading in the complete opposite direction he needed to go.

"Stop!" he yelled. "I need to get off! Please stop!"

The driver tried to hand Shane his change after he'd deboarded, but Shane waved him on.

He ordered a car from Grab instead. And then he waited.

And waited.

And waited.

When the Grab driver finally arrived, Shane was already twenty minutes late for the meeting. The stress he had kept bottled up released itself as a fizzle of embarrassment and defeat. What the hell was Corbett going to say when he found out Shane was late?

You know what, Shane thought. Fuck Corbett. Why had he booked this trip for Shane without any notice? Why hadn't he run it past Shane to make sure he had the goddamn time for it? Why had he given Shane no time to prep for the meeting? And why did Corbett call him in the middle of the night when he knew Shane had an early-morning meeting in a country he had never before been? The stress…it was all too much.

Shane tried finding a phone number for the pharmaceutical company, but he didn't see one on any of the information Corbett had given him, only the address and the names of the people he would meet.

The driver, a young Filipino with a thin mustache, asked, "Are you sure this is where you're going?"

"I think so. Why?"

"It's in Tondo."

"I don't know what that means."

The driver didn't respond. Shane watched the map on his phone. As the driver got closer to the destination, Shane looked up and saw what the driver meant: Tondo wasn't BGC. Groups of older Filipinos sat outside drinking. There was a pool table on the street. *On the street!* Thirty kids played basketball, using the jankiest of homemade hoops. The alleyways were narrow, with tattooed men sitting next to caged chickens, the air thick with the smoke of grilled meat.

As the driver pulled up to a building, several children ran to the car and peered inside at Shane, their hands cupped against the window, smiling. It was like a scene from a movie about a war-torn country.

"I don't think this is it," Shane said.

"This is the address," the driver said.

"You think a major pharmaceutical company would be located here?"

"This is the address," the driver repeated.

Shane took a deep breath. He wasn't sure what to do. The address on the map was indeed the same as the address on the papers that Corbett had given him.

"Okay then," Shane said, and he paid the driver. He eased open the door carefully so as not to injure a child. As soon as he stepped out of the car, kids wanted to fist bump him. He obliged. He thought maybe they wanted money, but they didn't ask for any. He was worried they might try to pickpocket him, but they seemed only to want to walk along beside him, as though he were a stray dog they'd befriended.

With a dozen kids surrounding him, Shane once again checked the address on the building against the one on the papers. The doors were shuttered with an accordion gate and a lock that looked like it hadn't been opened in fifty years.

Shane tried calling Corbett, but the call wouldn't go through. He sent Corbett a message, but it, too, was rejected. He must have been in a dead zone. He couldn't begin to fathom how bad cell service was in this neighborhood.

Shane took in his surroundings. Coaxial cables, strung from pole to pole, drooped like kudzu. The kids were getting restless. A few tugged at his shirt.

"Come, come," they said.

Shane was sweating again. The heat was unbearable. He was weak and shaky, and he felt sick to his stomach for missing his meeting. Fortunately, he still had plenty of time in Manila to straighten things out.

"Okay, okay," he said to the kids. "Where are we going?"

"Just *follow*," one of them said. He smiled at Shane. He was missing two baby teeth, waiting for the permanents to come in.

Everyone he passed, teenager or adult, wanted to fist bump or high-five him. Kids ran in front of him to dance. They led Shane into an alley. When a young woman, probably nineteen or twenty, emerged sweating from a kitchen to kiss his hand, Shane let down his guard. They were treating him with uncommon reverence, as though he were a man of distinction. The long lost king of Tondo.

The kids had wanted to show Shane off to the grownups. He was their catch of the day.

A boy yelled, "That's my mother!" and several kids laughed.

What the hell was going on?

What was going on, it turned out, was that Tondo wasn't the scary place it had been advertised to be. Maybe things were different at night, but in daylight? Shane was an exotic beast to be treated with reverence. For once, his pale Irish skin had caused him to stand out in a good way, even if, on a cellular level, it was a cause for worry, especially since he had failed to put on any sunblock before leaving the hotel.

An old man sitting in a small plastic chair motioned for Shane to come over and join him. He was holding out a drink for him.

"What is this?"

"Red Horse."

"Beer?"

The old man nodded. He motioned for Shane to join him, so he did.

Other men gathered around, from teenagers on up, some wearing basketball jerseys, some shirtless and tattooed. Children, creating an outer ring to the group, watched. The woman who had kissed his hand brought Shane a plate of food.

"Chicken adobo and rice," she said, and she stood waiting until he tried it. He was a man on trial. He set the beer between his feet. He picked up a piece of chicken and bit into it.

"Oh my God," he said. "This is so good. Best chicken I've ever eaten!" He wasn't lying.

The woman's eyes narrowed, as though her thoughts had turned to lust, and Shane felt himself blushing at the public flirting as the men around him, having seen what he had seen, laughed loudly. Children pointed at his reddening face and giggled. The old man handed him another beer, though he still hadn't finished the one between his feet.

As he raised the chicken leg to his mouth again, a chicken that was still very much alive walked aimlessly in the street, as though trying to decide what its options were, even though its fate had long been sealed.

Chapter 10

Shane woke up hours later in the plastic chair.

It was already dark. The old man remained next to him, but he also had fallen asleep.

There were more people out now, more kids playing basketball, more friends walking with their arms slung over each other's shoulders. Food stalls had popped open their colorful umbrellas as even more smoke filled the air. An old man walked by holding a bouquet of helium-filled balloons, some shaped like submarines, some like fish. A woman with a sign "Donation to the Blind" sang into a microphone as a man, possibly her husband, leaned against a speaker that was strapped to a four-wheeled cart.

A girl wearing a tube top stared seductively at Shane. She couldn't have been more than eighteen. Shane quickly looked away.

Instinctually, he patted himself down for his cell phone, wallet, and passport. They were all still on him. How long had he been asleep?

Just as he was beginning to stand, the old man woke up and motioned for him to sit.

"No, no, I need to go," Shane said. "You're very kind, though."

"You need to eat," the old man said.

"Thank you, but…I really should get going."

When Shane stood, he realized he was lightheaded. How many Red Horses had the old man given him? A chicken, chopped into quarters, sizzled on the grill nearest him. He looked up and down the street for the chicken he had seen earlier, but it was no longer there.

"I just need to get a Grab," Shane said.

After he ordered a car to come get him, he saw that he had several messages. He assumed they were all from Corbett wondering what the hell had happened, but most were weird local spam. The sole message on WhatsApp was from Hanh. It read: I found my passport. Thank you so much for your kindness.

Shane wrote back: Would you like to meet for coffee?

He lowered his phone and said to the old man, "Thank you for the beer. And the food."

The old man nodded. He took hold of Shane's wrist with one hand, leaned forward, and patted him on the arm with his other hand. His withered arms belied his strength. He let go of Shane's arm, shut his eyes, and dozed off again.

When the Grab car arrived, Shane slid into the backseat and the driver pulled slowly away, his eyes visible in the rearview mirror, quickly assessing the next thirty-four minutes of his life, as one should always do.

The driver had food in a bag in the passenger seat.

"Do you mind if I drop off?" he asked Shane. "For my family?"

Did Shane have a choice? What if he said no?

"Sure," Shane said, and the man smiled.

Not much later, the driver wheeled into a cemetery.

The cemetery was a neighborhood among the graves, with shops and basketball hoops and laundry strung between tombs. The dead were in concrete caskets, and the homes were tucked away in structures above or between crypts. Shane watched a woman, who was carrying a basket of clothes, climb up onto one of the coffins and then climb a ladder to a much higher crypt.

"The dead are dead," the driver said. "There are no ghosts here. I worry more about drug addicts."

Shane said nothing as the driver crept through the cemetery city, turning down one lane and then another, until he finally arrived at his destination.

"Keep your door locked," he said.

Three children ran to his car. Two cupped their hands and peered into the back window at Shane while the third child accepted the food from the driver's powered-down window. The driver reached out, ruffled the child's hair, and then powered the window back up.

"My children," the driver said.

Shane's phone buzzed, a message from Hanh, but he didn't read it. Even so, his heart sped up. When was the last time his heart had sped up from the first hint of something promising?

"How long have you lived here?" Shane asked.

"I was born here. We all were. My wife, too. We met cleaning tombs."

"Is that a job? Cleaning tombs?"

"Fifty pesos a month," the driver said, pulling away from his home.

Shane did a quick calculation: Fifty pesos was less than one dollar.

"How did you ever afford a car?" Shane asked.

"I made an arrangement," the driver said.

Shane didn't ask what kind of an arrangement, but he couldn't imagine it was a good one.

"We have to lease the land from the dead man's family," the driver said. "If we don't pay, a crime family will buy it."

"A crime family? You mean like a syndicate?"

"Yes." He stopped and turned around to face Shane. He smiled. "But how else could I live in a neighborhood full of movie stars and presidents?"

Chapter 11

"Thank you," Shane said and handed the driver three one-thousand peso bills – just over fifty U.S. dollars. Before the driver could process what he'd been given, Shane slipped out of the car and quickly walked away.

"Shane! Over here!"

It was Hanh. She'd agreed to meet him – but she had wanted to meet him for drinks, not coffee.

He craned his head until he saw her. She was dressed for a night out club-hopping, wearing a short red dress with spaghetti straps and tassels at the hem. The fabric was soft, like crushed velvet. Her shoes were high-heeled boots that laced up to look like fishnet.

At the sight of her, Shane felt extraordinarily old. He was already tired from his afternoon of Red Horse, from his ill-advised nap in the sun, from the confusion surrounding the meeting.

When he reached her, she said, "I'm happy you wrote back."

"Me, too."

"You don't look happy," she said.

"No, I am. It's just been a…" He thought of what it had been. "A strange day."

She poked out her bottom lip, a comic gesture of sympathy. Then she smiled.

"You're with me now," she said. "I'll cheer you up."

Shane was grateful when she led him to a pub instead of a rave. Several men turned to look at Hanh when they entered. The men were mostly white, probably expats, many coupled with a Filipina but still eager and hungry. It unnerved Shane, their insatiability, and the way Shane didn't exist for any of them. He was invisible. A non-entity in whatever calculation they were making.

Hanh both basked in and ignored the attention. She carried a very particular confidence that didn't acknowledge the inherent danger in any given room even though she must surely have felt it.

"Let's sit over here," she said, leading him all the way to the back corner.

How was it that only a few hours ago Shane had woken up in a chair in a part of Manila that was as exotic as anything he could have imagined, a place out of time – and now he could have been in a nice Chicago suburb, reading over a menu that served cheeseburgers with ridiculous names and jalapeno poppers and potato skins for appetizers. A Starbucks was probably around the corner.

Shane ordered a vodka tonic and Hanh ordered a Mojito de Mayon.

"Oh. You're serious," Shane said.

"Very serious," Hanh said.

"Okay then. So it's going to be that kind of a night." Shane laughed.

Hanh said, "How was your day? Tell me what happened."

"I need a drink first."

Once their drinks arrived, Shane deftly took her through his day, beginning with his inability to find his meeting, up until his driver bringing him to a cemetery.

"His family lives there," Shane said. "It was the strangest thing I'd ever seen."

Hanh considered this. "You couldn't find the meeting?"

"It didn't exist," Shane said. "It's like it had never existed." The neon lights inside the restaurant triggered something in him. He felt overcome with a reckless enthusiasm. "And I can't get hold of my business partner to let him know," he said loudly. He shrugged and laughed. He felt simultaneously defeated and elated. There was something invigorating about an epic failure.

"But *you*," Shane said. "You found your passport. Where was it?"

"It was under my bed," she said. "You were right. It was under something."

"Under your *bed?* I was thinking more like under a room service menu."

"I must have dropped it and kicked it under there. But don't change the subject," she said, pointing at Shane. "What do you think happened? Maybe you had the wrong address?"

"Maybe," Shane said. "I don't know. Doesn't matter. I don't want to think about it anymore."

He ordered another drink. To his surprise, Hanh was ready for another, too.

"One more for her, too," he said to the bartender. To Hanh, he said, "Thanks for meeting me out. For real. It's kind of you." He tried not letting self-pity seep into his voice, but it was inevitable. He smiled.

"You're cute," Hanh said, smiling.

"Oh, no," Shane said. "No, no." He wagged his head. When was the last time a woman had paid him a compliment, though? At least a few years by now. He missed it. "When did you say you had to go back home? Sunday?"

She nodded. Then she leaned in closer and said, "Take me somewhere."

"Where do you want to go?"

She shrugged. "I've only been to the U.S. and here. And Vietnam, of course. You've probably been everywhere."

"Actually, I haven't. Canada and Mexico. And here."

"Really?"

"Really."

"Let's go somewhere. Let's escape," she said.

"Where?" he asked.

"I don't know. Hong Kong? It's close."

"Hong Kong?" He thought about it. Until now, Hong Kong had only been a place he'd seen in movies – Bruce Lee movies when he was a kid; Wong Kar-wai movies as an adult. It was a neon-soaked dream, not a place he would ever actually find himself. But why not?

"Sure, let's go to Hong Kong!" he said.

The drinks arrived. Was he serious? Was *she* serious?

"Let's have a few more of these," Shane said, lifting his glass, "and then see what we think."

He clinked his glass against hers.

"Dzô!" she said.

"Cheers!" Shane said.

Chapter 12

After leaving the pub, Shane and Hanh hit a nightclub and danced until they were dripping with sweat, their clothes drenched. There were days in one's life that never seemed to end, and this was one of them. Already, his afternoon in Tondo seemed years ago. A Super 8 movie from a past life. The cemetery was a fever dream. When he and Hanh burst out of the club, sweating and drunk, they collapsed against each other, laughing. The music still thumped in his chest like a myocardial infraction. He had trouble catching his breath.

"Look!" he said, pointing to a bar across the street. They needed quieter surroundings, a place to deescalate. They headed over.

Hanh ordered another elaborate cocktail for herself. It was frightening how someone her size could keep pace with someone Shane's size.

Shane checked his phone again. Still nothing from Corbett.

"No word?" Hanh asked between sips from her straw. Her wet hair was matted to her forehead. Even her eyebrows glowed.

They were sitting in a curved booth in a darkened corner. Shane was slumped on his side of the booth. He shook his head.

"I'll call him from the hotel tomorrow," Shane said.

"There's at least a ten-hour time difference," Hanh said. "He'll probably be asleep. You want to call him tonight?"

Shane pulled at the wet shirt suctioned to his body to give himself some air.

"He knows I'm here," Shane said. "It can wait. It's not like I haven't been trying."

Hanh said, "You like him, don't you? He's your friend."

"He saved my life," Shane said. "He took me in at my lowest point…offered me something no one else would have."

"You sound like a stray dog." Hanh was teasing, but she must have seen the emotions brewing up in his eyes because she quickly asked, "What did he offer you?"

"A second chance."

Hanh nodded.

"Tell me about yourself," Shane said. "I'm tired of talking about myself." He smiled.

"An American? Tired of talking about himself?" She laughed.

"Imagine that!"

Hanh said, "My mother died when I was seven. Car accident. My father, he's a modest man. Humble. He drives a motorbike taxi. If I wanted to go to college, I had to go on scholarship. My father was a child during the war. He said that American soldiers would earn his trust by giving him chocolate bars. He says that whenever he eats Hershey bars now, he thinks about old Saigon and American soldiers." She leaned across the booth, placing her head on Shane's shoulder. "I'm hungry. Are you hungry?"

"No? Yes?"

"I know where we should go."

"Where?"

Ten minutes later, they were standing in line at Jollibee, and Shane was ordering something called Jolly Spaghetti.

"This is maybe the most disgusting thing I've ever seen," he said when they sat down with their food. "Is that *hotdog* in the spaghetti?"

"Looks like hot dog," Hanh said.

"What did you get?"

"A Chickenjoy Meal Deal."

Hanh reached over with a fork and plucked out a chunk of hotdog for herself.

"Mmmmm. Delicious," she said.

"God help us," Shane said.

They ate in monastic silence, the too-bright lights giving them an otherworldly hue. Certain he looked twenty years older, Shane longed for the more-forgiving lights of the pubs. Even the nightclub, with its seizure-inducing strobe lights, would have been an improvement.

Hanh reached over and wiped sauce from Shane's mouth. The sauce on the napkin was orange. No doubt it was one-hundred-percent artificial.

"There," she said. "Better."

After one last nightcap at yet another bar, they ended up standing outside her room at the Manila Hotel.

"General MacArthur and his family lived here during World War Two," Hanh said.

"Is that a fact," Shane said. He stepped close to her until she was almost against him. "History buff?" he asked, smiling. "You know about General MacArthur, do you?"

"How will you know the future if you don't know the past?" she said.

"A therapist would say that past behavior predicts future behavior," Shane said.

"There you have it. History isn't random. The future isn't, either."

"This is damned sexy," Shane said, and he meant it. He leaned in to kiss her, but she put up her hand.

"I want our first kiss to be in Hong Kong," she said.

"Really? Why not Manila?" He tried not to show his disappointment.

"I've always wanted to go to Hong Kong. It'll mean more to me."

"If you always wanted to go to Hong Kong," Shane said, "why didn't you go to Hong Kong instead of Manila?"

"Because I didn't want to go alone." She smiled. "It's silly, I know."

Shane considered this. He put his hands on her shoulders and said, "Okay. Hong Kong it is!"

"There's a one p.m. flight tomorrow. I checked."

Shane looked at the time on his phone. It was already two a.m.

"I better get back to my room, I guess," he said.

Hanh smiled. "We're going?"

"Of course!"

Hanh looked like she might cry.

"What?" Shane asked. "What's wrong?"

"I'm just happy. That's all." She pushed him away, playfully. "Now go," she said, pushing him again.

"Shouldn't we book the flight together?" he asked. "So we're not sitting apart?"

"If the plane's full," she said, "we'll make up a story about why we have to sit next to each other."

"Okay," he said, backing out of her room. "Sleep well."

She closed the door slowly, as though she didn't want to let go of the sight of him – until she did.

Chapter 13

Shane woke up the next morning surprisingly refreshed and, more surprisingly, sober. Maybe dancing for hours on end had purified his blood. Perhaps there were restorative qualities in Jollibee's food that he wasn't aware of. The entire night had been a plunge of adrenaline to his heart. Upon waking, he wasn't even sure how much had actually happened, but when he checked WhatsApp and saw a message from Hanh reminding him to book his ticket for Hong Kong, he realized that the best memories of the night were indeed real.

Still nothing from Corbett, though.

He tried calling from his hotel phone but received a recording letting him know that his call could not go through.

He checked Corbett's personal Facebook page to see when it had last been updated, but he hadn't posted anything since their lunch on Lake Martin when he'd posted a photo of one of the alligators with the caption, "Celebrating with a friend." Corbett kept his list of friends hidden, and the post had received only three likes. For a guy as congenial as Corbett, three likes was a dismal showing. But maybe he didn't collect friends the way other people did.

His friendship with Corbett had been an unexpected development at this late stage in his life. As a child, Shane had been a loner, the sort of kid who could entertain himself for hours with Hot

Wheels, concocting imaginary worlds out of pillows and blankets. The rich people – the ones who owned the Rolls Royce Silver Shadow – lived high up on a down-filled mountaintop while the poorer folks, those who owned cars with missing wheels, lived hidden in the rippled cotton landscape that ended in a steep cliff at the end of the bed. In his teen and young adult years, Shane's friends were mostly women, a select few who enjoyed independent films and books by Camus and Sartre. But now, with his Hot Wheels buried in a city dump and all the pretentious bullshit of youth long in his past, Shane had become friends with the kind of man he used to look down on – a slick, good-looking, fast-talking businessman. He was no longer the weird outsider with fringe interests. He was with the popular kids now.

Shane was starting to get worried – he hoped everything was okay back home – but he had more urgent things to tend to, like getting his ass to the airport.

Life was a series of strategically-placed landmines. Shane had come to the Philippines begrudgingly, and now, less than forty-eight hours later, he was falling in love.

Don't get your hopes up, Shane told himself. Keep your expectations in check.

He couldn't help himself, though. He was giddy. He smiled at the prospect that his life was about to irrevocably change. The thought of having to go back home and watch his neighbors endlessly pace their immaculate lawns with their leaf blowers, the thought of other people's silly home repair projects penetrating the bubble of his own home, their sawing, their hammering – all of it filled him with dread. Before leaving his room, he made a decision. In whichever direction the next few days led him, he wasn't going to resist it.

Chapter 14

At Ninoy Aquino International Airport, security teams circled the area. They were dressed in bulletproof vests and armed with shotguns, automatic machine guns, and high-powered rifles. One of the men met Shane's eyes, and Shane quickly looked away.

Shane was standing by the China Airlines line, waiting for Hanh. The area was busy and hot. Shane felt sweat roll beneath his shirt.

"Come *on*," he said under his breath, checking the time on his phone.

As the window started to close for checking in, Shane feared that this would be one more disappointment in a long life of disappointments. First, he braced himself for Hanh not showing up, and then he accepted it as fact. Of course she won't! he thought. Why would she?

But then she appeared, and he felt shitty for questioning her word.

"I'm so sorry!" she said. "Traffic was awful!"

"It's okay," Shane said. "Take a deep breath. Everything's okay."

"Are we going to be late?"

"I don't think so," Shane said. "We've got plenty of time."

Hanh looked tired, and she wasn't wearing any makeup. She was still beautiful. She kept turning away from him when she caught him looking at her, fidgeting with her carry-on, making sure she had her passport.

In line, Shane said, "Show me your passport photo, and I'll show you mine."

"No," she said firmly. She shook her head. "Bad picture. I look terrible."

"Impossible!" Shane said. "Here, let me see."

He was flirting, but when he held out his hand, she stuffed the passport into her purse. "Please, no," she said.

"Okay," he said. He was surprised that his feelings were hurt. He was only trying to be playful, nothing more, and he'd been rebuffed. Their first setback.

Shane hated how sensitive he could be. He'd always been that way, as far back in grade school when a teacher's gentle teasing might cause his eyes to water.

When it was their turn at the airline's check-in counter, the young woman behind the computer motioned for both of them to approach her. When Hanh hesitated, the woman motioned again. Clearly, she had identified Shane and Hanh as a couple, and there was no reason that they shouldn't check in together, especially since seating assignments hadn't yet been made.

"Passports," the woman demanded. She was Chinese and all business.

Shane and Hanh surrendered their passports.

Hanh asked if they could sit together, but the agent ignored her. She typed furiously, looked frustrated by what appeared on her screen, and then typed in some more.

Shane and Hanh exchanged looks, trying not to laugh. The agent's seriousness was almost comical.

The agent printed a boarding pass, stuck it in a passport, and, without looking up, handed it to Shane. Shane opened the passport to check the boarding pass, but instead of looking at the boarding pass, he zeroed in on a peculiar visa stamp. It was a departure stamp from Oslo, Norway, dated only a few months ago. The stamp was hunter green with drawings of two sailboats. At first glance, Shane thought the sailboats were pine trees. There were stamps from other countries, too. Thailand. Cambodia. Singapore. The passport wasn't Shane's; it was Hanh's. Both passports had blue covers.

Hanh snapped the passport out of Shane's hands. She looked angry. Instead of waiting for Shane, she began rolling her luggage toward the international departure gate.

"Hanh!" Shane called out. "Hold up!"

But Hanh kept walking. Nothing was making sense.

A security guard, dressed in paramilitary gear, stepped to one side of him while a large man in a blue suit stepped up to the other side.

"Sir? Please come with us," the man in the suit said.

Shane hesitated.

"I have a flight to Hong Kong," Shane said. "And I need my passport back."

The agent behind the computer handed the passport to the man with the blue suit, who tucked it away inside his jacket's inner pocket.

"I'm sorry," Shane said, "but what the hell is this about?"

The security guard took hold of Shane's arm and forcefully guided him to follow the man in the blue suit. Until now, Shane had been superficially aware that he was in a foreign country, but the reality was setting in that he had no special rights here, and that his anger would only make matters worse.

"It's okay," Shane said. "I can catch a later flight. It's okay."

But both men ignored him as they led him into a room at the end of a very long corridor, far enough away that no one would ever know he was there. It had all happened so fast that no one would likely remember a man being escorted away. It was just another thing happening on the periphery, like children playing on the floor, dogs sniffing for drugs, or the pilot pausing to check his phone after a long flight from God only knew where.

Chapter 15

The room was small and hot. Shane tried fanning himself with his own damp shirt by repeatedly pulling on the fabric and letting go, but it was useless. The man in the blue suit had told him he would be back soon, but an hour later he hadn't returned. The security guard remained in the room, a machine gun slung over his shoulder, his right hand resting on the handle of a holstered pistol.

Shane had sent Hanh a message about his detainment, but she hadn't written back. By now, the flight to Hong Kong had already boarded. The passengers had probably been instructed to turn off their phones. He checked Corbett's Facebook page, but the page had been deactivated.

When his phone buzzed from a notification, Shane's heart sped up, but it was just Alyssa, his cat sitter, on Messenger. She'd sent him a photo of Larry with the word "goofball" written under it. In the photo, Larry was on his back and looking up at Alyssa. He started typing a message – he wanted her to drive to their office and find Corbett – but halfway through his message, the guard walked over and snatched Shane's phone from his hand.

Shane wanted to protest, but he said nothing. Whatever misunderstanding was taking place, it would resolve itself sooner than later. Better to remain calm and patient.

When the door opened, two men entered – one wearing a black polo shirt with the letters NBI in yellow letters across his heart, the other wearing a bullet-proof vest with NBI in white letters across his chest.

The man in the bullet-proof vest was holding a shut laptop while the man in the polo shirt did all the talking.

"My name is Angelo Flores, and this is James Cortez. We're from the National Bureau of Investigation. Do you mind?" he asked, pointing to the only other chair in the room.

Shane said nothing.

Angelo Flores sat. He set his phone on the table and activated the app to record them. He said, "There seems to be an issue. We hope you can clarify a few things for us."

"Sure," Shane said. "I'll try."

"The man you met earlier, the man who brought you to this room, he's head of airport security."

"Okay."

"He was alerted ahead of time that you would be coming to the airport."

Alerted? What the hell did that mean? Shane waited for more, but he could feel the pulse in his throat.

After a pause, Angelo said, "Do you know what the NBI is?"

"I'm assuming you're like the FBI?"

Angelo smiled. He looked up at his partner, who did not smile.

"Yes," Angelo said, returning his gaze to Shane, nodding. "The FBI."

"Okay, so…I guess I'm confused," Shane said. "Have I done something wrong?"

"We're hoping you can shed light on that for us," Angelo said.

"I mean…I'll try," Shane said.

"You've been in Manila for less than two days, correct?"

"Yes."

Shane ran the past two days through his head but couldn't think of anything he'd done wrong. Had someone in Tondo accused him of something? Had the Grab driver assumed Shane was rich and alerted someone to shake him down?

"And now you're going to Hong Kong," Angelo Flores said, stating a fact.

"Yes."

"Why so little time in Manila?"

"I was supposed to have a meeting with a pharmaceutical company," Shane said, "but when I got to the address yesterday, the company wasn't there. Maybe it was never there."

"And you flew halfway across the world for this meeting with a company that doesn't exist?"

"I flew halfway across the world for a meeting with a company I *thought* existed. It wasn't until I showed up at the address that I learned there was no such company. Not at that address, at least." There was a pause. "Is that…illegal?" Shane asked.

"What do you do for a living, Mr. Doyle? Your name *is* Doyle, yes?"

"Shane Doyle, yes. I'm co-CEO of an advertising and marketing company in Lafayette, Louisiana."

Angelo Flores cut his eyes to James Cortez, who stepped forward and opened the laptop.

The frozen image on the screen was of Shane sitting behind a desk. The scene behind him was of a plate-glass window that overlooked the Manhattan skyline. Shane recognized the desk. It was the one he had sat behind in that grim vacant storefront in Abbeville.

Angelo reached over and pressed play.

The video wasn't, as he was expecting, a commercial for a carpet store. The chyron at the bottom of the screen read, "Shane Doyle, CEO of Wunderkind." The video alternated between shots of Shane speaking in his Manhattan high-rise office and happy, idealized families socializing in front of their mansions or piling into their luxury SUVs. The voice was Shane's, but the script was entirely different. Shane couldn't follow the details, but it had something to do with pension plans and virtual currencies.

When it was over, Angelo reached over and shut the laptop's lid.

"That *is* you, correct?" Angelo said. "Shane Doyle?"

"I mean…yes, that's me," Shane said, "but the video's a hoax. The filmmakers asked me to do a commercial for a carpet store, but they…I don't know what the hell this is. They edited it to make it look like I'm someone else."

"Carpet?" Angelo asked. "I don't see any carpet."

"It's a fake commercial," Shane said.

"But that *is* you. We can agree on that, yes?"

"Yes and no," Shane said.

He experienced a kind of paralysis, an inability to articulate himself. Ever since he was a child, his capacity to speak would disappear whenever he got nervous. To his teachers, Shane's jumbled words only confirmed for them his guilt, however flimsy and arbitrary their charges against him were.

His survival depended now upon his ability to speak lucidly. He took a deep breath.

"What's this all about?" Shane finally asked, slowing down, trying to wrap his head around their accusation, which remained elusive. "Let's say I *did* make this commercial. I didn't. But let's say I did. What's the issue?"

"You don't dispute that this is you," Angelo said.

"I don't dispute that it's me," Shane said, "but I dispute what I'm saying. I dispute the content. It's all been manipulated." In the fog of his thoughts, he remembered something that one of the filmmakers had said. "They mentioned AI. I'm sure that's how they used my voice but changed the words. *Some* of the words are things I actually said, but the context is different here."

Angelo laughed. His partner looked increasingly displeased. The airport security guard in the room remained noncommittal.

"You admit that this is you," Angelo said.

"It's me, yes," Shane said. "But I didn't say any of those things in that way. And it wasn't for whatever the hell Wunderkind is."

"Please stand," Angelo said. When Shane didn't stand, Angelo repeated himself, "Please stand."

The pulse in his neck…he could hear it in his throat now. "May I call my embassy?" Shane asked. "I'd like, as a United States citizen, to call my embassy."

"Maybe later," Angelo said, "but not now. Please stand."

Shane stood. His legs were weak. He was fifty-five years old, a grown man, and yet he felt like a child – the same fears, the same desire to weep at his helplessness.

"I don't know what's going on," Shane said. He sounded weak. Pathetic.

"Please face the wall," Angelo said. "Go on. Face the wall."

Shane did as he was told.

"Please place your hands behind your back," Angelo said.

Shane had feared these would be Angelo's next words.

"Go on. Behind your back now," Angelo said.

Shane obliged, but he was pleading with them. "This is a horrible mistake," he said.

The cuffs tightened around his wrists. He wasn't sure who had put them on him – Angelo or James.

Angelo said, "You have the right to remain silent. Any statement you make may be used for or against you in any court of law in the Philippines. You have the right to have a competent and independent counsel preferably of your own choice. If you cannot afford the services of counsel, the government will provide one for you. You have the right to demand physical examination by an independent and competent doctor of your own choice. If you cannot afford the services of a doctor, the state shall provide one for you. Do you understand these rights?"

The familiarity of the words gave Shane some small relief even though he knew that they shouldn't. They wouldn't have given him any relief back home, and yet here, right now, he thought, *The way things work here isn't so unlike the U.S. And the men speak English.* There was, he knew, a strong bond between the two countries, like half-brothers who had grown up in different families, thousands of miles apart.

"Yes," Shane said. "I do."

Angelo picked up his phone from the table and shut off the app that had been recording them.

As Shane was being led out of the room, he said, "I checked my luggage." He offered this information as though it were an urgent matter. "Will someone get my luggage before it gets sent to Hong Kong?"

Four armed officers stood in the hallway, ready to escort Shane. Their presence didn't scare Shane as much as his failure to imagine that they had been standing there waiting for him. What else was he failing to imagine?

"Don't worry about your luggage anymore," Angelo said.

"Okay," Shane said as he was led through an employee-only exit, which led to the tarmac, where a white police van waited for Shane, idling in the heat. Behind the police van were three more official-looking cars, all black. Several news crews stood behind a metal barrier. Five men with shoulder-mounted video cameras filmed Shane as he was led to the van.

Shane said to the van's driver, "Who do they think I am?"

He turned to look back at Shane. "You're a big deal," he said. He smiled and said, "Big shot!"

"I need your help," Shane said, but the man didn't reply. "Please," Shane said.

The man faced forward, his comportment that of a hearse driver as he pulled down the gear shift and accelerated, maintaining the same speed as the car ahead, all the while ignoring the dead man accompanying him.

Chapter 16

Shane sat in an interrogation room at NBI headquarters in Manila. One wrist was cuffed to the table. With his free hand, he was able to drink from a water bottle. When the door finally opened, a woman walked in and sat down across from him. She was mid-forties and wore a navy skirt with a white blouse and navy blazer. She introduced herself as Reyna Dela Cruz.

"I'm your attorney," she said, opening a briefcase and shuffling through some papers.

"I don't know how this works," Shane said. "Can I call someone back home? Don't I get to choose an attorney?"

She pulled out a single sheet of paper and read it over. She still hadn't looked directly at Shane. "You declined to choose your own attorney," she said.

"No, that's wrong. I haven't declined. Can I see that?"

She showed him the document.

"That's not my signature," he said. "Do I get a phone call?"

"You declined your one phone call," she said.

"What are you talking about?" he asked. He could hear the desperation in his voice, the tightness in his throat. "I didn't decline my phone call, and I didn't decline to choose my own attorney."

Reyna Dela Cruz finally looked up, meeting Shane's eyes for the first time.

She said, "From here, you'll be taken to a pre-trial detention center."

"What did I do?" Shane said. "What are the charges against me?"

"Your company defrauded dozens of people out of their money. In at least one instance, the victim killed himself."

"What company? I work in advertising."

"The investment firm."

"No, no. Nope." Shane shook his head. "I was just an actor. Actually, I wasn't even an actor. I was a last-minute replacement. The commercial is a fraud. They used AI to piece it together. *I'm* the victim here."

Reyna opened a laptop and spun it around for Shane to see. It was a LinkedIn account that listed Shane as the CEO of Wunderkind. She reached over, selected another tab, and showed him a website for Wunderkind that featured a photo of Shane on the "About Us" page.

Reyna said, "I could show you more, but..." She shut the laptop.

"This is insane."

Ignoring Shane, Reyna said, "You should probably know that the man who killed himself was the nephew of a cabinet member."

"What are you saying? What does that mean?"

"This is a Catholic country, Mr. Doyle. Family is important here."

"I understand that," Shane said, though he knew next to nothing about the Philippines.

Reyna put her papers back into her briefcase and shut it.

"Is this it?" he asked.

"Where you're going, you should be very careful."

"Look," Shane said. "I need you to contact the U.S. Embassy for me. Do they even know I'm here?"

Reyna said, "I'm sorry, but the facts of this case aren't in your favor. You've been accused of defrauding many people, one of whom is now dead. You were shown a video in which you are identified as the CEO of the company that defrauded these people. You acknowledged that the person in the video is in fact you."

"This can't be happening," Shane said.

"In the Philippines, you can't steal nearly a billion pesos and expect to walk away from it."

Reyna slid her briefcase off the table and walked toward the door.

"What's next?" Shane asked. "When's the trial?"

"On rare occasions, there's a trial a few weeks from the day of the arrest. Sometimes months. Sometimes years. But more often than not, the trial date never arrives."

Reyna knocked on the door, the door opened, and Reyna left the room without looking back.

Shane felt dead inside. His exhaustion was like a weighted blanket draped over his head and hanging down all around him, the way children dressed as ghosts. His will to keep going was questionable.

After being fingerprinted and photographed, after all the necessary reports and paperwork were filed, Shane was brought outside to yet another transport van. In the distance, an older man wearing a suit watched him. He was a large, imposing man surrounded at a distance by his own foot soldiers. Was this the cabinet member who Reyna Dela Cruz had mentioned? The sun was setting behind the man, making it difficult to see his features. He was a silhouette. Shane wanted to call out to him but was afraid that it would be misinterpreted as an aggressive gesture, and that the men carrying machine guns would respond in kind.

Shane saw the man nod, as though to indicate that he'd seen enough, and then Shane was forced into the transport van. The van was the centerpiece of a motorcade, complete with sirens and blocked traffic, cops on motorcycles whizzing ahead to stop cars on side-streets from pulling in front; after the van had passed the motorbike cops, they would whiz by again. It was hypnotic to watch, like bees flying into and out of a hive.

"Where are we going?" Shane asked, but no one answered him.

Chapter 17

When they arrived at the detention center, everything happened quickly: the van door slid open, Shane was pulled out into the heat and light, and he was marched into the facility.

Shane was brought to an open-air room with a long wooden table. It resembled a third-world laundromat, except there were no machines.

Several guards surrounded him as one frisked him. The only thing distinguishing them as guards was their gray polo shirt with a patch on the arm.

An old guard asked Shane what he was in there for.

"I don't know," Shane said.

"What did you do?" the old guard asked.

"Nothing," Shane said. "I didn't do anything."

The guard's face was covered in old acne scars. Around his neck was a skinny bungee-like strap that held a pair of cheaters. He put them on and examined a dot-matrix print-out. Shane hadn't seen continuous-feed paper in over thirty years. This gave him a chill for what it suggested about their penal system.

"Fraud that resulted in death," the old man said, reading. "Murder," he said, looking up over his glasses at Shane.

"Not murder," Shane said. "No. They think I'm someone I'm not."

"Quiet, murderer," the old man said.

Shane obeyed. He felt the pressure in his eyes, the tears trying to squeeze out, but he fought them back.

He was taken to another area, where he stood in front of a dingy bedsheet backdrop. A man with a camera walked over and handed him a handwritten sign to hold. It had his name and prisoner number on it. The man took Shane's photo.

Shane had to give up his shoes. In return, he was given slippers.

Next, Shane was escorted into the pre-trial detention center, paraded past prisoners who watched him with nothing less than hate. Not only was he the odious new prisoner, he wasn't even one of them. He was white.

Some of the prisoners looked out onto the courtyard through prison bars, but hundreds of the prisoners weren't cuffed and roamed free. They wore basketball jerseys and jeans. Or they were shirtless. Some wore jewelry, several chunky rings on their fingers and chains around their necks. The detainees outnumbered the guards and looked as though they could easily overtake them. Shane wasn't sure why they hadn't.

Overcrowded, the detention center was a cross between a jail and a slum. Extension cords drooped across walls like Christmas garland, plugged into older, even more-frayed extension cords. The whole place smelled faintly of piss and sweat and black pepper and garlic and burning rubber. If hell on Earth existed, this place was surely it.

Shane was led to a barber under a blue tarp roof, where he was ordered to sit on the stool. No sooner had he sat than the barber ran his electric razor over Shane's head, shearing off his hair in long stripes as a few dozen prisoners pointed and laughed. A man wearing a Michael Jordan jersey bent over laughing, covering his mouth with his hand. When the barber finished using the electric razor, he took out a straightedge and scraped away the stubble. Shane could hear the sound of it, like two pieces of Velcro pulling apart, over and over.

"Newbie!" someone yelled, and several others took up the chant: "Newbie! Newbie! Newbie!"

Next, Shane was led to a water pump where he was told to pump a bucket of water for himself. From there, he was led to an outdoor concrete cubicle, where he was ordered to strip down and shower. Completely naked, he scooped water out from the bucket and tossed it onto himself, rubbing with his hands as one guard and several prisoners watched. When he reached for his clothes, the guard said, "More," and the prisoners laughed. Shane continued washing until the guard made a gesture with his head indicating that he could get dressed now.

Another guard introduced Shane to his cell leader, a prisoner named Jose. He was probably younger than Shane but looked older. He could have been forty or sixty. Jose was in charge of where Shane was to sleep, when he could leave the cell, and when he could eat. His cell was 250 square feet and housed seventy inmates.

How the hell was this even possible? Shane wondered.

The cell had wooden shelving, floor to ceiling, on either side of the room. The shelves were where the prisoners, packed sardine-like, lived. They slid in and out of their designated space on their assigned shelf with no room to spare.

Jose pointed to the uppermost shelf. There was no ladder to reach it. Shane had to figure out how to get up there by holding onto one of the upright two-by-fours and then climbing up it by placing one foot on a shelf on either side of the room. The problem was that his legs didn't stretch that far and that there were no surfaces where people weren't resting. He kept losing his balance and falling.

The first time he fell, several detainees laughed. Then they sat up or leaned forward to watch. Shane was the night's entertainment.

After four failed attempts, Shane grabbed hold of the upright two-by-four and climbed it as he had seen people climb trees. Sweat stung his eyes. The heat and the stench of the room – human body odor and unfamiliar food – made him want to vomit, but he kept it together as he hoisted himself into his slot on the top shelf.

Shane wasn't sure how he was going to make it through the night, let alone however many days or weeks or months it would take to clear his name.

Shane never considered the possibility of his resolve being tested, and he never imagined how little or how much it would take to break him into a million tiny pieces, but he would have plenty of time to learn the answer. Five years, to be precise.

PART TWO

Chapter 18

Four years before his trip to the Philippines, Shane stood in line at Walgreens pharmacy in Lafayette, Louisiana, hoping to get stronger pain pills. The pills weren't for him; they were for his wife. It was a weekend, and Cheryl's doctor wasn't available. Her pain had become unbearable, and the pain pills she'd been given weren't working. Shane had wanted to take her to the emergency room, but Cheryl refused to go. She was dying. She wanted to die at home, not in an anonymous, fluorescent-lit room surrounded by chaos and neglect.

Shane had been waiting in line for twenty minutes while person after person in front of him droned on to the woman behind the counter, mostly about ridiculous things, things that *weren't* matters of life or death, and Shane wanted to scream at them to hurry the fuck up. When he finally got up to the counter, Shane tried explaining the situation – how his wife was dying, how her pain pills weren't strong enough, how there was no way to contact her doctor – but even as he spoke he could hear how insane his request sounded. How unhinged he probably looked. How much he sounded like a junkie.

"Is there any way to give me a stronger pain pill and, I don't know, I could bring the prescription to you tomorrow?" He pulled out his card from his wallet to show her that he was a licensed therapist. He said, "I mean, I'm *almost* a psychiatrist." He tried smiling.

He wasn't almost a psychiatrist, but in that moment it sounded true enough. He worked in the same office suite with a psychiatrist, after all. Many of his patients were also the psychiatrist's patients.

"I'm sorry," the woman said. "I wish I could help." She had short hair, bleached, almost a pageboy cut. Her eyes were rimmed red. Probably just waiting for her smoke break.

"May I speak to a pharmacist?"

The woman smiled. She looked sympathetic.

"I wouldn't recommend that," she said. "He'll get the wrong idea and…" Her eyes panned the store. Shane followed the movement of her eyes, only to land on a security guard standing by the selection of blood pressure monitors.

Shane sighed. "Got it," he said. "I'm sorry. My wife is dying."

"I'm so sorry," the woman said. "I wish I could help." She looked like she meant it, too. Her eyes seemed to be communicating something to him.

Outside, as he sat in his car, eyes wet from tears, someone knocked on his window.

It was the woman who had turned him away at the pharmacy.

Shane rolled down his window.

"Unlock the passenger door," she said.

"Why?"

"There are security cameras all over. Just…unlock the door."

Shane obeyed. The woman slid inside and handed him a bottle of pills. OxyContin.

"These aren't from the pharmacy," she said. "These are mine. There are only a couple in there, but…I hope they help."

"Are you sure?" Shane asked.

She nodded.

"Oh my God, thank you, thank you!" Shane said. "You have no idea how much this means! *No* idea!"

She handed him a doctor's business card. "If you need more, go here. Be sure to tell him I sent you. My name's on the back. Just show this to him."

"Why are you doing this?" Shane asked.

"I know when someone needs help. And you need help." She took hold of his hand and squeezed it. "Okay, I need to get back inside," she said. "Kiss me."

"I'm sorry…what?"

"For the security cameras. Just…kiss me."

He leaned across the center console and kissed her. The woman took hold of his face and kissed him longer and more passionately than he was expecting. Then she opened the door and walked back to work.

Chapter 19

Shane's wife Cheryl died the next morning, and everything for the next few days became a blur as he picked out a coffin, chose the clothes Cheryl would be buried wearing, contacted Cheryl's side of the family, and arranged public notices of her death, which required writing an obituary.

While on his way back from the funeral home for the second time in one day, the grief finally arrived, unplumbed and infinite, mutating like a virus. He pulled over and cried. He couldn't stop. There was a fleeting moment when he wasn't sure he would ever stop. For the first time since he was a child, the ability to quit crying was out of his control. Like breathing. Like blood flowing through his veins. He wasn't sure how he was going to get through the open-casket viewing and then the funeral.

"Goddamn it," he said and punched the car's ceiling.

When the tears finally relented, he pulled from his wallet the business card that the girl with the pageboy haircut had given him, and he drove to Dr. Russell Duchamp's office.

The office was tucked away in an industrial park, a neglected mid-century building with a parking lot full of spiderwebbed cracks in the cement. Even so, there were a few dozen people waiting to see the doctor, including several men and women pacing and smoking outside.

When Shane was finally called into the examination room, two hours after he had arrived, Dr. Duchamp came in and said, "Cash only. If you need an ATM, there's one in the lobby."

He had a jazz musician's beard, what they called a soul patch. His face had old acne scars that gave his skin a kind of glow.

He looked up from the chart and said, "Do you have a referral?"

Shane handed him the business card. When Duchamp saw Kylie's name, he smiled.

"She's a good one," he said.

"She is," Shane agreed.

Duchamp wrote a scrip, tore it from his pad. He held it up with his forefinger and thumb. "You'll get this after you pay at the front desk. Don't get it filled at Walgreens or Walmart or Target or any supermarket, you hear? Go to one of these." He handed Shane a list of pharmacies Shane had never heard of.

Duchamp reached into his pocket and pulled out a dozen business cards.

"Write your name on these and give them to people who are, um, *in need* of Oxy. If any of them come in and give me one of these cards, you'll get an extra twenty pills for free next time you're in."

Shane nodded. He had no intention of coming back. He just needed to get through the next few days – days he dreaded and couldn't imagine but had to push through nonetheless.

Duchamp reached out and shook Shane's hand. "It's been a pleasure."

Chapter 20

Shane shook two Oxys from the bottle and tossed them back, chewing instead of swallowing. They numbed him just enough that he could make it through watching his wife's coffin being lowered into the ground. The pills made him feel as though he were floating from one horrific scene to the next. A pleasant emptiness washed over him in waves. To friends and family members, he probably looked numbed or in shock, appropriate reactions to what was happening.

That night, Shane considered swallowing all the pills in the bottle. There were at least fifty Oxys. He poured them out onto the kitchen table and spread them apart with his hand. He wanted to take all of them but didn't have the courage. Instead, he chewed up two more.

The next day, he took three Oxys. Instead of chewing them, he used Cheryl's pestle and mortar to grind them up, the same pestle and mortar she had used to make curries for Thai and Indian food. Shane ground the pills into dust and then snorted them off the chopping block.

How many more pills did he have? Forty, give or take?

Okay, okay, he thought. I'll stop when I finish this bottle.

It was like every other compulsion he had experienced. It would run its course, and then he would move on to something new. That's what he believed. And so when he ran out of pills, he told himself to buck up and deal with it, but he couldn't focus at work.

"Did you hear what I just said?" a patient asked one day, sitting in the armchair across from him.

Shane nodded. He hadn't heard. He'd gone back to work too soon, thinking the distraction would be good for him, but he couldn't stop thinking about his wife in the ground. He kept having nightmares that she had woken up in the coffin only to discover that she had been buried alive. When he wasn't distracting himself with some kind of horror scenario that involved Cheryl, he obsessively thought about getting more pills.

"What did I say?" the patient asked, quizzing him. He was a truck driver, an addict, who was experiencing a depression out of which he didn't think he could escape. His name was Bill Boltz. He had introduced himself as *Bill Boltz, like nuts and bolts, except with a z.*

Shane shook his head. "I'm sorry," he said. "My wife died last week."

"Oh, man, I'm sorry," Bill said.

Shane stared vacantly above Bill's head, unable to meet the man's eyes.

Bill leaned forward and took hold of Shane's hands.

"What're you taking?" he asked.

"Nothing," Shane said. He shook his head.

"I'm a fucking addict, asshole," Bill said. "Don't shit a shitter. What're you taking, man?"

Shane jerked his hands away and stood. He walked behind his desk and flipped through his calendar.

"I think we should reschedule," Shane said.

Bill said, "Nah, it's good."

"What do you mean?"

Bill hoisted himself from his chair and said, "I think you know what I mean." He sighed. "Look, it's nothing personal. I like you. But you're just not in a good position right now to help me."

Shane cocked his head, trying to convey that he didn't have any idea what Bill was talking about. But he *did* know.

After Bill left, Shane leaned back in his chair and listened to the sound of his breath. He had never felt so much relief at a client leaving.

Bill had been the last appointment before lunch, so Shane cancelled the rest of the day's clients. He didn't want to be there. He didn't want to be home, either. Too many reminders of Cheryl. Since her death, he had been sleeping on the couch, avoiding the bedroom.

His office was a two-man practice: on one side was his office, and on the other side was Dr. Gus Fellowes's office. As a therapist, Shane couldn't prescribe drugs, but Gus could. He was a psychiatrist. And drug reps were always shuffling in with samples.

The office had shut down for lunchtime. The receptionist locked the door on her way to Chick-fil-A. The building was a no-nonsense structure built in 1957. It still had the original water fountain. The bathroom had silver stall dividers dulled by age. Shane didn't want to replace any of it because of how well it unlocked his clients' memories, reminding so many of their own grammar schools. For many, walking into the building was like stepping inside a snow globe of their own past. No amount of therapy could unlock the past as easily.

Shane walked to the rear exit and opened the door: Gus's car was gone. He owned a Maserati Quattroporte with the vanity license plate: T RX. Next to Gus's empty parking space sat Shane's car, a Nissan Altima.

Shane walked back to Gus's office and tried the doorknob. It was unlocked.

He stepped in and looked around. On the desk sat his prescription pad. The pad pulsed like a beating heart, but it was just Shane's eyes throbbing from the speed of his pulse. He scanned the room for samples. He just wanted a few Oxys to take the edge off.

"Need something?"

Shane spun around. It was Gus's assistant nurse.

"I'm just…" He was just *what?* "Ah, hell, you caught me!" Shane said and laughed. "I was going to steal his copy of the DSM for a few hours."

The nurse, whose name was Rachael, motioned for him to follow her. Shane obeyed. She shut and locked the doctor's door and then led Shane to a small consultation room with a bookcase. She pulled the thick book from the shelf and handed it to him.

"Don't forget to bring it back," Rachael said.

"Of course." Shane carried the book back to his office. On the way, he opened it up and pretended to search for something, but the words were mysterious hieroglyphics, and his heart pounded from the suspicion he had raised.

He cancelled his afternoon appointments and went for a drive, but his destination was already predetermined: Duchamp's.

There were even more people waiting in the parking lot. A woman confided to him that she'd been waiting for thirty hours already. Furthermore, there was a security guard – an off-duty cop – to make sure the clients remained civil. Shane was embarrassed that he had to be here among junkies since his needs were for a different reason. Grief management.

"Hey you!" It was Kylie from Walgreens. "You made it!" she said.

"Second time," Shane said.

"How's your wife?" Kylie asked. "I hope the pills helped."

"She…" Shane couldn't bring himself to say the words aloud.

Kylie stared at him, confused.

"She died," Shane said.

"Oh no," she said. "Fuck! I'm so sorry."

Shane rubbed his hand over his face.

"Here," Kylie said and shook a pill from the bottle. She handed it to him. "You're looking a little rough. You can pay me back later."

"Thank you. You have no idea how much I need this."

"Plus the ones for your wife."

"What?"

"You can pay me back later. This one plus the ones for your wife. No hurry."

Shane didn't say anything. Was she serious?

"You want a tip?" Kylie asked.

Shane waited.

"Start giving out those business cards he gave you. You get enough people to come here, he'll put you on a list. Once that happens, you just go to the security guard, and he'll take you straight to the receptionist. None of this camping out in the parking lot bullshit. The more clients you get him, the sooner he'll see you. I'm on the VIP list." She grinned. She was missing an incisor.

"That's good to know," Shane said.

"See?" Kylie said. "I'm your friend." She stepped closer and said, "Resistance is futile."

Chapter 21

Shane and Kylie began meeting up at Duchamp's office together, first as friends – but then they started driving to Shane's house afterward to hang out. Sometimes they had sex, but it felt more like a way to pass time than anything intimate.

"You loved her," Kylie said one afternoon as she lay in bed naked, shaking four Oxys from the bottle onto her palm. She gave two to Shane. The other two she stared at in her palm, as though they were objects with magical powers. Which, Shane supposed, they were.

"How did you meet?" Kylie asked.

"In college. Film Arts class. We sat near each other."

"What are the odds that your soulmate just sits down near you?"

Shane couldn't tell if she was serious or screwing with him.

"Film Arts. So…did you want to be a director?" Kylie asked.

"No," Shane said. "I wanted to be an actor. I was in plays in high school. Read about Stanislavski's methods. Read his essays. I really wanted to study at Lee Strasberg's school in New York. If you wanted to learn method acting, that was the place."

"So what happened? Didn't work out?"

"I gave it up," Shane said. "It was just a silly dream."

"I like older men," Kylie said. "By the time they get to me, the worse is already behind them."

“Can you promise me that?” Shane asked.

“I promise nothing.”

He reached over, removed the two remaining pills from her palm, and took them, too.

Chapter 22

Shane had been a psychologist for over twenty years, but he was starting to wonder if he had ever done anyone any good. Even before his wife died, he had begun feeling as interchangeable as a postal carrier. When he was an undergraduate, his interest in psychotherapy had been sparked by a short passage about the Scottish psychoanalyst R. D. Laing in a psychology textbook: "We are all murderers and prostitutes – no matter to what culture, society, class, nation, we belong, no matter how normal, moral, or mature, we take ourselves to be." Laing treated mental distress as a journey, often transformative, full of insights deeper than anything a prescription drug or treatment could offer. Shane was especially fascinated by Laing's community project where patients and therapists lived together. How better to understand a patient than to tear down the wall between them?

Shane hadn't given much thought to Laing in years, but what if Laing was right? What if Shane had become just another drive-thru therapist, offering the same menu of unhealthy crap as every other therapist?

"You okay?"

Shane opened his eyes. He'd been drifting on a raft of ideas about R. D. Laing, starting to fall asleep.

Dr. Gus Fellowes stood in the doorway.

"Yeah," Shane said. "Yeah-yeah. Just…long day."

Gus said, "Well, don't mind me. I just came to get that right there." He pointed at the DSM on Shane's desk and began walking toward it, but then he noticed a pill bottle on Shane's desk. He picked it up and read the prescription.

"Whoa," he said. "These yours?"

"Back injury," Shane said, straightening up, trying to wake more fully.

"Eighty milligrams?" Gus said. He looked up from the bottle. "Who's your doctor? You really shouldn't be taking that much."

"Really?" Shane said. "Hm. That's what he prescribed for it."

"God, no." Gus read the label more closely. "Duchamp? Is he an orthopedist? Never heard of him."

"I think he's new to the area," Shane said. "I was just following his orders. But maybe that's why I'm so, I don't know, out of it all the time."

Was he sounding convincing? Could Gus see through his bullshit?

Gus nodded. Set the pill bottle back down. "Seriously," Gus said. "There are other medications you can take. You probably should see someone other than this Duchamp guy. If you need a referral, let me know."

Shane nodded. "Will do."

Gus looked around. The room was darker than usual. Just a desk lamp.

"I'll let you get back at it. Saw a whole bunch of clients out there waiting for you."

"Always busy," Shane said and forced a smile.

The first client who came in had lost his job due to an injury. He had a long red beard and thick red eyebrows, and he wore a cap with a sewn-on patch advertising a seed company. His name was Cole.

"In the seed business?" Shane asked.

Cole looked confused. Shane remembered now. He'd seen him before. A gambling addict. The injury was a new development.

"Dude. I just got done saying I spent twenty-five years working IT."

"Oh yeah," Shane said. "Sorry." It was coming to him now: the injury.

"How are you dealing with the pain?"

Shane leaned back in his chair. "Not well."

"I know a doctor you should see," Shane said. He opened his desk drawer and pulled out a business card. He wrote his own name on it and then handed it over.

Cole studied the card. "Duchamp? What kind of doctor is he?"

"Pain management. If you go there, just hand them this card. It's a referral. You'll get right in."

Cole looked up from the card. "He's good? This Duchamp?"

"Best I've seen," Shane said.

On his way home, Shane stopped off at one of the mom and pop pharmacies on Duchamp's list to get his own prescription filled. It was the sort of place that depressed the hell out of Shane but that his wife Cheryl would have loved. She had loved businesses that existed out of time, sealed in amber, left behind. The pharmacy, dusty and dimly lit, was full of crutches and walkers and leg braces and toilet seats, none of which looked particularly new. Boxes for humidifiers had turned brown with age. A rotating rack for paperback books held a few Louis L'Amour novels, a Jacqueline Susann novel, and a dozen

Harlequin Romances from another decade. All of it brought on an unexpected melancholy that settled deep in Shane's chest. He was afraid he might start crying.

Shane's hands shook as he turned over the prescription.

An old pharmacist looked at the prescription, looked up at Shane over his half-glasses, and then looked back down at the prescription.

Shane knew the man was judging him, but he also knew that the man probably needed to fill these prescriptions to stay in business. How else could he compete with Target or Walmart?

Shane spun the rotating book rack with a finger as he waited for the old man to unlock a cabinet that held the Oxy. The pharmacist ran his fingers across the labels of several bottles until he landed on the one with the correct quantity and milligrams. He locked the cabinet and brought the bottle to the cash register, where he bagged it, stapled the top of the bag, and then rang it up.

Outside, Shane ripped open the bag, pulled out the bottle, opened it, jammed his thumb through the seal, and shook a few into his mouth as cars rolled by and the world continued to spin with or without him. He could breathe again.

Chapter 23

Kylie called Shane at work.

"I'm out of Roxy, and my car isn't starting," she said. "I need to get to Duchamp's."

"I'm at work," Shane said. "Call Uber."

"Don't be a dick," she said. "Come and get me."

"I told you, I'm at work."

"Stop it," she said. "You can leave. You can do whatever you want."

"I can't. I have to hang up now. Okay?"

When Kylie said nothing, Shane hung up.

Two minutes later, Shane's assistant poked her head into his office and told him that he had a call.

"She says it's urgent," the assistant said. His assistant's name was Rose, and lately Shane felt an air of judgement emanating from her. "I think it's the same woman who just called."

"It is," Shane said. "You can put her though."

"You sure?"

Shane nodded.

"You want the lights on?" Rose asked, looking around the office.

Shane shook his head. Rose left, shutting the door behind her.

Shane picked up the phone, punched a red button, and said, "You can't fucking do this."

"Look," Kylie. "I helped you when your wife was dying. The least you can do is help me."

Shane felt his heart starting to pound harder. Really? That's where she was going to take this? To his dying wife?

"Okay. All right," Shane said.

"I'll be out front," she said. "We need to hurry. I'm going to tear my skin off. Seriously."

Ten minutes later, Shane pulled up and Kylie got inside. Her arms appeared clawed, like she really had tried tearing off the skin.

The entire way to the clinic, Kylie talked but Shane disassociated. He was afraid if she mentioned his wife again, he'd do something terrible to her. He was no longer sure what he was capable of.

The clinic parking lot had only a few stragglers.

"No!" Kylie said. "No, no!" She opened the door while Shane's car was still in motion.

"Jesus, hold on," Shane said, hitting the breaks.

Kylie jumped out and ran to the entrance. Shane watched her jerk the door to no effect. She wheeled around and began yelling at one of the stragglers, who told her to go fuck herself.

Shane got out of his car and tried to restrain Kylie, who pushed him away.

"They got fucking raided! DEA or FBI or some shit. God…DAMN it."

"Easy," Shane said. "We'll figure this out."

"You got any pills left?"

Shane did, but he wasn't going to part with them.

"No," he said. "We're in the same boat."

"Are we? Are we really?"

Kylie eyed him as though she didn't believe him. She took out her phone and began making calls.

One straggler watching from a distance said to Shane, "Bitch is *crazy!*"

Something about the way the man said what he'd said caused Shane to see this moment objectively, as though in a museum: a life-sized diorama for future children to observe. And then he imagined Cheryl glimpsing Shane's future without him, wondering how it had come to this.

"We need to go to Breaux Bridge," Kylie said. "I'll give you directions."

Shane tried holding onto the image of Cheryl, but it was out of grasp now. Gone.

"Okay," Shane said.

Chapter 24

Kylie led Shane to an abandoned gas station. He pulled around back, where there was a door to enter the service area of the building, where cars once rose into the air on hydraulic pillars and men wore blue jumpsuits and drank Pepsi Cola from the bottle. The gas station's façade was made of large, white porcelain panels.

"He's inside," Kylie said.

"Who?"

Kylie got out of the car before answering. Shane parked quickly to join her.

Kylie knocked on the door, and a man opened, looked around, and then motioned for them to come in.

"This is him?" the man asked, motioning with his head toward Shane.

Shane cut his eyes from the man to Kylie. What had she told him?

"We just need some Oxy," Shane said, "and we'll be on our way."

Even in the station's limited light, Shane was struck by how self-assured the man was. He had piercing eyes and a thick beard.

"Oxy?" he said to Kylie.

"I didn't tell him," Kylie said.

"Tell me what?" Shane asked.

"It's not Oxy," Kylie said.

The man walked over to one of the counters, where a leather shaving kit sat. He unzipped it and pulled out a bag of powder.

"What's that?" Shane asked Kylie. "Cocaine?"

"No," she said. "Not cocaine."

The man removed a spoon and a lighter. He handed the spoon to Kylie.

"Are your hands steady?" he asked.

"Fuck," Shane said. "*Heroin?*"

"Bingo," the man said. He scooped out the heroin from the baggie and placed it on the spoon, and then he lit the spoon.

Shane watched the powder liquefy. And then he watched the man insert what looked like a small cotton ball onto the spoon before placing a needle into ball and, pulling back the plunger, filling the syringe with the liquid. He shook the syringe and tapped it with his fingernail, then pushed the plunger forward.

"I need some money," the man said.

Kylie looked at Shane.

"Are you serious?" Shane asked.

"It's cheaper than Oxy," Kylie said.

"That's not what I mean," Shane said.

He waited for Kylie to say more, but she didn't. He sighed, removed his wallet, and asked, "How much?"

"Twenty."

Through the garage door's windows, he saw the parking lot of a convenience store across the street. He thought he recognized a man in the parking lot. A client.

Shane handed the bearded man a twenty dollar bill.

Kylie moved to a couch that sat against a wall. There were still old fuse boxes on the floor, jars of Goop to clean grease, spark plugs.

Shane watched the man take hold of Kylie's arm, searching for a thick vein.

Kylie said to Shane, "Don't watch."

"Why?"

"It's private," she said.

Shane turned and looked out the window again, waiting for his client to emerge from the convenience store, but he didn't.

"Your turn," Kylie said, her eyes barely open. She was high now.

"Nah, I'm good."

"Really?"

"Really."

"Go on home then," Kylie said. "I'll be fine."

"And how the hell are you going to get home?"

"He'll drive me," she said, motioning toward the man.

To Shane, the man said, "I don't use."

"Hm," Shane said, not without judgment.

"We go *way* back," Kylie said and laughed. "Trust me. I'm safe."

Are you? Shane thought. *Safe?*

Chapter 25

Shane pulled across the road and parked in the convenience store parking lot. Attached to the store was a casino. This explained Cole's presence.

When Shane stepped inside, he saw Cole seated at one of the two tables near the fried chicken counter. He was sipping coffee, a scroll of scratch-offs in front of him.

Cole adjusted his seed cap. Did he say he worked in IT? Shane couldn't remember. What he *did* remember was giving him Duchamp's card.

Cole had initially come to Shane because he was a compulsive gambler – video poker and scratch-offs, mostly – but the last few times he'd come to see Shane, Shane had had a hard time concentrating. Instead of probing deeper, he asked Cole questions he could have asked anyone about any subject. *How does gambling make you feel? What impact is it having on your life? What kind of relationship did you have with your father?*

What good had Shane done this guy? None. And the truth was never clearer than now.

"Cole?"

Cole looked up. "Doc?"

"I'm not actually a doctor."

"You're not?" He seemed genuinely surprised to learn this.

Shane shook his head. "I'm not a psychiatrist."

Cole just stared at him. Then he broke into a smile and said, "Just fucking with you, doc."

Shane forced a smile. "So…what's going on tonight?"

"What do you mean? Am I in trouble?"

"Nah. I just meant…what are your plans?"

"My plans?"

"Yeah. Were you planning to gamble tonight?"

Cole shrugged. "Already started." He motioned to the scratch-offs. "What's going on? You following me?"

"No, just happened to see you." He motioned with his head to a door beside the cash register area. "What's next door?" Shane asked.

"Video poker."

"Well," Shane said. "What're you waiting for?"

Cole cocked his head at Shane. "You okay?"

Shane leaned forward and placed his hands on the table. He said, "I feel like everything up until now has been bullshit. I've been wasting your money. I need to take this journey with you. So here's what I'm willing to do. I'll front you tonight. We're going to push it, as far as you can take it."

Cole considered the offer. "Like giving a kid a pack of cigarettes to cure him of smoking."

"Sort of," Shane said. "But I'll be right there with you. Each time you put down a bet, I'll put one down, too."

"Damn," Cole said. "You off your meds?"

Shane shook his head. He was grinning now, probably looking manic.

Cole finally reached out to shake Shane's hand. "Fuck yeah," he said. "Let's do it."

Cole pushed himself up from his chair and started heading toward the door for the casino.

"Not here," Shane said. "Lake Charles. I'll drive."

"Oh, you're *serious*."

"Leave your car here. We'll get it afterward."

On his way to the parking lot, Shane found the two Oxys he'd stashed in his wallet and swallowed them dry.

R. D. Laing had said, "Experience is the only evidence." And Shane needed that experience to do his job. Laing had been right when he said that we were all murderers and prostitutes.

Well, Shane thought, *we're all gamblers, too*

An hour and change away, Lake Charles was where the casinos were, like Golden Nugget and L'Auberge. The way Shane saw it, Cole needed Shane there. His patient was swimming out into deeper waters, and Shane was the only one with a life preserver. But in order to save him, Shane needed to try to kill him. Wasn't that how it always was? Arsenic was the cure for heartworms. Mercury was the cure for syphilis.

For a city known for its gambling, Lake Charles was probably the unluckiest city in Louisiana. Plans for a new naval station with a fleet of six hundred ships was scrapped after the end of the Cold War. The city was assaulted by a hurricane in 2005, and then two more in 2020, topped off by yet another in 2021. There were only so many times a city could fall to its knees and then stand back up.

The casinos were the city's only beacon of hope.

The night began at the blackjack table in the high-limit room, hour after hour of dealt cards, most of them under the dealer or bust. The losses came fast and hard. Shane was blurry eyed by three in the morning, barely able to add up his hand.

"I'll be at the roulette table," Shane told Cole.

"I'm running low," Cole whispered to Shane.

"I'll bring more chips," Shane said. "Hold tight."

Shane had already taken out the maximum amount from the casino's ATM. He'd gotten a cash advance from his credit card, too, the equivalent of what he had remaining in his savings.

At the roulette table, Shane placed chips on red 19, over and over. He committed to it. Even after losing ten thousand dollars in fifteen minutes, he knew with each loss that his odds to win were increasing. It was simple math. Where people went wrong was shuffling money around the board. No, just make a commitment and stick with it.

When Shane placed another thousand in chips on red 19, the croupier said, "Again!"

"Ride or die, baby!" Shane said, grinning.

The croupier spun the roulette wheel and then spun the ball in the track. This was the moment when Shane could feel adrenaline running like ice through his veins. This sensation, along with the possibility of winning, was why he risked losing a thousand dollars, over and over.

When the ball finally settled into black 22's pocket, Shane felt a momentary urge to cry. Because he had crossed a line. Because he knew he was too far in now to stop. They called roulette the devil's game because when you added up all the numbers, the total came to 666, and there was no reason to believe the devil wasn't watching and laughing right now.

At one point, to no one, Shane said, "Where's this going?"

He looked across the room at the blackjack table but didn't see Cole.

He didn't want to leave the roulette table because he knew the second he didn't place a bet would be when the ball landed on red 19. But, as Cole's therapist, he had an ethical responsibility for his patient's safety.

"Sir?"

Shane jolted upright. "What?"

"You can't sleep at the table." It was the croupier looking with concern at Shane. He cut his eyes toward someone across the room. Shane groggily looked over, saw two security men, and then looked back at the croupier.

"I'm good," Shane said.

When the croupier spun the wheel, Shane gathered his few chips and walked away. He looked around the room but still…no Cole.

After circling the casino several times, Shane went out to the parking lot. He called out, "Cole! Cole!"

And then he found him, hunched over near the trunk of a car, vomiting.

"You okay?" Shane asked.

"Where were you? Where'd you go?"

"I got distracted," Shane said.

"Did you get more chips?"

"Bit of a cash flow problem," Shane said. His heart was thumping. He was feeling the anxiety that Cole felt. This was why he was doing this. To step into Cole's life. His *skin.* To fully understand what troubled the man. It was like poking around under the hood of a car whose engine grinded when you turned the key but wouldn't start. R. D. Laing would have been proud.

"I can't think," Cole said. "I can't get my thoughts to slow down."

"Yes you can," Shane said, crouching next to him and putting his arm over his shoulders. "Trust me, you can."

Shane thought of his own father's late-in-life hoarding, how there came a point when the old man must have felt his life slipping beyond his control, how he must have reached a point of knowing he would never have control again unless he burned it all down and started over.

"I know where we can go," Shane said.

Cole nodded.

"Okay," he said. "All right."

An hour later, Shane was pulling behind the decrepit gas station with the large, white porcelain panels.

"What's this?" Cole asked.

"You need something to take the edge off," Shane said. "You need some medicine."

The two men made their way to the service area's back door. Shane knocked.

The man with the piercing eyes and thick beard answered. He stared at them a moment and then stepped aside to let them in.

Kylie was passed out on a decrepit couch.

"She okay?" Shane asked.

"She's in a good place," the man said.

"I need you to set my friend up," Shane said.

"And you?"

Shane hesitated. He thought of his empty bank account. He thought of where his mind had gone tonight, the place where his father sat waiting for him, surrounded by empty soda cups and used straws and random bricks of Styrofoam and empty pill bottles and cellophane-wrapped snacks from years ago. This was never about Cole. This was about trying to understand his own father.

The revelation was a punch to the center of his chest. His lungs felt expired of air.

"Yeah. Me, too," Shane said.

There was another couch, a smaller couch, that the bearded man motioned toward. Shane and Cole obeyed.

"Money first," the man said.

"Right," Shane said and removed his wallet. He handed over enough for the two of them.

"Who first?"

"You go," Cole said.

Across the room, Kylie moaned and repositioned herself.

"You sure she's okay?" Shane asked.

The man said nothing. He tapped heroin out onto the spoon and then lit the spoon. Shane watched the flame, mesmerized, hypnotized.

Within minutes, Shane was floating as he watched what had just happened to him happen to Cole, and he felt at one with his client. Cole was him, and he was Cole. It was a breakthrough in their sessions – sessions that, until tonight, had been going nowhere.

To the bearded man, he said, "I didn't catch your name."

"I didn't throw it," he said.

Good one, Shane thought, shutting his eyes and smiling. He could feel himself being pulled under, and there was nothing, not a damned thing, he could do about it.

Chapter 26

Year One in the Manila detention center, Shane spent most of his days feeling sorry for himself, wondering how one man could have had such unrelenting bad luck. He was also afraid for his life every second of every day. He was afraid to ask the guards for anything because asking usually resulted in harsher punishments, more duties, or verbal abuse. He wondered if anyone on the outside was trying to help him. He wondered why Corbett hadn't traveled to the Philippines to work with the U.S. Embassy on his release. Or maybe he had but no one had told Shane. He wondered what had become of his cat, Larry, and what his sitter, Alyssa, must have thought of him. He spent a lot of time worrying about things that were trivial, but he didn't know yet that they were trivial.

Year Two, Shane spent every moment trying to figure out how he'd ended up in the detention center. Hanh had turned him in, obviously. And she was surely associated with the Vietnamese men back in Abbeville, who produced the fake commercial. The three of them had set him up. This wasn't an amateur operation. There was a genius at the helm. As much as Shane resisted it, all roads led to Corbett since Corbett was the one who had recruited the men in Abbeville, since Corbett was the one who had sent Shane to Manila.

Shane's obsession with piecing together the plot had distracted him from the very real dangers around him. After a minor incident over food, Shane lost his eye in a fight that involved another detainee shoving a spoon into the lower outer corner of his eye while four men held him down. He heard the spoon enter, the nauseating sound of a plunger at work, followed by Shane's own squeals of horror and pain before he went into shock.

Year Three, Shane was denied surgery for a basal cell carcinoma that was growing on his temple, the same place where he'd already had a much smaller pea-sized lump removed. The new lump was the size of an acorn. It was ugly and foreboding, but it also earned him some respect with the other detainees. Perhaps they were afraid of what it portended, the way still air and a noiseless sky sometimes portended the arrival of a tornado that would lift an entire city, spin it around in the air, and then drop whatever was left of it.

Year Four, Shane trained with the Sigue Sigue Sputnik gang. One of their members, a young man named Ethan, remembered Shane from the day Shane had visited Tondo. Shane had spent the day drinking Red Horse with the gang member's grandfather, Shane had shown the old man respect and kindness, and so Ethan offered Shane the gang's protection. In time, Shane became the gang's personal experiment. Could they turn a scrawny, old white guy into a killing machine?

Shane accepted the challenge.

He allowed Ethan and the others to push him to limits of his physical capabilities – and then he let them push him some more. In only a few months, Shane was all muscle, no body fat, and he had a face that other detainees, especially new detainees, avoided looking at for fear of a confrontation. With a skull-thin face, a mysterious growth, and only one eye, Shane wasn't anyone you'd want to fuck with. He also let a man named Alon tattoo him.

Alon had made his own tattoo devise using an electric razor, a battery, a sewing kit, a lighter, a toothbrush, and a razor – and with this primitive device, Alon covered Shane's arms and chest with elaborate images Shane described to him.

To celebrate Shane's induction into the gang as an honorary member, the Sigue Sigue Sputnik boys found the man who had removed Shane's eye and, using only their thick and dirty fingers, removed both of the perpetrator's eyes. Afterward, Ethan found Shane sitting alone on the floor, meditating, and he held out his fist for Shane. Shane fist-bumped Ethan, and then Ethan opened his fist, revealing the two freshly-removed eyes.

"Take them," Ethan said.

Shane held out his hand and accepted them. Only a few years ago, Shane would have felt horror at the sight of the eyes and unfathomable guilt at the pain that the gang had inflicted on this man. He would have worried about retribution. But today? He felt nothing. He felt no pity for the man to whom the eyes belonged. And he'd been in more fights than he could count – dozens of assaults to his person, including sexual assaults at night while his cellmates feigned annoyance instead of outrage. Fear, Shane had learned, had become a useless response.

Throughout the detention center, there were drains for the water run-off from typhoons. On his way to eat, Shane dropped the two eyes into one of the drains and kept walking. The eyes would likely make their way to Manila Bay, only to be nibbled on by a school of milkfish, whose fate would be a bed of ice in a wet market, only to be sold, marinated, fried, and served with longanisa sausage, scrambled eggs, and garlic rice – a fine breakfast for a man whose only reprieve between home and work was this moment right here, his few deep breaths of solitude, thankful that he could provide for his family, followed by a prayer for the dead.

On the third month and fifth day of Year Five, with no prior warning, Shane Doyle was processed and released. He had made it out. Like fucking Lazarus, he thought as he stepped out of the detention center. He'd risen from the ashes. He was alive! And he was going to find the motherfuckers who had put him here, even if doing so killed him.

PART THREE

Chapter 27

Shane Doyle was sixty years old when he was released from the detention center. The case against him never even made it to trial.

An official from the American Embassy was waiting for Shane to take him to a hotel in Manila for the night before driving him to the airport in the morning for a flight back to Louisiana.

The official, who had probably seen only older photos of Shane, winced at the sight of him. He introduced himself to Shane as Henry.

"You can sit up front," Henry said, but Shane ignored him and slid into the backseat. "Okay then," Henry said, shutting the door.

Henry jogged around the car and got into the driver's seat.

"You okay back there?" he asked.

"I'm fine," Shane said.

"Let me know if it gets too cold."

"I haven't felt cool air in five years," Shane said.

Henry said nothing.

From his window Shane watched people going about their business – driving, walking, laughing, singing. He couldn't have explained what was running through his mind if he tried. In part, it was the realization of how the world had continued on without him. For all intents and purposes, Shane had ceased to exist. In part, it was how his own world had shrunk to the size of the detention center, and how all of his daily concerns involved the other detainees and the guards, along with whatever diseases ran rampant, the fights he tried to avoid, the rats that were always there in the kitchen: Shane's world had tightened into a fist.

At a stop light, Henry handed Shane an envelope.

"What's this?"

"Two thousand in cash," Henry said. "To help get you back on your feet."

"Two grand?" Shane laughed through his nose. What did that come out to? About a dollar a day?

"It's not much," Henry said, "but…"

He let the word linger.

Shane said, "Why was I released? Did Phil Corbett have anything to do with it?"

"Who?"

"Phil Corbett. My business partner."

"No. Wasn't him. Remember a man named Luke Bradfield?"

"No."

"Expat living in Dumaguete? Retired cop?"

Shane shook his head.

"Apparently, he sat next to you on the final leg of your flight."

Oh shit. Shane did remember now.

"You have *got* to be kidding. He contacted you?"

"He saw the story in the news right after you were arrested," Henry said. "Remembered talking to you. He got in touch with the Embassy. It was only because of his persistence that the Embassy pursued the matter."

Shane pulled his wallet from his back pocket and searched inside. Sure enough, the cop's napkin was still there: Luke Bradfield, his email, his WhatsApp phone number, and his local number. Son of a bitch!

Several miles later, Henry said, "Your first flight is at one a.m. I'm thinking we should get to the airport no later than eleven."

"Okay. Hey. You guys ever find the woman who came with me to the airport? Hanh?"

"No," Henry said. "We didn't."

"Are you still looking?"

Henry said, "Someone is, I'm sure."

"But you don't know for certain."

"No," Henry said. "It's a cold trail."

"I'm sure it is."

Henry said, "I bet you'll be happy to get the hell out of the Philippines."

Henry was looking in the rearview mirror at Shane. Shane nodded.

"You can say that again, brother," Shane said.

Chapter 28

In his hotel room, Shane took a hot bath – the first time he'd been in an actual tub in over five years. With his toes, he kept adding more hot water each time the water became tepid. He sat in the tub for an hour. And then he started crying.

He let go, crying as loud and hard as a child. He was aware of the sounds he was making, the bathroom's tile walls echoing, the noises like an animal he'd never before encountered.

He never thought he'd be free again. Each day in that place had been like a year of torture. He was always looking behind him, always unsure who he could trust, his trial date a distant mirage.

Shane let himself cry in the tub because he knew he was never going to cry again. This was it, he told himself. Get it out now and then move on.

When he stopped crying and stood from the tub, he felt renewed as the water dripped from him. He felt baptised. He moved slowly, arthritically, careful to raise his leg high enough to clear the tub's edge. He toweled himself off. He looked at his naked self in the bathroom mirror and, in this new context, under soft, pleasant lighting, didn't recognize himself. The tattoos, swirling from one image into another, were a personal journal: chess pieces, a globe of the world hoisted by fingertips, an eye with a razor held up to it, the shadow of a hand, the head of a female robot, a scorpion, a cowboy riding a bomb, an old bicycle – a hallucinatory churning of memories. All told, there were seventy-five tattoos, seventy-five memories.

Shane looked twenty years older than when he entered the facility. He was unrecognizable with the missing eye and the growing tumor. The years between fifty-five and sixty were often cruel under the best of circumstances, but these five had shaved off an indeterminate number of future years.

His phone was still miraculously capable of charging after five years. He checked his bank balance. He still had a few thousand and change in savings. His mortgage bill had been on autopay, so it was possible he still had a house. His checking account had long been closed, likely from lack of funds thanks to IRS seizures. His Apple credit card had automatically renewed and was stored on his phone, paying his monthly phone bill, which, in turn, was paid by his bank. His passport, mercifully, was still valid.

Shane didn't have much by way of resources to work with, but he had enough.

He would need new clothes; he would need a backpack for traveling light. His luggage, tagged for Hong Kong, was never returned.

Shane got dressed. He ordered a Grab for the airport.

When he opened his room's door, he made sure Henry from the Embassy wasn't in the hallway.

By the time Shane took the elevator down to lobby and stepped outside, a car was already waiting for him. The driver was probably Shane's age. According to the laminated ID hanging from his rearview mirror on a lanyard, his name was Manuel.

"Mind if I sit up front?" Shane asked.

Manuel studied Shane's face. The missing eye. The ominous lump. Then he glanced down at the tattoos on Shane's arm. Shane followed Manuel's gaze to one tattoo in particular, the one on his hand: a satellite with the word "Sputnik" arched over it. A gang tattoo. Above the tattoo was his wife's name. Cheryl.

Honor your loved ones. Remember the dead.

Manuel nodded. Shane slid in, shut the door.

"Airport?" Manuel asked.

"Airport," Shane said.

"Where are you going?"

"Anywhere but here," Shane said.

Manuel eased into traffic.

Shane took one last look at the hotel. A smarter man would have stayed. He would have stuck to the plan. But Shane couldn't. Across one of his ribs was tattooed "We are all murderers and prostitutes." R.D. Laing wasn't wrong. The thing was, most people didn't act on their impulses. They kept their cravings tamped down. Even as a child, Shane knew he wasn't *most people.*

The majority of the room lights in the hotel were off. Henry was probably sound asleep, silicone earplugs inserted and sleep mask on, dreaming about his beautiful life. And why shouldn't he? Shane almost envied the poor son of a bitch.

Chapter 29

Shane caught a late flight to Dumaguete-Sibulan Airport. In Dumaguete, he took a Grab to an Airbnb, where he slept restlessly, woke up too early, and paced his room until eight a.m. The entire night, he heard dogs barking, motorbikes, animals rustling through trash, and karaoke.

His first stop when he left his room was a local pharmacy, where he bought an eyepatch. Outside, he tore open the packaging and put it on. Using his phone's camera, he looked at himself. The patch covered the knot of scar tissue and a good amount of the tumor. No sense scaring the shit out of people from whom he needed answers.

Next, he started walking. Most businesses were still closed, but a few were open, like fruit stands, milk tea kiosks, and open air restaurants serving breakfast. The air smelled of grilled pork.

A young woman, tired or bored, stood in front of her empty restaurant, staring off into the faraway.

"Excuse me," Shane said, and the woman, trance broken, smiled at him. She wasn't fazed by his appearance. She started to get him a menu, assuming he was there to eat. Shane didn't have the heart to tell her that he had only wanted to ask her a question, so he followed her inside and took a seat. He felt something below the table touch his leg. It was an old matted dog attracting horse flies.

Shane ordered a bowl of lugaw, a kind of rice porridge. He was used to eating very little and probably wouldn't be able to finish an entire bowl of anything. How many times in the detention center had he been served rotten fish? There was a time someone found ground glass in the rice, scaring everyone off the most frequently served dish. Shane had trained himself to go days without eating.

When the food was served, Shane said, "Excuse me, but…is there an area where expats go? Is there a bar or a part of town?"

"Ground Zero," the server said.

"Ground Zero. What's that?"

"Restaurant. They sell coffee there. And western food." She looked down at his porridge. "Do you like it?"

"It's very good, yes," Shane said.

She smiled. "You like Filipino food?"

"I do," Shane said.

This made her happy. She was probably in her forties but looked like she had lived a hard life.

"Do you live here, or are you visiting?" she asked.

"I came here five years ago for work," Shane said, "and I never went home."

"Oh, you must like it!" she said.

Shane smiled and nodded. He wasn't going to tell her the truth.

When she left him alone, Shane ate a few more spoonfuls of porridge before calling it quits. He didn't want her to think he didn't like it, so he fed the rest of it to the dog that had been panting eagerly under his table. When the dog finished, he brought the bowl back up to the surface. The woman would be pleased to think that Shane himself had licked the bowl clean.

He left a good tip. He knew many expats railed against the whole concept of tipping, fearful that Filipinos would come to expect tips – but fuck those people. Shane had no patience anymore. What he felt inside him was a percolating rage. If anyone ever berated him about leaving a tip, he would likely knock the asshole to the ground and start kicking him repeatedly in the ribs.

This was the imaginary scenario Shane was unspooling in his head as he marched toward Ground Zero. He caught himself speaking out loud more than once, his anger at a situation that hadn't even occurred seeping out, his private thoughts verbalized.

Was he going crazy?

Was he already crazy?

He remembered clients who had said to him that when they went crazy they *knew* they had gone crazy but couldn't do anything about it. They were helpless in the face of something stronger than them.

Shane wasn't convinced he was crazy yet, but he knew that after spending five years where he had spent five years, he was no longer the Shane Doyle he had once been. This was a fact. The old Shane Doyle was dead. The new Shane Doyle was blinking his remaining eye in the morning's light, his eyepatch already collecting sweat from his forehead, the tumor pulsing and angry, blood running through his veins like gasoline: it wouldn't take much to go up in flames. All he needed was the right motherfucker to say the wrong thing to him. And a part of him welcomed it.

Chapter 30

Shane had not been steered wrong: Ground Zero was flush with expats.

He thought the sight of so many foreigners – Americans, Australians, Brits – would be comforting after five years of being surrounded by Filipinos, but he tensed up instead. They had lived their lives, oblivious to Shane's plight – all, that is, except for Luke Bradfield.

He hadn't texted or called Luke, hoping to see him in the flesh. He'd already imagined how it would play out: Shane would come upon him in Ground Zero and wait for the look of recognition; Luke, a large man, would slowly register who he was looking at and then, standing, grinning, maybe even crying, lock Shane in a bear hug; and Shane, willing himself to keep it together, would thank Luke in person for saving his life.

Shane approached the first table where a foreigner sat alone with a cup of coffee as he scrolled through his phone.

"Excuse me," Shane said. "Do you happen to know Luke Bradfield?"

The man peeked up over bifocals. He was clearly taken aback at the sight of Shane. Shane would have to get accustomed to this response. Even with the eyepatch, he was a fright to someone who wasn't expecting him.

"No, I'm sorry. I just got to town. Looking for a place to live," the man said.

Shane nodded and continued on to the next table. And the next.

When he approached a gathering of men – five of them, all in their sixties – Shane stepped up and made his inquiry.

The men regarded each other before a man with a white goatee cleared his throat and looked around. Voice low, he said, "You're not here to cause trouble for his family, are you?"

"God, no," Shane said. "No, no. He helped me out with something big. And I just came here to thank him."

"Sounds like Luke," the man said.

Another guy, bald and liver-spotted, said, "Hey, you're that guy. Shane Doyle. Right?"

Shane nodded.

The bald man said, "I saw you when you came in. Thought you looked familiar. But only in a vague kind of way."

Shane said, "So, you know what he did for me."

The goateed man said, "You haven't heard."

Shane waited.

"Luke died two weeks ago," the man said.

"Two weeks ago?"

The man nodded. "He was obsessed with your case. Kept a banker's box full of news articles, did his own research."

"What did he die of?" Shane asked.

The bald man said, "Heart attack. Happens to a lot of us. There used to be ten of us. The ranks are thinning."

One of the other three men, a man wearing a shirt that advertised Chang beer, said, "You've got a hell of a story. You want to sit down for an interview? We're vloggers."

The goateed man said, "We're kind of local celebrities."

All the men laughed at this. But it wasn't an ironic laugh. They were serious.

The Chang beer man said, "What do you say?"

Shane registered all the mini-tripods lying across the table, the iPhones, the chargers.

Shane said, "I'm sorry for your loss," and walked away.

Chapter 31

Shane found the house and knocked. It was a small house, nothing like the monstrosities that filled American neighborhoods.

A Filipina answered the door. She wasn't afraid or wary. She smiled and said hello. Her hair was pulled back, and her eyes were large and sad.

"My name is Shane Doyle," Shane said. "I met your husband once. I met Luke on a plane and…"

The woman's eyes widened. "Shane Doyle?"

"Yes."

"Please, please, come in. Come in."

Her name was Angel. Shane followed her into their house. The first thing he saw was a framed photo of Luke on a table with unlit candles surrounding it. He imagined the nightly ritual of lighting the candles, igniting the grief all over again. Nighttime was always the worst. The grieving hours.

"Sit, sit," Angel said. "Wait here."

She returned minutes later with a glass of murky liquid.

"Do you like buko juice? It was Luke's favorite."

"I do," Shane said. "Thank you."

He took a sip. It was coconut milk and sugar, way sweeter than his palette was accustomed to.

"I met your husband only once," Shane said.

"I know," Angel said, smiling. "He told me about meeting you. And when he saw your photo in the paper, he recognized you. He knew you were innocent."

"I owe him everything," Shane said. "I'm so sorry for your loss."

Angel said, "He called you his last big case." She got up and left the room, returning moments later with a banker's box. Shane could tell by her expression that the box was heavy, full of papers.

"Please, here," Shane said, standing and taking the box from her. He set it down on the floor. "May I?" he asked, and he removed the lid. It was filled to the top with news clippings, notes, letters.

"You should have it," Angel said.

Shane said nothing. He was mesmerized by its contents. Inside this box: his fate…but also the key to his freedom.

He wanted to start going through it right there, but out of respect he put the lid back on it and said, "Thank you." He looked over at Luke's photo. He hoped Shane's case had given meaning to the man's last five years instead of being a burden. "Where is he buried?" Shane asked.

"I'll take you," Angel said.

Shane didn't want to leave the banker's box behind – he had an irrational fear of someone taking it – but he had no choice as they were taking Angel's scooter. Shane would ride on the back of it.

The cemetery wasn't far away. The gates were still open when they arrived. Angel pulled slowly into the entrance. The grounds were clean, well-tended.

When Angel parked the scooter, Shane said, "I went to a cemetery in Manila where families live. When I was in the detention center, I heard stories from men who'd grown up there. Children playing in crypts. Mothers sleeping on their own child's tombs. I don't know, but I think that would have given me nightmares," Shane said.

Angel smiled. "You of all people should be afraid of the living, not the dead."

Shane couldn't disagree with her.

They walked down a long row of cemetery plots until they came upon Luke's. Angel crouched and brushed away fresh dirt that had blown onto the marble slab. He looked around, making sure he wasn't being followed.

"Was he Catholic?" Shane asked.

"He was. Are you?"

"I was raised Catholic," Shane said, "but…" He let the thought linger. He didn't want to be rude.

Angel moved from a crouch to her knees. She shut her eyes. Her lips moved as she prayed. And then she made the sign of the cross.

"Amen," Shane said.

"Amen," Angel said, holding out her hand for help.

Chapter 32

Shane half-expected his escort from the U.S. Embassy to be waiting for him at his Airbnb, but no one was there. The escort had been assigned to make sure Shane could safely leave the country without any snafus, but since Shane had chosen his own course of action, the Embassy probably cut bait on him. It wasn't as though Shane was a criminal. Not yet, at least.

In his room, Shane opened the bankers box and settled in for a long night, removing all the papers and sorting through them. When it got too muggy in the room in the early afternoon, Shane fetched himself a beer from the fridge and took off his shirt. He no longer recognized his own body – not just the tattoos or the scars but also the old-man skin itself, as translucent as wax paper.

Shane held the bottle to his forehead to cool down before continuing.

What Luke had pieced together was that the fraud Shane had been accused of committing was large in scope, much larger than Shane had thought. Tens of millions of dollars had disappeared. Maybe more. Wealthy businessmen, mostly in Southeast Asia, had lost everything overnight. The crime that Shane had been arrested for involved a man named Juan Ramos of Makati. He had walked into the middle of Makati's main street and shot himself in the head. He was the cabinet member's nephew, which, in turn, gave his suicide more exposure than many of the others.

A man in Chiang Mai, Thailand, poisoned himself.

A man in Ho Chi Minh City, Vietnam, jumped from the fifteenth floor of his condo.

There were other businessmen who died that week – all because their fortunes had disappeared overnight. Asia was a saving face culture, and losing that kind of generational wealth was likely more shame than a person could bear. There were thresholds to humiliation.

The most curious death was a man named Charlie Leung. He had traveled from his home in Hong Kong to Phnom Penh, Cambodia, where he was found dead in his hotel room. But he had not killed himself. He was murdered. And it appeared to have been some psychosexual murder, in which he was naked and tied to his bed. Security footage confirmed that he had been visited that night by a woman, most likely a prostitute, though she had disappeared after leaving the hotel. She had become a ghost.

Luke had begun a correspondence with Charlie's brother, Lei.

According to the letters, Lei moved from Hong Kong to Phnom Penh with the hope of finding the woman who had murdered his brother. Shane read the letters chronologically, and with each letter, Lei's cognitive abilities were increasingly impaired. It was some real *Flowers for Algernon* shit. The final letter read simply, "I just want someone to help me. Lei." It was as though someone had been slowly poisoning him.

I just want someone to help me.

Jesus.

Shane recognized his own desperation in this stranger's letter. How many times before Shane knew if anyone cared about his plight had he had the same thought?

And what was the coincidence that the same man was helping both of them?

The letter was dated two years ago.

Shane fell asleep that night sitting upright in an armchair, papers scattered around him. On an end-table sat five empty beer bottles. On his lap, a newspaper from Hong Kong with Charlie Leung's photo on it. He was smiling, and there were mountains in the background – happier days.

When Shane woke up the next morning, he ventured out to buy a backpack and a small carry-on duffel bag, a few T-shirts, and two pairs of cargo shorts. He bought underwear, a toothbrush, toothpaste, and deodorant.

Back in his room, he stuffed the contents of the banker's box into his carry-on and the rest of his belongings into the backpack.

Who was Charlie Leung? And why had a prostitute murdered him?

Unlike the other deaths, Charlie Leung's offered a mystery that might actually lead somewhere. Shane's flight wasn't until morning, so he spent the night, suitcase open, reading about Mr. Leung, trying to crawl inside his head, the way he would crawl inside his patients' heads, the way a method actor would crawl inside a character's head. Unlike the others who had died, Charlie had been born poor. He was the outlier.

While standing on a street corner, waiting for his Grab car, a white cat rubbed against his leg. His own cat Larry was surely dead by now. His cat sitter likely surrendered the old man to a shelter. It wasn't her responsibility, after all. He wouldn't blame her.

"Go," Shane said to the white cat rubbing against his ankle. "Go on now." When he nudged the cat away with his leg, the cat hissed and backed up.

The Grab driver arrived, and Shane slid into the backseat. He booked a flight to Phnom Penh through Manila. There were no direct flights.

Of all the horrific events in Shane's life these past five years, the thought of Larry dying alone in a shelter, unable to process why his life had come to this, was the thing Shane would never get over. There was no sin more painful than betrayal. Shane had come to this epiphany the hard way.

Chapter 33

All Shane knew about Phnom Penh and Cambodia was what he remembered from the news. Pol Pot. The Khmer Rouge. The Killing Fields. Genocide. It was a country that had had someone else's foot on its neck for centuries – until recently. He couldn't begin to imagine what that did to a people or how a country overcame such horrors.

At the Phnom Penh airport, the immigration officer placed a sticker-document across an entire passport page and then stamped half of another page. They weren't fucking around.

He exchanged some of his money to Cambodian riel, though he had learned on his layover that they used U.S. currency, too. He bought a SIM card for his phone.

Dozens of men competed for his attention, offering to give him a ride. "Where are you going, sir?" "This way! This way!" "You pick the price!"

Shane surveyed the crowd until he found the only man not making a pitch. He was standing in the back, smoking a cigarette.

"How much for a ride into the city?" Shane asked.

The man wrote a price onto a ticket: $12.

"Okay," Shane said.

"Where?" the taxi driver said, cigarette still in his mouth. "Show me." He pointed to Shane's phone.

Shane pulled up a map and showed him, and then the man started walking away, motioning for Shane to follow him. Shane was expecting a car, but the man took him to a tuk-tuk. It was old and long, plenty of room for several people and luggage, but there were no seatbelts, and Shane felt conspicuously exposed, despite fabric drooping over his head.

The driver weaved in and out of the thick, unruly traffic, occasionally driving in the break-down lane. More than once, motorcycles zipped up beside them, the rider looking in at Shane.

"Be careful," the tuk-tuk driver said. "Your phone."

"Gotcha," Shane said, tucking his phone out of sight. He kept his feet on the top of his carry-on and his backpack strapped to his back as he leaned forward to accommodate the cumbersome hump.

The smell of car exhaust was overwhelming, dizzying. The air shimmered from the fumes. The roads were pot-holed and ambiguously marked. People used sidewalks to park their cars and scooters.

When the tuk-tuk arrived at his condo and after Shane unloaded his duffel bag and backpack, he tried handing a few dollars to the driver for a tip. The driver shook his head and drove away. At first Shane thought his refusal was something about the culture that he didn't understand until he saw his own reflection in the condo building's front door.

In a country with a history of unthinkable atrocities, where landmines still maimed and killed civilians, the driver had taken pity on him.

Chapter 34

Shane ventured out into the night.

Phnom Penh felt like America's Wild West – a city of speakeasies tucked away, secret entryways, alleys that spiraled into themselves. The people with whom Shane tried to speak weren't unfriendly – in fact, many were friendly – but they regarded him with caution and wariness, children of the traumatized nation that they were.

Some men gave off darker vibes, watching Shane from a great distance as he approached and then continuing to watch him as he passed – eyes hooded, intentions barely concealed.

Tuk-tuk drivers aggressively petitioned him for business. Sometimes as many as a dozen at once would accost him, all yelling out to him, trying to make eye-contact as they put out their hands to welcome him aboard.

Shane took one such tuk-tuk to Lei Leung's address. The last letter that Lei had written to Luke Bradfield was over two years ago now, but the return address was a starting point at least.

Phnom Penh was beautiful at night – the building's lights, the river, the unholy mix of ancient and modern. Occasionally, Shane would catch a whiff of garbage or sewage, the sweet-awful smell of death and dying. But then it would be replaced by the smell of food cooking nearby, possibly outdoors, and he'd hear voices, musical and sharp at the same time – the Khmer language.

The tuk-tuk driver dropped him off on a street near the river. Shane paid up. Unlike the previous driver, this man accepted a tip, offering silent gratitude, before driving quickly away.

The address was for a place called No Joke Coffee. It was still open, but there were no customers. Shane didn't see any other entrances, so he went inside and walked up to the barista, a young woman, who was looking at something on her phone. When she saw Shane, she smiled – but it was a shy smile.

"Hello," Shane said. "I'm looking for…" He hesitated a moment before changing his approach. "I'm sorry, do you speak English?"

"Yes, bong," she said. "But not good." She smiled. She covered her mouth with her hand.

"It's okay," Shane said. "I don't know any Khmer." She was cute…at least twenty years younger than him. She wore braces. In his younger days, he might have flirted with her – subtly, perhaps too subtly. But his flirting days were long over. He couldn't imagine a circumstance in which he would ever flirt again.

"Coffee?" she asked.

"Sure," Shane said. "Black."

She was meticulous and serious when she worked. When she brought him his drink, he said, "Do you know a man named Lei Leung?" He didn't have a photo of him, only one of his brother, Charlie. "He's from Hong Kong?"

"Oh yes," she said. "He live here." She pointed at the ceiling. There must have been apartments upstairs.

"Perfect!" Shane said. "And how can I find his apartment? I didn't see a door outside."

She pointed to the entrance to the back room. A long piece of translucent plastic, cut into strips, separated the front from the back.

"There is stairs," she said. "But he never come home anymore."

"Oh?"

"He stay out all night."

Shane sipped his coffee, waiting for more.

She said, "I see him walk up and down riverside."

"Walking?"

She looked like she was trying to find the right word. Then, from behind the counter, she walked like she'd been drinking.

"Drunk?" Shane asked.

"No, no."

"Drugs?"

She nodded.

"Do you know where he goes?"

"Try Funkytown." She said this without a hint of irony.

"Funkytown?"

She nodded.

"Thank you." He paid for his coffee.

When she smiled at him, she covered her mouth again.

As soon as he stepped outside, he began to sweat. The heat was merciless.

He wished he was young again, still optimistic about the world, but he was neither young nor optimistic, and he had to make peace with those two sad facts.

Chapter 35

In addition to serving cans of Angkor and Krud beer, Funkytown offered large balloons filled with nitrous oxide. The bartender manned the tall, skinny tank that stood near the cash register. He looked like a man waiting for an opportunity to make a balloon animal.

No one was drinking beer. Beer was subterfuge, probably stocked in the cooler to justify the license hanging on the wall. Instead, each person in the bar had their own balloon, from the couple all the way down at the end of the bar to the half-dozen patrons spread amorphously across two long sofas. They leaned against each other like marooned jellyfish, drifting in and out of sleep, occasionally bringing a balloon to their lips and sucking in. *Hippy crack*, one of Shane's patients had called it – a heavy-lidded college student who couldn't get his shit together and probably never did. Nitrous Oxide would send you to that other, sweet place, but you were unlikely to rob a liquor store to get your next fix.

"Balloon?" the bartender asked. He was a short man whose eyebrows looked like they had been tattooed on. His hair was black and shiny, too perfect, like the snap-on hair of an action figure.

Shane held up a finger to indicate one balloon. He laughed when the bartender delivered his order.

"This is great," Shane said. "This is perfect."

He paid the man and then took a hit from the balloon.

When he was in college, he and his roommates would buy boxes of miniature nitrous oxide canisters at Discount Den. Back then, you could ask the cashier for a box of whippets and a pack of reds while you paid for your Talking Heads CD that came in longbox packaging. Shane hadn't thought much about any of this since the eighties, and now here he was in Cambodia of all places, in a roomful of men and women frying their brain cells with impunity.

The first hit of the balloon caused Shane to feel like he was strapped inside of a space shuttle, twirling toward a dreamscape. He kept rubbing his face before realizing that has rubbing his face. Several times, gas would seep from the balloon, like a gentle fart, and Shane would smile.

"Another balloon?" the bartender asked.

"No, I'm still full," Shane said and laughed at his own joke.

The bartender, smiling, nodded.

Shane remembered seeing *The Third Man* on campus with Cheryl, one of their first dates, and he remembered the two of them laughing too hard at the scene where the old man selling balloons approaches Major Calloway and Sergeant Paine, both of whom are trying to remain inconspicuous, and asks, "Balloon?" It was the way that Major Calloway and Sergeant Paine turned away from the balloon man, like a pair of dogs in trouble for rooting around the trash, that had caused them to laugh the hardest.

After the movie, he and Cheryl went to a random keg party and ended up making out inside the closet of a house full of people they didn't know. He still remembered the poster in the bedroom; it was the blown-up image of U2's *Boy* album cover – the haunted boy's eyes following them as they walked across the room.

Someone tapped his arm; Shane opened his eyes. It was the bartender. He was smiling.

"You fell asleep," he said.

"Did I?"

"Everyone falls asleep here," he said.

Shane motioned with his head toward the couch.

"Softer landing," Shane said.

"You fall from barstool," the bartender said, "you crack head open. Like an egg."

The bartender laughed. In another country, Shane might have thought the man was laughing at him, but there was no indication of cruelty in the man's eyes.

"Like an egg indeed," Shane said. He leaned forward. "You know a man named Lei Leung by any chance?"

The bartender's smile faded. He stared at Shane a good while before tipping his head toward the sofas. "Over there."

"Oh!" Shane looked over at the group on the two sofas, but he wasn't sure which one was Lei.

"Problem?" the bartender asked.

"No, not at all," Shane said. "But tell him I'm here. It's a surprise. Hey. I've got another question. Don't take this the wrong way, but…are your eyebrows tattooed on?"

The bartender laughed and walked away, swiping his wet rag across the bar.

A few minutes later, Shane watched the bartender text someone. And then he saw one of the men on the couch – a man whose back had been facing Shane – turn around and look at the bartender and then look at Shane.

Goddamn it.

When he saw Shane looking at him, he turned back around and took another long hit on his balloon. And then he let go of the balloon, watching it fly wildly above them until, limp, it landed on a young woman who was sound asleep.

The bartender said, "Mr. Lei would like to buy you a drink."

"You serve liquor?" Shane asked, and he remembered an old joke: *Liquor in the front, poker in the rear.*

A drink miraculously appeared in front of Shane. Where had it come from?

"What is this?" Shane asked.

"It's from Mr. Lei," the bartender said, causing Shane to wonder if he'd asked the right question.

"Bottoms up," Shane said and took a drink. "Hey, that's good."

A few hours and one balloon later, everyone had filed out, except for Lei, the bartender, and Shane.

Shane knew it would have been more prudent to have remained clear-eyed, and yet he was being true to the teachings of R. D. Laing. He would meet Lei for the first time on Lei's level. Like the undercover cop who mainlines heroin to prove he's not an undercover cop, Shane was as messed up as, if not more than, Lei.

The bartender said, "Five dollars."

"Oh, I already paid," Shane said. "Remember?" But when he looked down and saw a full balloon in his hand, he realized that he had been given yet another one. "Okay, okay," Shane said. "This is tricky," he said, reaching into his pocket for the money while trying not to let go of the balloon. He found a five and handed it over.

He needed to take a piss. He wasn't sure how he could piss while holding a balloon. But he also wasn't sure where to put the balloon while he went to the restroom. Maybe he could hold it between his teeth. Pinching its open end, he stood from the barstool but tumbled backwards into a wall. As soon as he slammed against the wall, he let go of the balloon, and it flew absurdly away from him.

The bartender ran around the bar to help him.

Suddenly, the bartender's face was as close to his own face as a lover's.

"Have I asked you about your eyebrows?" Shane asked. "Are they tattooed on?"

And that was all he remembered until he woke up later, his wrists and ankles cuffed with plastic zip cuffs.

The bartender was behind the bar, but Lei was sitting across from Shane and leaning forward.

"When did you get out of prison?" he asked. "Answer me. When the fuck did you get out of prison, and how did you find me?"

Chapter 36

"What?" Shane asked, squinting, looking around.

"You look like shit," Lei said. "What is this…some kind of disguise?" He reached over and snatched off the eyepatch but cringed when he saw the knot of scar tissue instead of an eye.

The sleep was so deep that Shane was disoriented, waking into a moment of his life that did not compute. He couldn't have said how old he was or where he was sitting. He didn't remember that he was in Cambodia. He didn't remember five years in a detainment center, thinking he would die there. He didn't remember Corbett or any of his life back in Louisiana. But then, like an old TV that used vacuum tubes, ghosting images from Shane's past began to appear, and then slowly it came back into focus. And then the anger rose up inside him, the primal need for vengeance. He felt it in his gut and in his chest, righteous and famished, the way another person might have felt the Holy Ghost's spirit dwelling within.

Lei said, "I'd recognize you with or without your stupid eye. I hope that's a brain tumor," he said, reaching out and touching the lump on Shane's temple.

"Skin cancer," Shane said.

"Melanoma?" he asked, hopeful.

Shane shook his head. "Probably basal cell."

"Too bad," Lei said.

The bartender delivered a fresh cup of coffee for Lei, who sipped it as he stared through the steam at Shane.

"When did you get out of prison?" Lei asked again.

"I was never in prison," Shane said. "It was a detainment center. I was never brought to trial. The whole thing was a sham. But I'm sure Luke explained all of this to you."

Lei's expression changed. "Have you seen Luke?"

"Luke died a few weeks ago," Shane said. "I just met his widow."

Lei was trying to process the news.

"The last correspondence I saw between the two of you," Shane said, "was a few years ago."

"You're reading our private shit?" he asked.

"Luke's the reason I'm free now. And the reason I'm here is to find out what happened to your brother," Shane said. "Someone fucked me over. Ruined my life. And your brother is dead. Look, I'm doing this with or without your help."

Shane was still experiencing the effects of the nitrous oxide and whatever had been slipped into his drink. He had to focus; he had to remain lucid. His mouth was dry. His tongue felt like a toad sleeping in his mouth.

"Do you mind?" Shane asked, raising his cuffed arms.

Lei pulled a Swiss Army knife from his pocket, and he opened the miniature scissors on it. He snipped free the plastic cuffs around his legs first, and then those around his wrist. He shut the scissors and placed the knife back into his pocket. Up close, he looked like he hadn't slept in months.

"Here's what we're going to do. I'm going to give you my WhatsApp number," Shane said. "I have all of Luke's research. I'll tell you everything I know. I'm going to help you. Okay?"

Lei nodded. Then he started crying. The guy was a wreck.

Shane said, "I need some sleep, though. So let's meet up later. Does that work?"

Lei nodded again.

"I'm sorry about the cuffs," he said.

"Why do you even have zip-ties?" Shane asked.

"I don't," Lei said. "He does."

Shane turned to the bartender, who was closing out the register.

Lei said, "He's in the kink scene here. Spankings, rigging, restraints."

"Oh." Shane smiled. "I'm lucky I didn't get flogged then."

Lei forced a smile. He said, "I'm sure that's still a possibility, if that's your thing."

Shane shook his head. "Six o'clock tomorrow," he said. "Where do you want to meet?"

"Gerbie's," Lei said.

"Where's that?"

"Google it."

Shane stared at him. He sighed and said, "Come clean. No balloons, okay?"

Lei said, "I'll try. But no promises."

Chapter 37

Shane had his first uninterrupted sleep since leaving Manila. He had dreamed the recurring dream about the spoon that had scooped out his eye, removing it from his skull like an olive from a jar, but in the recurring dream Shane tries having the eye, which he has been carrying with him for years, surgically reattached, only to realize that the surgeon has attached it upside-down, and Shane has to walk through life seeing the world as though through a kaleidoscope, and when he takes a step onto a crosswalk, trying to negotiate a busy street, he experiences vertigo and falls to his knees as cars barrel toward him.

Shane awoke with a start, catching his breath.

Jesus!

There was no Aircon in his room, only a fan, but it was still more pleasant than any day – any *second* – that he had spent locked up. Last night's buzz had finally worn off.

Shane got up, showered, and dressed.

He took a tuk-tuk to a place called Gerbie's, a sandwich and salad shop that also sold coffee. The food looked healthy – the exact opposite of the kind of place he'd have expected Lei to recommend.

Shane sipped his coffee as he waited for Lei. When it became apparent that Lei wasn't going to show up, Shane ordered a steak sandwich and stared out the business's large round window at the endless stream of scooters and tuk-tuks. On the other side of the road were merchants selling food and kitsch. It was the yin and yang of street vendors: delicious, authentic food on the one hand, mass-produced junk that would eventually find its way to a landfill on the other hand.

Fucking Lei. Where was he?

Shane paid up in American dollars but received a combination of American dollars and Cambodian riel in change. Determining if the change was correct required the kind of higher math Shane wasn't capable of.

According to letters Lei had written to Luke, he had been searching for the prostitute who had killed his brother, but Shane had already decided that this wasn't going to be his approach. The way to go about it was to recreate Charlie Leung's final days, to experience those days for himself.

R. D. Laing had famously blurred the line between psychiatrist and patient, especially at Kingsley Hall, where he and his patients lived together. But what if Shane took Laing's approach one step further and actually stepped inside of Charlie Leung's life, as much as was possible, recreating the dead man's final few hours, second by second, as closely as he could? What if Shane experienced what Charlie had experienced? Was there any other way, except through deep empathy, to understand the motives of another human being?

Start from the beginning, he told himself.

What did he know about Charlie Leung?

Thanks to Luke, he knew a hell of a lot. He had Charlie's credit card receipts for his short stay in Phnom Penh. Among the many things the receipts told him, Shane knew where Charlie had eaten the night before he died. The FiveFive Rooftop Restaurant.

A tuk-tuk was parked outside Gerbie's, so Shane slipped inside and showed the driver on the phone's map where he wanted to go. The driver nodded and accelerated.

After a few minutes, Shane looked at the map and saw that the driver was taking him in the opposite direction.

"Wrong way," Shane yelled over the traffic's noise.

The driver held up his hand and waved it, as though saying, *Relax, I know what I'm doing.*

Shane believed him at first. Shane didn't know which streets were one-way and which ones weren't. He didn't know the traffic patterns. Perhaps it was faster to take a roundabout way than heading straight toward the destination. But as Shane watched the dot on his map move further and further from the river, he knew he had been lied to.

The driver turned around and smiled at Shane, motioning again with this hand to please be patient. The man was old enough to have survived Pol Pot's genocide campaign. For all Shane knew, the man himself had fought in the Khmer Rouge army, the very mention of which might still evoke the worst nightmares in everyday citizens.

The driver turned down an unpaved road, driving quickly, raising his hand periodically as though he could read Shane's mind.

Then he pulled into the wide-open grounds of a temple. It was paved like a parking lot, but there were no cars, and weeds had broken through the concrete.

The driver, slowly angling through the parking lot, weaved between temple buildings. At long last he pulled up to an outbuilding that looked like it might have been an open air dining area for monks but was now just shelter. At the far end of a picnic table sat Lei.

The driver stopped and motioned toward Lei.

When Shane started to pay, the driver shook his head. *Don't worry.*

Lei rested his elbows on the wooden table. When Shane approached, Lei said, "He's going to wait here for you," and tipped his head toward the driver.

Shane sat across from Lei.

On the table, a spoon and a lighter. In the spoon: black tar heroin. Shane saw it regularly in Manila. It didn't take much money to buy off a guard in the detention center.

"I see now why you couldn't make it," Shane said.

Lei shrugged. He said, "Cambodia is the worst place for a drug addict. Or the best place, depending on your point of view."

"Is that a fact?" Shane said.

"Damned straight," Lei said. "Whatever you want. Molly. Ketamine. Diazepam. I can get you a hundred pills for three bucks. One hundred and ten milligram pills. Put a couple under your tongue and let them dissolve into your capillaries. Sublingually."

"I learn a new word every day," Shane said.

"Sounds like cunnilingus," Lei said. "Go on. Say it. *Sublingually.*"

Shane said, "I'm good."

"One week, you're putting Diazapam under your tongue. A week later, you're shoving them up your ass."

"Like most things in life," Shane said.

"Ain't that the truth."

Shane hated to admit that he was intrigued. "Where do you get this stuff?" he asked.

"Anywhere. Walk into a pharmacy, see if they have it. If they don't, go to the next pharmacy. Sooner or later, you'll find your poison. Quickest way? Ask your driver." He nodded toward the tuk-tuk driver.

Shane mopped sweat from his brow with his forearm. They were sitting in the shade, but it didn't matter.

"I woke up this morning thinking about Charlie," Lei said. "I'd pushed him out of my head. And then here you are, telling me shit I hadn't thought about for two years."

Lei picked up the lighter and flicked it a few times. He stared at the black tar, eager to cook it. There was only so long you could put off the inevitable.

"You want to share?" he asked. "I'm not selfish."

"How about we hold off until we're done talking," Shane said.

Lei took a deep breath, his eyes not leaving the spoon. He said, "You're not going to find her. That ship sailed years ago." He looked up. "The whore, that is."

"Then what are you still doing here?" Shane asked.

"Do you know how much Hong Kong costs these days?"

"Was your brother supporting you?"

"He was supporting everyone," Lei said. "His wife, his kids, our mother, me. Even a few cousins."

"And your father?"

Lei shook his head. "He died when we were kids."

"Didn't your brother have other investments? How did he lose everything in this one deal?"

Lei laughed. "My brother wasn't an investor. He didn't grow up in that culture. We grew up poor. Hand to mouth. My brother was a gambler. He made a lot of money early on with a few lucky investments."

"How'd he get the money to invest?"

"He got involved with triads."

"Triads?"

"Organized crime. Hong Kong has its own La Costa Nostra."

"What was he involved with? What kind of crime?"

"Smuggling chemicals to the U.S. and Canada. Sometimes Europe."

"Chemicals?"

"Shit that makes methamphetamine and MDMA. You know…ecstasy, molly. But once he started making money with his investments, he wanted out. Which isn't, as you can imagine, easy. He had to pay the Triads a monthly fee to stay out of it."

"And when he lost everything…"

"Money or no money, he still owed the Triads. And now that he's dead, the debt doesn't just go away. His wife Song owes it. Or maybe I would have owed it if I'd stayed. Maybe I still do. Who knows."

Shane wasn't sure what to think about a man who left his brother's wife and her kids in the wind. Would he have done the same thing? Or would he have spent the rest of his life being a martyr?

"You feel guilty, though, don't you?" Shane asked.

"What do you think? Song's living in a cage home now. I don't know about the kids."

"What the hell's a cage home?"

"It's what it sounds like," he said. "You ever hear of Google? You should try it."

Lei stared at Shane a good while before flicking the lighter and heating up the spoon. After the black tar turned to liquid, Lei pulled a cigarette from his shirt pocket.

"Want one?" he asked. "Last chance."

Shane shook his head.

Lei dipped the cigarette into the liquid and then lit the cigarette.

Shane leaned back. The black tar's vinegar smell was pungent, causing Shane to squint and blink. It also made him nostalgic. The gravitational pull toward self-destruction was a strong one.

Lei's eyes were becoming unfocused, his lids heavy.

Shane thought of the night in the abandoned gas station. Kylie asleep on the couch. The bearded man's eyes glowing as he lit the spoon. Cole watching the powder metamorphose into liquid, as mesmerized as a disciple watching water turn to wine. It had been a critical point in Cole's attempts at recovery, a nudge into the abyss.

"You shouldn't keep the driver waiting," Lei said.

Shane nodded.

"Don't die here," Shane said.

"Here's just as good a place as any," Lei said. He tried smiling.

"Believe it or not, I've been where you're at. It started with Oxy. Then I started scoring heroin wherever I could get it. Lost my job. Lost my friends. One night, I went into cardiac arrest. I was lucky. I was in a grocery store when it happened. I was buying a carton of orange juice with a handful of change I'd been saving."

"And now look at you," Lei said. "Not exactly a ringing endorsement for sobriety."

"Getting even motivates me," Shane said.

"And what happens when you catch the bad guys? What'll motivate you then?"

"I'll worry about that bridge when I reach it."

Shane hoisted himself up from the picnic table, walked back to the tuk-tuk, and got inside.

The driver did a U-turn and headed across the parking lot, but just as he was about to cross over onto the unpaved road, a dozen kids ran out in front of the tuk-tuk, blocking him. The kids were anywhere from four years old to twelve. Half of them jumped into the back of the tuk-tuk with Shane. At first Shane thought they were playing, but then the oldest kid, sitting across from Shane, kept lurching forward and and landing on Shane's thighs with his palms. Shane realized the kid was trying to locate Shane's wallet.

"Stop it," Shane said, but the kid kept doing it.

The other kids giggled as they touched Shane, also searching for something valuable under the guise of playing. They were a clever bunch.

When the teenager tried touching Shane's eyepatch, Shane swatted away the kid's hand.

"Give them something," the driver said, speaking English for the first time.

"Really?"

"They have nothing," the driver said. "They need food."

Was the driver in on it?

Probably.

Shane sighed loudly for the driver's benefit. He didn't want to pull his wallet free while the kids surrounded him, so he motioned for them to get off the tuk-tuk first. When they didn't move, Shane asked the driver to explain to them that he would give them some money if they deboarded and stood the fuck back.

The driver spoke rapidly to them. The kids got out of the tuk-tuk but remained close.

"Back!" Shane said.

No one moved.

Shane lunged toward them and yelled it this time: "*Back!*"

They understood Shane and gave him a wider berth.

Shane removed a handful of bills. He told the driver what he was going to do and what he wanted the driver to do, and as soon as Shane crumpled the bills and threw them, the driver took off.

Shane could see in the side mirror the driver looking at him. And he could see that the driver wasn't pleased with a man who didn't have the dignity to hand money to kids, throwing it instead, the way you toss scraps of bread to pigeons. But Shane wanted out of there. He had developed a second sense in Manila for when things were about to turn ugly. The moment right before things shifted, the room would become eerily quiet. Or Shane would notice a subtle look exchanged between two cell mates. Or someone would whistle to get somebody's attention, and a shiver would ripple through Shane. He didn't know whose eyes may have been watching him now from behind bushes. He didn't know if any of the kids had knives. He didn't know anything about this country except for the dark cloud that had hung over it for centuries and, for all Shane knew, still might.

Chapter 38

Shane went to dinner that night at the FiveFive Rooftop Restaurant.

He didn't bother showing anyone who worked there a photo of Charlie Leung. No one would remember a man who had eaten dinner at the restaurant five years ago, even if any of the staff still worked there, and it was unlikely that they did. But that wasn't the point, anyway. The point was to step into Charlie's shoes; the point was for Shane to see the man's final two nights through his own eyes.

Shane compared the menu prices with the credit card bill. To rack up a bill that high, he would have had to order enough food to sample several items from each course. It was hard to imagine him doing that alone. But it was also hard to imagine him inviting to dinner a party of people in a city in which he knew no one. No, he had probably invited the prostitute, likely a bargirl who spoke English.

Charlie Leung had just arrived in Phnom Penh earlier that day, so he must have gone straightaway to a bar to find a woman he could invite to dinner. Lady X, Shane thought. Lady X must surely have gotten curious when Charlie ordered so much food. Maybe her curiosity was piqued before then; maybe it was when they showed up at such a nice hotel and then took the elevator up to the rooftop instead of to his room.

When the server arrived – a woman so young that she would have been only thirteen or fourteen the night Charlie died – Shane asked her what the most popular entrees were.

"I'll take those three then," Shane said.

The woman laughed, thinking he was joking.

"No, really," Shane said, smiling. "I'll take those three."

Shane's appetite still hadn't returned after his release. Maybe it never would. Even his favorite food back home – crawfish étouffée – didn't inspire any cravings.

When Shane's food arrived, the other patrons – couples, mostly – stole glances at him. Who was this one-eyed monster covered in prison ink? A quick look from Shane, and they turned their attention back to their own food.

The skyline was beautiful. The river, the temple, the lights from a distant casino. He imagined Charlie standing at the edge, drink in hand, staring out over the city.

Shane's eye kept returning to the temple that sat only a few blocks away. Had Charlie been a Buddhist? Did he believe in a higher power? As the river shimmered from the city's lights, Shane felt for certain that Charlie Leung knew he was going to die. Charlie wouldn't have left his family with nothing. Shane was willing to guess that there was a life insurance policy in Charlie's name, and if Charlie had killed himself, his family wouldn't collect anything. But if he arranged for someone to kill him, they might get twice the policy's amount. Double jeopardy. But if this was the case, why was his family, as Lei suggested, living in poverty now?

Charlie must have laid out his plan to the prostitute over dinner. Based on the amount of the bill, there was probably wine – expensive wine – to loosen her up, to get her to consider the proposition. He was treating her to an extravagant meal; he was wooing her to consider the unthinkable.

Shane ate very little. He asked for the food to be boxed up.

He imagined what it would be like knowing with certainty that tomorrow he would be dead.

He had tried on more than one occasion to kill himself during the five years of his detainment, but there was never any certainty that it would work. And, obviously, it hadn't. If anything, he spent five years living in utter uncertainty. Would he make it one more day, or would he try to end it all? And if he tried to end it, would he succeed?

Outside, with his food boxed and bagged, Shane strolled toward the river, but when he saw a monk sitting outside the temple smoking a cigarette, Shane walked toward him.

The monk looked up at Shane. When Shane hesitated, the monk offered him a cigarette.

"No thanks," Shane said, shaking his head. "Would you like some dinner?"

The monk was leaning against a waist-high brick wall. The top of the wall was wide enough to set up the food. Charlie opened each box to reveal it all to him, the scallops, the lamb chops, the tenderloin skewers.

The monk looked up at Shane and smiled. Then he laughed at his good fortune. At long last here was the positive karma the monk had been taught to expect. He pinched the lit end of his cigarette, snuffing it out, and rested it on the wall's ledge.

Shane found the plastic forks and knives, and he gave them to the monk.

The monk speared a chunk of tenderloin and brought it to his mouth. As he chewed, he shut his eyes.

"Pretty damned good, isn't it?" Shane asked.

The monk motioned for Shane to eat.

"No, no," Shane said and patted his stomach. "Too full."

The meal had depleted a good chunk of Shane's bank account. He had enough for another flight, a few nights in cheap accommodations, and street food – but not much more.

Shane leaned against the wall, facing the temple, as the monk ate. Inside was an enormous statue of Buddha. Was it unusual that no one was there praying, or was that par for the course?

As Shane started to leave, the monk put his hand on Shane's shoulder. Then he put his hands together and bowed, expressing his gratitude to Shane.

"Of course," Shane said, and again he tried imagining what it would be like to know that this was your last full day on earth. "Enjoy," Shane said to the monk before turning and walking away.

Chapter 39

Shane reached Riverside. The tuk-tuk's brake lights gave the night a cinematic quality. He stood on the side of the businesses, looking across the street at the Mekong boardwalk, where small children, seemingly belonging to no one, ran up and down. A night ferry floated on the river. Shane had read that there were party boats that cost sixteen dollars per person with unlimited beer and food. Sixteen dollars! Why, he wondered, did anyone live in America where it cost fifty dollars a day just to park your car in a city like Chicago?

The street hustlers approached Shane to sell him their services. Did he want a ride somewhere? Did he want a woman for the night? Did he want to go to the Killing Fields tomorrow? Or maybe to one of Pol Pot's prisons? They could pick him up first thing in the morning, they told him.

"No, no," Shane said, wagging his head.

An old woman in dirty clothes approached with a bag of...*something.*

"Twenty dollars," she said.

"What is it?" Shane asked.

"Hash," she said.

Shane took the bag from her and examined its contents. He still wasn't sure what it was, but it definitely wasn't hash.

He gave the bag back to her.

"No," he said.

"Fifteen," she said.

"No, I'm not interested."

She smiled, revealing missing teeth, and then showed off her ancient body with its loose and crinkled skin. "You like?"

By his calculations, she probably had been a child during Pol Pot's reign of terror. Her parents might have been killed by the Khmer Rouge. Undoubtedly, she had been displaced from Phnom Penh, if she had grown up here, along with two million others, leaving the city to the ghosts until the survivors were allowed back in four long years later.

Shane removed his wallet and gave the woman a twenty dollar bill. He waved away the proffered hash, and when she tried sidling up next to him, he gently held her back and said, "Please, no. Thank you. But no."

The episode had unnerved him. When he thought of Lei lighting the spoon, he felt the old hunger returning, his thoughts beginning to spiral. At the end of the spiral were two words: *fuck it.*

He approached a tuk-tuk driver and said, "Pharmacy."

The driver pointed to a pharmacy only fifty yards north of where they stood.

"No," Shane said. "Not that one."

The driver's eyes lit up. He knew what Shane was looking for without being told. He motioned for Shane to get in.

The breeze that came into the tuk-tuk from its speed was a welcome reprieve from the brutal humidity.

The driver drove through intersections without a care for other cars, motorbikes, or tuk-tuks.

"Easy there, Steve McQueen," Shane said, but the driver ignored him.

On a nearly empty street, far from the tourists, the driver pulled over. The street was dark. At first Shane feared the driver had misunderstood him, but then he saw it: the green cross, inside of which was a chalice with a snake wrapped around its stem.

Shane paid the driver.

"Wait for me?" he said.

The pharmacy was small. An old man stood behind the counter. He looked up from his phone when door opened. He said nothing.

Shane approached the counter. A Chinese lantern hung from the ceiling, a halfhearted nod toward an aesthetic.

"I need something for pain," Shane said.

The pharmacist nodded. He pulled from the shelf behind him a box of Paracetamol.

"No, something stronger," Shane said.

The pharmacist returned the box and pulled another from the shelf. Tramadol.

Shane made a face, shook his head.

The pharmacist tried again, this time bringing morphine to the counter.

"How much?"

He sized Shane up. "Fifty," he said.

Shane laughed. He pulled a ten dollar bill from his wallet. The pharmacist eyed the other bills peeking out.

"I need the rest of it for the driver," he said and pointed out the plate-glass window.

The pharmacist took the money. He put the morphine pills into a small brown-paper sack, stapled it, and handed it over.

Half-an-hour later, back in his room, Shane removed the blister packs of pills and studied them. One by one, he popped the pills from their blisters.

Shane's heart sped up when he lifted one of the pills to his mouth.

Sublingual, he thought.

He set the pill down onto the fleshy pink flesh of his under-tongue, a part of his mouth that resembled a tiny intestine. He lowered his tongue over it to generate the heat required to melt the pill.

He thought he was starting to feel something, a warming of his blood, when he brought his cupped hands to his mouth and tried spitting it out. The pill was stuck there, though, wedged in an uncomfortable way and unmovable. He reached into his mouth and pulled it out. He scooped up the remaining pills, carried them to the restroom, and dropped them into the toilet. Instead of flushing, he removed the bum gun from its fixture and he sprayed the pills. They circled the toilet water, spinning around and around, all the while dissolving. Once they had disappeared into nothing, Shane flushed.

Drained, he lay in bed and listened to his heart pounding, the intake of each breath, the breathing out. Everything else was so quiet, he might have been dead. But he wasn't. And soon enough other people who had hoped he was dead would learn the truth – that he was alive. He was fucking alive.

Chapter 40

Shane woke up early, eager to put together the day's itinerary based on Luke's notes. Luke had been in touch with Charlie Leung's family in Hong Kong, which was how Luke had ended up with phone records, bank ledgers, and credit card statements. That they trusted an American living in the Philippines spoke to Luke's authenticity and sincerity, not to mention his doggedness.

From what Shane could piece together, Charlie had taken out ten thousand U.S. dollars from a bank in Hong Kong, one thousand at an ATM at the airport in Phnom Penh, and another ten thousand at a branch of his bank in Phnom Penh. That left a remaining balance of five hundred dollars in his account. Three weeks earlier, his bank account had had over five million in it.

Shane knew what it was like to lose everything, but Shane's losses had come over time and were self-inflicted. Charlie Leung's losses came at the snap of a finger. Discovering five million dollars missing from a bank account must have felt like watching a skyscraper unexpectedly collapse: the inexplicability of something so colossal and permanent suddenly gone.

In addition to buying food, Charlie Leung had visited a medical supply store in Phnom Penh. That explained the restraints found at the scene of the crime. These were hospital bed restraints used for a patient's safety, not sex shop restraints for fetish-friendly couples, but there was little distinction in how the restraints worked. Charlie probably didn't want to risk raising any red flags with airport security either leaving Hong Kong or arriving in Cambodia. At the very least, he probably didn't want to be embarrassed should anyone check inside his carry-on.

Shane wanted to see the medical supply store and the bank branch for himself, but he couldn't stop thinking about his life insurance theory. Before he started retracing the dead man's footsteps, he wanted to talk to Lei first – before Lei got too fucked up to talk to him.

All the way to Lei's apartment, Shane was certain his theory was correct, that Charlie had hired the prostitute to kill him so that his family could collect twice the amount of money. The simplest explanation was most likely the correct explanation. Occam's razor.

With pieces of the larger puzzle beginning to fit together, Shane entered No Joke Coffee feeling more enthusiastic than he'd felt in years.

The barista looked up and smiled at him.

"I'm back!" he said.

"Hello. Coffee? Black?"

"Yes! You remembered! I didn't get your name last time."

She looked confused.

"What's your name?" he asked.

"Boupha," she said, looking embarrassed. She smiled then put her hand over her mouth, hiding her braces. "And you? What's your name?"

"Shane."

"Shane," she repeated. "Nice to meet you, Shane."

"Nice to meet *you.*" As he waited, he stared at the shredded plastic shower curtain that hung between the café and the residential part of the building. He willed Lei to appear, but no one came through the curtain.

"Have you seen Lei today?" Shane asked.

"No."

"Hm. Do you mind?" He motioned toward the shower curtain.

"No," Boupha said.

"Be right back!"

Shane hustled up the stairs to Lei's room and knocked several times. When no one answered, Shane tried the knob. It wasn't locked. He opened the door and walked inside. Two cockroaches ran in opposite directions.

The room was tiny, and yet it appeared large for its conspicuous lack of belongings. Some dirty clothes on the bed. A pair of shoes. A bag of rice by a rice cooker. The garbage, however, had begun to pile up – takeout boxes, fast food bags, empty plastic bottles for flavored milk or water. A faint sewage smell pervaded the room, coming from the drain in the bathroom. Lei's DNA was everywhere in the form of hair strands. Several strands clung to the shower wall, looped like its own foreign script. A single strand of hair clung to the bar of soap, like a man hanging from the edge of a cliff. Several clumped by the drain. Strength in numbers.

Shane shut the door and walked back downstairs to the café.

"Not there," he said and he pushed through the curtain.

His coffee was waiting for him.

Boupha said nothing.

It was too early for Funkytown. Had Lei even come back here last night?

Shane paid his bill. It wasn't much, but he also had to start keeping track of how much he was spending. His money would eventually run out. And then what?

"Anything you can tell me about Lei?" Shane asked.

Boupha said, "He always sad." She offered a smile to counter her words.

Shane considered the country they were in, the horrors it had seen, fucked over by everyone, including the worst atrocity imaginable by their own people: auto-genocide. The city he was standing in had been evacuated, empty for years. A ghost ship of unspeakable horrors. And yet here was Boupha, full of hope in her café, making flat whites and iced lattes, remaining upbeat and smiling, always smiling.

"If you see him, tell him I stopped by? Okay?"

"Okay," Boupha said.

Shane tried smiling, but he didn't have a good feeling. Whatever optimism he'd felt upon entering the café had drained away like a bloodletting, leaving him uncertain about the future.

Chapter 41

Shane used the same ATM that Charlie had used, taking out some cash for himself. He scooped the money out of the tray and stuck it in his wallet. The sight of his significantly-diminished balance caused his stomach to ache. It was the same knife stab of a spasm he had experienced nearly every day in the detention center.

When Shane turned around, the tuk-tuk driver from yesterday was parked at the curb. He called out to Shane.

"Tuk-tuk?" he asked. "Where are you going?"

Shane didn't believe in coincidences, but in a place like Phnom Penh, where the hustle was real, he assumed tuk-tuk drivers actively motored around looking for repeat customers. It wasn't as though Shane – pale, Irish, and one-eyed – didn't stand out in the crowd.

"Okay," Shane said. "Same place as yesterday."

The driver nodded.

"Same place," he repeated.

Though Shane had been in Phnom Penh for only a few days, he was already familiar with various routes, and the sight of a particular business instantly oriented him – Brown Coffee, Texas Chicken, Tiger Sugar. They were heading south on Rue Pasteur No. 51.

No one stopped at four-way intersections. In America, the result would have been a multi-car accident, but here scooters and tuk-tuks and cars swam around each other while barely slowing down. It was a miracle of intuition, something sorely lacking in the west.

The exhaust fumes, however, were another story. Shane doubted any vehicle here had ever been inspected. The air was a wavy vapor-fueled hallucination. Shane was feeling lightheaded until his driver hit a pothole and Shane's coffee jumped from its cup, drenching his cargo shorts.

"Fuck," Shane said.

"Almost there," the driver said, mistaking the object of Shane's displeasure. His knowledge of English seemed to improve with each encounter. Was it only yesterday that the driver had pretended not to know the language?

The tuk-tuk zipped down the unpaved road and then into the temple's paved lot.

Shane could see someone sitting on the picnic bench where Lei had sat yesterday, but he wasn't sure it was Lei. Whoever it was, they were sleeping. Shane didn't want to startle a stranger, so he asked the driver to stop at a distance.

Shane slid out and slowly made his way toward the table.

"Lei? Is that you?"

The closer he got, the more concerned he became that something was wrong. The man was slumped over, but he wasn't sleeping.

"Jesus Christ," Shane said when he reached the bench. The man was indeed Lei. And he wasn't breathing. As soon as Shane touched him, he realized Lei was dead – and that he had most likely been dead for hours.

Shane looked around. There was no one here except for the tuk-tuk driver, who was talking on his cell and smoking a cigarette. Shane saw in the distance the kids again, only this time there were some older kids with them, bulking up the pack. Instead of one teenager, there were at least five now.

Shane was closer to the tuk-tuk than the kids were by half.

Shane picked up the spoon that Lei had been using to cook the black tar heroin and ran to toward the tuk-tuk. His right leg had been injured in a fight in Manila, stomped on by a man who had accused Shane of stealing his instant noodles, and although Shane was running as fast as he possibly could, the kids ran faster.

Shane yelled out for the tuk-tuk driver to pay attention.

When Shane slammed himself inside the tuk-tuk, his knees on the floorboard, he yelled, "Let's go! Let's go!"

But the driver didn't move.

"What the fuck are you doing?" he asked. "Let's go! C'mon!"

The kids arrived and circled the tuk-tuk. Gone was the ploy that they were just playful children. There was menace in their eyes now. Shane's life meant nothing to these kids. Anything was possible.

And then Shane remembered that the driver had seen Shane by the ATM; that he had *miraculously* appeared out of nowhere; that his English was better than he'd been letting on, begging the question: what else had this man been concealing?

The older kids began reaching into the tuk-tuk, trying to feel where Shane's wallet was by touching him.

Shane swatted the kids away. The youngest kids tried climbing onto the tuk-tuk as a distraction, but Shane pushed them off. One of the kids hit his head on the ground and started crying, prompting the older kids to become more aggressive.

"Get the fuck away," Shane said.

When the next teenager reached inside, Shane punched him in the face, breaking the kid's nose. He felt bone give way under his knuckles as blood sprayed down the kid's face. The boy looked confused as he reached up to touch his face to see what had just happened.

Another teenager tried climbing into the tuk-tuk. Shane grabbed him by the hair and slammed his head into the metal pole that held up the tuk-tuk's awning. He slammed the kid's head several times and then pushed him out of the tuk-tuk. The kid lost his footing and fell.

Shane took the spoon and reached around the driver's head, grabbing the man's hair with one hand and pressing the spoon against the bottom of the man's right eye. He pressed in so hard he thought he might actually pop the eye out before he could issue the threat.

"I swear to god I'll fucking blind you if you don't get us out of here."

When the driver didn't do anything, Shane pressed harder and yelled, "Go! Go! Go!"

The driver let out a moan from the pressure of the spoon and accelerated. The acceleration threw Shane back against the seat as the tuk-tuk ran over the fingertips of a felled child. Shane still had a grip on the man's hair, pulling his head back in such a way that watching the road was probably impossible. Shane finally let go and said, "I'll fucking kill you if you don't get me out of here right now."

The driver pulled out of the temple parking lot and onto the unpaved road.

Shane glanced behind them. The kids, not expecting Shane's resistance, didn't follow. He wasn't proud that he had injured any of them, but they were all still alive and so was he. It was everyone's lucky day – except for Lei's.

The driver and Shane didn't speak on their way back to the heart of the city. Shane reached up and straightened his eyepatch. He checked the tumor to make sure it wasn't weeping. When his eyes met the driver's in the rearview mirror, the driver looked away.

Before exiting the tuk-tuk, Shane leaned forward and whispered into the driver's ear, "I don't want to see you again, okay? If I see you again, I'll kill you. Understood?"

The driver nodded.

"Say it," Shane said.

"Yes," the driver said. "I understand."

"All right then."

Shane got out. He paid for the trip. He knew that the man's betrayal was because he needed money to survive. Or maybe it was to support a bad habit. Whatever the reason, it wasn't personal. And so there was no good reason to stiff the guy.

The man was wary as he took the bills.

"Keep the change," Shane said and headed inside his building. It wasn't until he stood at the door to his room that he realized that he was still holding the spoon. And that his hands were shaking.

Chapter 42

Shane wasn't without blame for Lei's death.

Lei's brother's murder had led Lei to self-medicating, sure, but Lei had long ago put aside any hope of solving what had happened to him. He'd apparently been willing to live with those ambiguities as long as he could maintain a state of altered consciousness.

Shane's presence had woken the dragon.

In an earlier life, Shane would have felt guilt. Guilt was a moral emotion rooted in empathy, but what had empathy ever gotten him? No, Lei was a means to an end. The point wasn't to find what had happened to the man's brother; the point was to find out who had destroyed Shane's life. Empathy only blurred the end goal. Sure, Shane wished it hadn't happened and he acknowledged that his appearance in Phnom Penh may have been the catalyst, but he didn't feel any guilt.

Once in bed, Shane fell into a deep sleep, startling awake at the sense that someone was in the room with him. But no one was in the room. It was just the lingering ghosts of his time locked up. In the detention center, people would steal from you while you slept. They would pickpocket you. They would sometimes sexually assault you, several men pinning you down as you awoke into a world that was worse than any imaginable nightmare.

Shane steadied his breathing. And then he got up and showered.

Shane would never take a shower for granted ever again. Or the privacy of a toilet. Or clean clothes. Or a bed. You begin to think that these things are a right, things that everyone should be afforded, but they're not. They're a privilege. And like other privileges, they can be stripped away in a second. Breathing wasn't even a right. How many men had he known whose right to breathe had been taken from them?

Shane headed out for a drink. A few yards past Brown Roastery, there was a narrow alley with signs of life – spiral staircases made of wrought-iron, people walking into and out of businesses, motorbikes and tuk-tuks zipping past him.

Shane headed down the alley. A few tourists looked over to smile, saw Shane's face, and quickly turned their heads, pretending to look elsewhere.

He found a tiny, family-run convenience store with a variety of fruit spread out on a blanket, a restaurant serving Cambodian food, a narrow sake bar, a speakeasy, a Korean bar with pink neon lights inside and K-pop on the flat-screened TVs, a burger joint, a craft beer bar. The street coiled like a snake, winding tighter and tighter, like an ouroboros, the ancient serpent that eats its own tail. Shane kept walking, past an art gallery, past an American themed-restaurant, past a restaurant advertising grilled frog. His shirt was heavy from the humidity as sweat poured freely from his pores. He ended up at a small Vietnamese-owned bar whose hand-painted sign out front read, "Thank You for Finding Us."

He had indeed found them.

Shane sat at the four-stooled bar and ordered a bottle of Heart of Darkness, a beer brewed in Ho Chi Minh City. He appreciated the irreverence.

"Where from?" the woman asked, smiling. She was probably in her forties. Two children were sitting nearby doing homework. The girl had a Hello Kitty backpack.

"Louisiana," Shane said. "America."

"America!" the woman said. "Very nice!"

"What's your name?"

"Vinh."

"Nice to meet you, Vinh. I'm Shane. It took a while to find you." He motioned to the bar. "This place, I mean."

"Last bar," she said. "Not many people make it here."

"Too bad." He took a swig of his beer. He was grateful that there were no nitrous oxide balloons here – just beer, a laminated page of appetizers, and some basic mixed drinks. "You ever been to America?" he asked.

"No," she said. "Expensive."

"That it is."

"Have you been to Vietnam?" she asked.

"No," he said. "Maybe one day."

"How long flight?" she asked. "From America?"

Shane smiled. "Long," he said.

He thought about the flight from Louisiana to Manila, the conversation he'd had with Luke. Luke had been trying to warn him.

Do things like this always happen to you? Luke had asked. *You meet a man at a bar and go into business with him the next day. Two years ago you burn down everything in your life, and now you're CEO of a successful company about which, by your own admission, you know nothing. You show up to interview a couple of guys and end up in a commercial. From where I sit, you're living a charmed life. And now you're flying to the Philippines to meet a company about business…even though you're a small outfit in southern Louisiana. I hate to break it to you, but most people aren't this lucky.*

What Luke was trying to tell him was that these were red flags. He was a cop, after all. By telling him "most people aren't this lucky," he was saying, "Watch your ass."

He thought of Hanh in Manila and the two filmmakers in Abbeville. Were they the engine that ran the operation, or was it his old partner Corbett who ran the show?

Corbett had played Shane to perfection. He had seen a hole in Shane's life, and where another man might have been sympathetic, Corbett saw opportunity. And Shane had handed the information to him so easily. The recent break-up. The career upended. The downturn in his life. And Shane had fallen so easily for the false friendship that Corbett had offered. The fake handshakes. The deceptive back slaps. There was a term for Corbett: dark empath.

From here on out, no one was to be trusted. *No one.*

Shane finished his beer and ordered another.

"How long you been here?" Vinh asked.

"Just a few days."

"How do you like it?"

Vinh's kids, deep into their homework assignments, were no older than some of the kids who had tried to rob him today.

"It's an adjustment," Shane said.

Vinh looked like she didn't understand. "My English," she said and shook her head.

"I like it very much," Shane said, revising his sentiment.

And this was true if he could freeze this particular moment right now and seal it in amber. He felt content sitting there at the last bar in the spiral, just the four of them. If every day could be like this moment, he would be fine. But he kept thinking about Vietnam and how Tam, Kenny, and Hanh fit into the equation.

"Where are you from in Vietnam?" Shane asked.

"Saigon," she said.

Same as Hanh.

"What's it like there?" Shane asked.

"Very busy," she said and laughed. "Many people."

"More than here?"

Vinh frowned and nodded, as though to say, *you have no idea.*

"I have a question," Shane asked. "Is Hanh a common name?"

"Hanh?"

"Yes, a woman's name. Hanh. Are a lot of women in Vietnam named Hanh?"

"Yes. Very common," she said. Then she gave Shane a sly look and said, "You know Vietnamese woman named Hanh? You have girlfriend?"

"Me? No, no. I'm single."

Vinh leaned closer. Teasingly, she said, "No girlfriend? Handsome man?"

Shane smiled, enjoying the flirting, but then his smile faded and he shook his head. He waved his hand, as though to say, *Please, no.*

The children were watching. They were young enough to sense a shift in the air, the way a stream of sunlight could suddenly reveal all the room's dust motes, thousands of specks dancing like visible atoms.

"I'm sorry," Vinh said.

"No, no, it's okay. It's not you."

"Are you mad?"

"Not at you, no. You're lovely."

Shane smiled at the children to reassure them that everything was okay, but they quickly looked away, knowing everything wasn't.

Chapter 43

Drunk, Shane made his way to Street 104, a popular area for sexpats. The men who walked in and out of the bars were Shane's age or older, mostly Brits and Aussies, decked out in sweat-soaked tank tops, cargo shorts, and flip flops, stinking of cigars and fungal infections. There were a few Russians, intense and humorless, wearing shiny designer shirts and silk pants. Their shoes, with gold-toned studs and crystal embellishments, probably ran several thousand bucks retail. Shane didn't hear any American accents. Cambodia was a longer flight from the U.S. and therefore a less likely destination. Regardless, Shane fit right in – inebriated, damaged, older-looking than he actually was. He had found the street of wounded souls.

Loud music thumped from several bars. Restaurants overflowed with customers seated outside on tiny plastic chairs. Beer was poured into glasses full of ice.

Shane waited for a gap between a stream of scooters before crossing the street. He turned off Street 104 and walked until he found a less-populated area. He couldn't stop sweating. His eyepatch was moist again.

Shane entered the only bar that didn't have any customers, only bargirls – and only two bargirls at that.

They both came over to him, one on each side, taking his arms and leading him to the bar.

"Buy us drinks?" the one on his left said.

She spoke English. At least three words.

Shane turned to the one who hadn't spoken and said, "Tell me about yourself."

She smiled and moved closer, pressing against his arm. She didn't speak English.

Shane ordered three drinks, but once they came, he led the bargirl who spoke English to a table near the front entrance. The other bargirl started to follow, but Shane held up his hand and smiled, trying to look apologetic. She stuck out her lower lip, fake-pouting, and took her drink to the bar.

"What's your name?" Shane asked.

"Chan," she said. She looked twenty, twenty-one. She took a drink and giggled. She wore braces. Her makeup was too heavy. She'd have been prettier without it.

"Slow night," Shane said. "No people."

"Always like this," she said. "Prettier girls in other bars."

"What do you mean?" Shane asked. "You and your friend are pretty." He was flattering her, trying to warm her up.

She giggled and said, "Not pretty, no." Nervously, she finished her drink and showed Shane the empty glass. "Please?"

"Okay, sure."

"And one for my friend?"

Shane sighed for comic effect, pretending to be put out. "Okayyyyy, I guess," he said. "Since you twisted my arm."

Chan ran to her friend, pressing against her, the two them laughing. Her friend turned around and said to Shane, "Thank you!"

Well, Shane thought. She knows two words of English. Maybe he'd misread her, after all. Misreading people had been his fatal flaw. What the hell kind of person became a therapist when all their instincts about people were wrong?

When Chan came back, Shane said, "Drink up. I want to take you somewhere."

He clinked his glass against hers and tipped it back until the ice hit his nose.

Done.

Chapter 44

Shane took Chan to the hotel that housed the FiveFive Rooftop Restaurant, but instead of taking her dinner, he led her to the front desk and asked for a room.

The man behind the counter was the manager, and he looked like he wanted to refuse Shane's request – his purpose for getting a room wasn't subtle – but the manager clearly had no grounds. He swiped a key for Shane and handed it over.

"Room 608, sir," he said.

"Perfect."

"Any luggage?"

Shane shook his head, further cementing his intentions.

Chan was oblivious to the interaction between the two men. She was taking in the whole of the hotel, likely the nicest place a client had taken her.

"Swimming pool?" she asked.

"Of course," Shane said. "Swimming pool. Sauna. Gym. The whole kit and kaboodle."

Shane took her hand and led her to the elevator, which dinged as soon as they were close.

"Hurry!" he said, pulling her, like teenagers on a date. "Before the door closes!"

In his drunken state, he momentarily forgot that this was a transaction. There was a split-second where this felt like his actual life, coming home from a date in a wild, lawless country that was still feeling its way out of decades of darkness. Shane felt like an outlaw. A gunslinger. An adventurer. He put his arm around Chan, and she leaned against him, and he thought, drunkenly, *This is all I've ever wanted.*

The elevator dinged, and the doors slid open. Shane was jarred back to reality. He was an old, broken man carrying out an operation. Nothing more.

Chan took off her shoes before walking into the room. *Buddhist*, Shane thought, slipping off his own shoes, not to be rude.

"I take shower?" she said. "Then you take shower?"

"No, wait," he said. "Later. Come here. Sit." He motioned for her to sit next to her on the bed.

Shane had seen the itemized hotel bill from Luke's box. On the night of his murder, Charlie had ordered champagne. He looked at the room service menu and found it – the most expensive bottle the hotel offered. It was the sort of gesture you'd make when you were going to end things, not when there was a chance you might be murdered.

Shane picked up the phone and ordered.

Chan looked nervous.

"Everything's okay," Shane assured her. "I'm just trying to figure something out."

Shane found a Miles Davis album on YouTube – *Ascenseur Pour L'Echafaud* – and he set his phone down on the bedside table. The opening trumpet notes were not what he was expecting. Haunting and disconcerting.

"It's nice," Chan said, but Shane didn't believe her. She said it just to say it.

When the champagne arrived, Chan relaxed.

Shane located a corkscrew by the minibar. He twisted it into the cork. He imagined his brothers from the Sigue Sigue Sputnik gang twisting a corkscrew into the eye of his enemy. When Shane pulled the corkscrew from the bottle, he saw the man's eye popping free, the champagne a geyser of blood from the empty socket.

Chan laughed as the fountain of champagne simmered down.

Shane poured two glasses. He offered a toast – "To life's mysteries!" he said – and Chan, unsure how to toast, giggled until Shane clinked his glass against hers and then motioned for her to drink.

"I have a question," Shane said.

"Okay."

"If I asked you to choke me, how much would you charge me?"

Chan thought about it. She said, "Same price."

"No, no. If I asked you to choke me until I died, how much would you charge me?"

"I don't understand," Chan said.

"You choke me," Shane said. "Right?" He mimed choking someone. "And then I die." He shut his eyes and stuck his tongue out. "I'm dead," he said. "How much?"

Chan thought about it. He expected her to say that she wouldn't do it. But then she said, "Five hundred."

"Five hundred dollars to kill me?"

She nodded.

"That's all?"

She nodded.

The thought chilled him. *Five hundred dollars.*

But then he had an idea.

He pulled one hundred dollars from his wallet and set the bills down next to his phone.

"I want you to kill me," he said.

Chan stared at Shane, as though reconsidering, and then she looked over at the money before turning her attention back to Shane.

"Okay," she said.

"Okay then. But let's finish the champagne first."

Chan smiled. She was enjoying the champagne.

"Cheers," Shane said and clinked his glass against hers.

Chapter 45

Shane didn't have any straps for Chan to restrain him. In lieu of restraints, he stretched his arms out, like a crucifixion, and asked Chan to place her knees on top of his biceps to pin him down.

The police report and autopsy indicated that Charlie Leung had been found naked, and suggested that he likely had been having sex with the prostitute (a fair assumption), but Shane didn't want to have sex with Chan. Shane realized as soon as Chan put her hands around his neck that this was a mistake of judgment. It was impossible to get inside Charlie Leung's head without the restraints and without having sex with Chan.

Chan dug her thumbs into Shane's windpipe, as he had taught her to do. Her initial reluctance morphed almost instantly into rage. It was as though she were choking every man who had mistreated her, every man who had kicked her out into the street without paying her, every man from her childhood who had ever touched her when they shouldn't have. Tears filled her eyes as she pressed even harder, funneling her entire body weight into the tips of her thumbs. She was determined to kill him.

Shane shut his eyes. He let down his guard. He tried to accept his fate, as Charlie Leung accepted his.

A long-forgotten moment came to him: he and his wife on the first day of spring, undergraduates, not yet married, not yet dating, stepping out of a university auditorium where they had just watched Ingmar Bergman's *Persona*, the sun startlingly bright and the grassy quad churning with sunbathers, hundreds of them, the air thick with coconut oil and Coppertone as the sea of bodies bronzed and burned. Cheryl had turned to Shane and said, *Heliophiles.*

What?

It's an organism that seeks out the sun.

Shane smiled. He fell in love with her right then and there, Liv Ullmann and Bibi Andersson still flickering inside his brain, the campus a Roman orgy of flesh and cheap beer, the world as promising as it had ever been.

He asked her what she was doing later, and she said, *Howling with my pack.*

Who's your pack?

Cheryl leaned close and, in a voice that sounded like Bela Lugosi, said, *Why, the children of the night! What music they make!*

Chan still had hold of his neck and was struggling to choke him, but Shane was too strong for her, and when he grabbed her wrists, he easily removed her hands – an option that had not been available to Charlie Leung.

Chan continued to struggle – she was surprisingly strong for someone who weighed well under a hundred pounds – but she was no match for Shane.

"Take the money!" Shane yelled, tired of fighting her. "Go on! Take the money!"

Chan finally stopped trying to reach for his neck. She rolled over onto her back, out of breath.

Shane was coughing from the few seconds that she had tried crushing his windpipe.

At some point during the struggle, the bucket of ice and empty champagne bottle had been kicked over. One of the champagne flutes had broken.

"Jesus," Shane said, still coughing.

Chan said, "I'm sorry." The rage had passed. She had returned to the submissive bargirl, afraid of upsetting her client.

"You did good," Shane said. "I just…I don't know. It wasn't right." He sat up in bed and rubbed his hands over his face. He let out a sigh that could have been an expression of his exhaustion for the last five years of his life. "I think I had too much to drink today," he said.

Chan rolled over, facing the money.

"Go on," Shane said. "Take it."

Chan slid the money toward her. She counted it.

"Thank you," she said. "I go now?"

"Sure," Shane said.

She patted Shane's thigh and said, "I go to temple now. I make merit for you."

He imagined Chan standing outside the temple, lighting a fresh candle with an already-lit candle.

"Making merit. Isn't that usually for the dead?" Shane asked.

She met his eyes for the first time since she had tried to kill him.

"Yes," she said, picking up her shoes. "You not die today. But maybe tomorrow."

Her prediction wasn't without value, Shane thought, as she bowed and left the room.

Chapter 46

Shane snagged a direct flight to Hong Kong for a hundred and fifty bucks. Despite the savings, Shane's bank account was nearly empty. Another problem he needed to remedy.

He landed in Hong Kong just before noon.

After checking into his hotel, he moved his documents from the duffel bag to the backpack. He wanted to reveal to Charlie's wife what he had found. He wanted to gain her trust.

Backpack on, Shane headed out for the day. He stopped first at a tea restaurant and ordered eggs, toast, and a pork chop. It was like stepping into the 1950s, with its round tables and short round stools, all surfaces a faded pastel: green or pink or blue. The walls were covered in Chinese calendars and mid-century photos and menus. A fan was mounted to the wall, oscillating, causing a chill to go up Shane's back each time the breeze found him.

Shane and his wife had bonded in college over their love of art house movies, and they continued, after they graduated, to pick up flyers for movies playing on campus – indie movies, foreign movies, cult movies. One of their favorites was *In the Mood for Love*, set in Hong Kong in the early 1960s, and he felt now like he had been chosen to be a background player in the movie.

He also felt the surprising blow of missing his wife. He had compartmentalized her death in such a way that he rarely dredged up grief at the thought of her. Those recent sucker punches of grief came during quiet experiences he knew she would have appreciated, like eating breakfast at a tea restaurant in Hong Kong.

He sipped his milk tea as he poured over Luke's notes. Luke had been in contact with Charlie Leung's widow, Song. Next to her name, Luke had written "an ancient dynasty in China."

Song Leung.

Shane committed her name to memory.

Song Leung, Song Leung.

And there were two boys, Xiao Dan and Tai.

In her last correspondence to Luke, Song admitted that she was almost out of money, and that she didn't know what was to become of her and her sons. She didn't mention anything about a crime syndicate or having to live in a cage home. He wasn't sure how reliable Lei's information had been, though Shane couldn't discount it. The first place to head was to Song's last-known address: the luxury condominium where she and Charlie had lived with their kids.

Shane paid for breakfast and strapped on his backpack. Several customers looked at him on his way out. They stared without pretext. Not only was he a foreigner, but he was an unusual-looking foreigner. He had been told that pale-skinned foreigners especially stood out because of a fetish for white skin (whitening cream was sold in every pharmacy), but Shane was also repulsive now. He was both sides of the coin: captivating *and* revolting. It was probably difficult to know how to feel about him. How did one reconcile two extremes?

Shane took a cab to Sunny Days Condominium, an upscale building with security and a front desk. The man behind the front desk, dressed in a black suit with a bow-tie, had a pencil moustache and tiny wire-frame glasses. Some sort of pomade made his hair shiny. It smelled antiseptic, the way men had smelled at the barbershop when he was a child.

"May I help you?" he asked.

Shane was acutely aware that he didn't belong here, what with his tattoos, the cheap clothes he'd bought in Dumaguete, the backpack. He glanced behind him and saw that two security guards were keeping eyes on him.

"I'm trying to find a forwarding address for Song Leung," Shane said. "I knew her husband, and I have some things that belonged to him."

"You have things that belonged to Mr. Charlie?" the man asked, intrigued.

"Yes," Shane said. "Papers. They're in my backpack. But this is the last address I have for her."

The man shook his head. "I'm sorry, but Mrs. Leung doesn't live here anymore. I can't help you."

"Oh. Okay. Do you think there's anyone else in the building who might know? Neighbors? Friends?"

The man reached up and smoothed his mustache. He stared myopically at Shane, as though looking passively through binoculars at a distant crime in progress.

"No, sir," he finally said. "I can't help you."

Shane nodded. "I appreciate it," he said, though he knew the man was lying. He *could* have helped Shane; he chose not to.

The two security men watched Shane as he walked from the front desk to the exit. They continued staring at him as he stood outside. When Shane walked a few yards down the sidewalk, the men stepped outside to keep him in sight. They wore earpieces, and one of the men was speaking while staring at Shane, as though narrating what he was seeing.

Shane walked further down and leaned against a wall.

And then he waited.

Each time someone exited the building and headed in Shane's direction, Shane would ask them if they knew Song Leung. Mostly, they ignored Shane. A few shook their heads. Even fewer spoke at all, saying *no* or *no, sorry*.

The guards eventually returned to their stations at the front of the building's entrance, out of Shane's sight. Shane probably looked unstable – crazy but harmless.

"Excuse me," Shane said to an older woman. She was in her seventies or eighties – old but spry, dressed for yoga and carrying a rolled mat under her arm. "Do you know Song Leung, by chance?" he asked.

The woman hesitated. She seemed intrigued.

"This is complicated," Shane said, "but I was accused of stealing her husband's money. Charlie's. But I didn't. My business partner did. Or maybe some of his associates did. I'm still trying to figure all that out. Anyway…" He paused to take a breath. He tried to read the old woman's milky eyes. He took a deep breath, waited a beat, and then continued. "I heard Song lost everything, and I want to help, but I don't know where she is."

"Who told you about Song?" the old woman asked.

"Her brother-in-law."

"Lei?"

"Yes."

"Where is Lei?"

"Cambodia. But he's dead now. Overdose. I'm sorry."

She shook her head. "Always trouble, that one." She sighed. "You knew Charlie?"

Only yesterday he had slipped into Charlie's skin, asking a prostitute to choke him to death to better understand the man himself. But did he really know him? Did *anyone* know Charlie Leung?

"No," Shane finally said. "I didn't learn about Charlie until…" How much should he tell her? "I spent five years in a detention center in Manila, waiting for a trial date. And then I was cleared of any crimes. An American police officer named Luke had been helping to clear my name. He was helping Song, too. But he died before I was released. His wife gave me all his papers." He reached around and patted the backpack. "And that's how I learned about Charlie."

He was talking too much, but he hoped honesty could unlock doors.

"You're a good man," the woman said. "I see it. But don't stay in Hong Kong very long. It might not end well for you."

Was she threatening him? Or helping him?

"You like yoga, do you?" he asked, smiling.

She nodded. "Have you tried it?" she asked.

Shane shook his head. There was so much in this world he hadn't tried.

"You should," she said. "The goal of yoga is liberation from suffering."

"Is that so?"

"Same as Buddhism," she said. "You look like you're suffering. You need something."

"You're not wrong," Shane said.

The woman stepped closer and whispered an address.

She said, "You'll find Song there. But don't stay here long. You've been warned."

She reached out and squeezed Shane's hand and then continued her journey.

Chapter 47

Shane was hustling to reach the address when he had a panic attack in the taxi.

"Pull over, please," he said.

When the driver didn't hear him, Shane raised his voice.

"Pull over! Now!" he yelled.

The driver pulled over. Shane handed the man too much money and got out of the cab. He was having difficulty breathing. Without checking to see if Shane was okay, the cab driver pulled away.

He was standing in front of Sun Wah Café. To the left of the café doors was a magazine stand that sold cigarettes, newspapers, and Chinese magazines about pets, cameras, and weddings. It was the sort of place he never saw anymore, and the sight of it sent him spiraling into a wormhole of nostalgia. Even the doors for the café, all glass and chrome, reminded Shane of times his parents had taken him to restaurants in downtown Chicago when he was a child.

Dizzy, trying to get a grip on his panic attack as fumes from a stopped bus saturated the air around him, Shane could well have been transported back to Wasbash Avenue of 1971. Time travel was no less credible as the last five years in a detention center had been, or the fact that he was presently in Hong Kong trying to locate a woman he didn't know who lived in a cage home. For just a moment – a half-second – time was as fluid as a river.

Shane took a deep breath and then walked inside the café.

The air-conditioning overhead helped center him. There weren't many customers, which also helped. He wriggled out of his backpack and set it down on the seat on the other side of his booth. After settling in, he ordered milk tea and a lemon tart.

As had happened at the other restaurant, Shane thought of his wife, Cheryl. The booth he sat in was made for two. He imagined her, instead of his backpack, sitting across from him. Mirrors covered most of one wall, creating the optical illusion that the place was much larger than it was.

He was feeling better by the time his milk tea and tart arrived, though a deep sadness had settled in. His and Cheryl's plan was to work hard, retire early, and then travel the world. She had made it to the *work hard* part. Together, they had taken inconsequential trips to places like Biloxi, San Antonio, and Little Rock.

Why was Hong Kong making him so goddamned sentimental? He would rather have kept his feelings pushed down, the way you held a living thing under water until it went limp, and then you could let it go and watch the water carry it away.

Shane sipped from a cup that advertised Black & White Milk. The plate with the tart had Chinese characters around the outer edge. The food and drink were sweeter than anything he'd ever have consumed before coming to the Philippines, but his body craved it now.

A man walking by stared at Shane. Shane nodded at the man. The man nodded back, then snatched Shane's backpack, ran to the door, and pushed his way outside.

"Fuck!"

Shane slid out of the booth with the aim to run after the man, but he hadn't paid and he could hear someone yelling at him, so he took a handful of bills from his pocket and tossed them on the table. And then he pushed through the doors, looking left and then right. He saw the runner already at the end of the next block.

Shane took off after him.

A bus had just released a dozen passengers, causing Shane to zigzag around them, ducking and weaving. He could still see the thief. The man was a Hongkonger or maybe Chinese. He definitely wasn't a westerner. He was a good twenty years younger than Shane. Shane felt old and sluggish by comparison, trying to gain speed but feeling himself slow down, his lungs burning.

Foot traffic was even heavier up ahead, and Shane thought he might be gaining on him. He wasn't sure he had enough stamina, but then his body shifted into another gear, and his strides lengthened.

He didn't know what hit him, but he fell sideways, rolling toward the street, barely stopping before a bus cruised by his head. Shane looked up and saw two men walking slowly away, older and wearing dress clothes, but they weren't office workers. And then Shane saw on one of the man's clenched fists a pair of brass knuckles.

Shane reached up and touched his jaw. Was it broken?

A few bystanders, speaking quickly in a language Shane didn't understand, helped him to his feet. They were appalled by the two men's behavior, pointing in their direction and talking passionately, animatedly, but of little use to Shane, who not only didn't understand them but could no longer see the man who had taken his backpack or either of the men who had blindsided him.

"Thank you," Shane said to the people gathered around him. He brushed himself off. Nothing was broken. He'd live.

As the crowd dissolved, carrying on with their day, an old man walked up to Shane and said, "Triad." He shook his head. "No good."

The man was older than Shane's parents, if Shane's parents had still been alive. The old man had probably been a teenager during the island's occupation under the Japanese Empire; seen the Brits control the island not once but twice. He wore cheap flip-flops. His big toes didn't have any nails. He was missing teeth. Mostly bald, he had a rim of close-cropped gray hair. The backs of his hands were all tendons and veins. He was inches from death. But in his cloudy eyes swam Hong Kong's history. He placed a hand on Shane's arm, said, "Be careful," and walked away.

Triad.

Lei was right about the Hong Kong mafia's involvement. Shane's appearance at Charlie Leung's old condominium must have tripped a switch for the man with the pencil-mustache behind the front desk. And Charlie had stupidly hung around the building all afternoon, giving plenty of time for gangsters to arrive and size him up from a distance.

The old man offering Shane advice was to be trusted. He was so old he might have had run-ins with the triads himself. But what could Shane do? He couldn't just fly home. He couldn't pretend the last five years hadn't happened.

He was a little banged up – he'd scrapped some skin off his elbows and palms – but the injuries were negligible.

He checked to make sure he still had his wallet.

He did.

He checked to make sure he still had his phone.

He did.

He brushed himself off one more time, adjusted his eyepatch, and started walking. Stasis was never a good option. He had a goal. And each step toward that goal would bring him closer to an answer. That was how therapy worked. And finding the motherfuckers who made him spend five years in hell? That was how retribution worked.

Chapter 48

The apartment complex looked from the outside like a bad acid trip: vertical rows of pastel colors now so filthy that the walls appeared to be melting; windows violated in every manor by air-conditioning units; clothes draped over railings and rusted bars, baking in the haze-drenched sun. There was so much chaos and grime going on with the exterior alone that it served as a dire warning for what to expect inside

The moment Shane stepped through the doors he was struck by how closely the place resembled his own living conditions as a prisoner in Manila. The cage homes were as advertised: long hallways stacked with cages, each cage barely large enough for one person. It was like a macabre pet store, but instead of dogs and kittens, there were people inside the cages sleeping or staring out with suspicion at the interloper. The cages were four by four by six feet. There was no sunlight. Wires were strung everywhere, each socket overloaded. A fire hazard if ever there was one. A few cages had Astroturf instead of a rug to give the illusion of life.

Shane squeezed his way through the narrow rows. It was nearly impossible for two people to pass each other. An old woman had to crouch down to where Shane's legs were so that she could find enough space to pass him.

Shane called out, "Does anyone know Song Leung? I'm looking for Song Leung!"

Most people stared vacantly at him from their cages. Many ignored him, lost in their own tasks – sewing, cleaning, watching a miniature TV. These were the city's workers – the streetcleaners and housekeepers and laborers.

Shane could see, as he passed some cages where the bed was made and framed photos of family members hung from the cage wires, the struggle to maintain some dignity. Meanwhile, an argument had broken out inside the area's communal kitchen. Shane couldn't understand what the argument was over; he only recognized the tone.

Over the next hour, Shane walked the lengths of ten floors. He wasn't sure how many more he could do today.

"Song Leung? Anyone? Song Leung?"

From what Shane had read on his flight here from Phnom Penh, the cage homes were a step up from coffin homes, which were even smaller and, as with the cage homes, as advertised: homes in the shape of (and barely larger than) a coffin. The world was indeed a needlessly cruel place – mercilessly cold and indifferent.

"I know Song Leung," a man said from inside his cage.

"Yes?"

"Up two," he said. "Right about here. But on other side." He pointed to the cage directly across from him.

"Thank you, thank you!" Shane said.

The man pointed in the direction of the stairwell.

Shane counted his steps to the exit. *Thirty.*

When Shane opened the door, he squinted from the light, blinded, unable to see anything for a moment. He could feel the scar tissue tightening where there had once been an eye – a reflex. Despite the old air-conditioning units he saw outside, it was stifling hot here. The stairwell gave no relief as there were no fans, only sunlight freely pouring in, offering nothing but heat.

Shane mounted two flights of stairs and took a deep breath before entering.

This time he was blinded by darkness and had to wait a moment for his eye to adjust. He counted off thirty steps and stopped. The man downstairs lived to Shane's left. Shane turned to his right and peered into the cage. "Song Leung?" he asked.

A woman looked up from a magazine and stared at Shane.

"Are you Charlie Leung's wife?" Shane asked.

"Go away," she said and returned to her magazine.

She was lying on a thin mattress. The cage wasn't large enough for chairs or a desk. It also wasn't large enough for her sons, who were conspicuously missing.

"My name is Shane Doyle. Does that mean anything to you?"

Song said nothing. She angrily flipped through the magazine's pages. She was a handsome woman with dark lines under her eyes, prematurely gray hair, and a downturned mouth.

"I can't promise anything," Shane said, "but I'd like to help you to get out of here. Did you know that your husband had a life insurance policy?"

If Song's anger had been at five, it was now at ten.

She tossed the magazine and spun around to face Shane.

"Yes," she said. "Of course I know!"

"So what happened?" Shane asked. "Did the insurance company have issues with it? Didn't they pay you?"

"Who the hell are you?" she asked.

"I'm Shane Doy…"

"Yeah yeah yeah. I mean, who *are* you?"

"I'm the man who was accused of stealing your husband's money."

At last, this news seized her attention.

"I'm the man," Shane continued, "who spent five years in a place worse than this..." – he motioned around him – "...waiting for a trial that never came. I'm the man who only got out of there thanks to a man named Luke Bradfield who lived in Dumaguete. I believe you know Luke."

"I did," Song said. "But then he stopped helping us. So I don't know if he was ever really helping us. Maybe he was made up, like the company my husband invested his money in."

"No, Luke was real," Shane said. "He was ill the last year of his life. And then..."

"And then what?"

"He died."

Song's face, which had been as tight as a fist, softened.

"How do you know?" she asked, unable to let go of her suspicion.

"Because I visited his widow," Shane said. "We went to his grave. Because she gave me all his research. Except that someone stole it this morning. Here, in Hong Kong. They grabbed my backpack and ran."

Song took in all of Shane, studying him as though he were an object she was about to sketch.

"Your brother-in-law? Lei?"

Song nodded.

"He overdosed in Phnom Penh. Just a few days ago."

Song didn't reveal any emotions. She looked like a person whose burdens had reached their maximum capacity, and any new burden would have to wait until she unloaded what she was carrying.

"How are you going to help me?" she asked.

"Let's talk about that life insurance policy first," Shane said. "I want to hear why you didn't get the money."

Song was a woman without options. She unlocked the cage door and reluctantly invited him into her home.

Chapter 49

The cage was barely wide enough for two people. The mattress was a narrow one, and Shane could taste Song's breath as she breathed. The home was part storage locker, home office, and bedroom. Colgate toothpaste rested next to a wedding photo in a frame, which leaned against a roll of toilet paper, which sat next to traps for cockroaches. Power strips were plugged into extension cords that ran out of the cage, probably plugged into even greater fire hazards.

Song listened to Shane tell his story, including details of his recent trip to Phnom Penh. So far, Shane wasn't telling her anything she didn't know, except that her brother-in-law had died.

As he talked, he tried not letting on that the cage was bringing him back to his own dark place of relentless physical assaults and disease and hallucinations, but he could feel his fingers digging into his thighs to keep his trauma contained.

"Tell me about the insurance money," Shane said.

"Triads took it," she said. "Charlie paid them monthly so he didn't have to work for them."

"Kind of the opposite of a membership fee," Shane said.

"When he died," Song said, "they said he needed to keep paying. When I collect the insurance money, they say if I give it to them, they'll leave me alone. They say all debts are paid."

"Except that it leaves you with no money," Shane said. "Where are your sons? And your mother?"

"My mother took my sons to Guangzhou."

"These Triads," Shane said. "Who are they? Where can I find them?"

Song looked confused by the questions.

"I want to talk to them," Shane said.

"No," Song said. "They'll kill you. These are bad people."

"They won't kill me if I have something to offer them."

"No," Song said. "I don't want trouble. I pay them. I'm free."

Never had the word free been so ironic.

"I understand," Shane said, "but you can't stay here forever. Is that what you want?"

Song was silent. Of course it wasn't what she wanted, and yet she hesitated.

"Just a name," Shane said. "I can fix this."

From the cage across the narrow aisle came a man's voice. "Fang Zhong," he said.

Shane pivoted. How many others had been eavesdropping?

The man was wearing a stained undershirt. His sparse hair defied gravity, as though someone had rubbed a balloon across his head.

"Where can I find him?" Shane asked.

"Casino in Macau."

Macau was the Vegas of Asia with dozens of high-end casinos.

"Which casino?"

The man shook his head and then turned his attention back to the water boiling on a hot pot. He opened a plastic tub of instant coffee and sprinkled some into a mug.

"Fang Zhong?" Shane asked.

Song said nothing.

"Look," Shane said. "I won't do anything to make your life worse. Promise."

"My brother-in-law," she said. "He was alive until he met you, right?"

Shane nodded.

Song had made her point.

"Okay then," Shane said. He stood up. As soon as he stepped out into the claustrophobic walkway, Song locked the cage and resumed her position on the mattress, pretending to read a magazine. "I'll let you know what I find out," Shane offered to anyone who cared to listen.

Chapter 50

Shane took the ferry from Hong Kong to Macau. There was an old area of Macau that looked like old Hong Kong, and then there was the Vegas part of Macau – gaudy, shiny, flush with tourists. After Shane exited the ferry, he headed for the bright lights and fountains and streets that looked like Hollywood sets.

He wanted to believe that he was a different man now than the night he had burned it all down in an abandoned gas station, but was he? He had flushed the morphine pills down the toilet in Phnom Penh, but what did that prove? The only thing it proved was that for one night he had willpower. In truth, all he needed was one pill to flip the switch, and then he wouldn't be able to stop. Whatever he was pursuing, his brain wasn't wired to let up.

In the first casino, Shane started by asking security guards if they knew Fang Zhong, but they shook their heads or ignored him, keeping their eyes locked on other things in the distance. He continued the same tactic in the second and third casinos. It wasn't that Shane expected to be led directly to Fang. What he expected was for word to get out that a distinct-looking white guy, a man with an eyepatch and a tumor, was looking for him.

And it worked.

Before he stepped foot into the fourth casino, two men approached Shane, stopping him before he could enter. They were the same two men from Hong Kong who had caused him to lose sight of the thief who had stolen his backpack. One was a heavyweight; the other, a bantam.

"You guys again," Shane said.

"You should go home," the heavyweight who had tackled him said. "Louisiana, is it?"

"You've done your due diligence," Shane said. "Do you want a gold star?"

"You're in over your head," he said, stepping toe to toe with Shane. He sounded American. Second, maybe third generation.

"Maybe, just maybe, I have something valuable to offer your boss," Shane said. "And maybe if he finds out that you cockblocked me, your buddy here is going to have to take you out on a fishing boat and toss you into the South China Sea. Do you want to put your friend here in that position?"

He shook his head. "Man, you've got balls," he said and laughed, but then he looked nervous, like maybe Shane had a point. He took out his phone and made a call. Was he speaking Cantonese? After a few exchanges, he hung up and jerked his head toward Shane, indicating for him to follow.

"I'm not getting into a vehicle with you," Shane said. "Give me an address."

The tackler looked like he'd had all that he could take of Shane, but then he gave him the name of the casino and told him a room number.

"Penthouse suite," he said.

Shane said, "Tell him I'm on my way."

The casino was a short walk. Fifteen minutes, tops. The casinos in Macau made the casinos in Lake Charles look like trailer parks.

Shane's sweat turned icy when he stepped into his destination and was hit by a blast of AC. He'd heard that casinos in Vegas pumped oxygen into the game rooms to keep the players lively – and, quite possibly, alive. The story was likely apocryphal, but Shane felt fully awake now, ready for action.

There was only one elevator for the penthouse suite.

The man who stood guard, after speaking into a walkie-talkie, allowed Shane to enter the roped-off area. By the look the guard was giving him, Shane was not the sort of guest normally allowed onto the elevator. The cargo shorts, for starters, were a red flag, but they were just one of many. The eyepatch, the unappealing lump, the prison tattoos: these were the culmination of a man who would trip multiple switches.

When the elevator bell rang for the suite and the door slid open, another guard escorted Shane into the suite itself, through the living area, where floor-to-ceiling windows looked out over Macau.

The skyline of casinos and hotels looked like something out of *Blade Runner*, the way one skyscraper was wider at the top, defying logic, or the way colored lights outlined every building. The future had come to fruition, the way it had been imagined in 1982.

The guard led Shane into one last room, an office, where an old man sat behind an enormous glass-and-steel desk, as futuristic as the cityscape behind him.

When the guard left, the man said, "I was told you're looking for me."

Fang Zhong was at least seventy – small but not frail. Shane feared showing any regret for coming here. Like a shark that can detect blood a quarter of a mile away, Fang had reached his current position by smelling weakness and doubt.

Shane said, "I'm not here in any kind of antagonistic position. I'm not here to threaten anyone."

At this, Fang smiled, as though any threat against him was laughable.

Shane pushed on. "Here's the thing. I have an offer for you that you'll find hard to pass up."

Fang said nothing as Shane had said nothing of value yet.

"May I?" Shane asked, motioning to the chair across from Fang.

Fang nodded.

"I assume you know who I am," Shane said, sitting. "I was falsely accused of a committing fraud against several very wealthy businessmen, including Charlie Leung. But it was my business partner, a man named Phil Corbett and three Vietnamese, who committed the fraud. And by my calculations, they got away with over two hundred million dollars."

"And you want our help to find the money?"

"No. I want your help finding Phil Corbett. If I find him, you can have the money. And you can have his business partners' money. That's my promise."

"What else do you want?"

"I want to give Song Leung the value of her husband's life insurance payout."

Fang said nothing.

Shane said, "I have a degree in Social Work, not Math, but a two million dollar investment for a two *hundred* million dollar return…I'd say that's pretty damned good." He smiled. He had to be careful. He didn't want to oversell it. He said, "And that's how I'd look at it – as an investment. Not a concession."

Shane was careful not to present an offer that could result in losing face. He had learned this the hard way when he was locked up. You never wanted to box someone in; you never wanted to humiliate someone. More than once Shane had watched someone die after causing someone else to lose face. It was about honor and dignity. If you lose that, you lose everything.

Shane said, "The two million is for my services, and I'd like to gift it to Song Leung."

Fang said, "I'll help you find your business partner. But you won't get the money until you hand him and his associates over to me."

Shane considered this. On the one hand, it was perfectly reasonable that Fang shouldn't have to pay anything upfront. On the other hand, he had hoped to wrap things up with Song Leung before moving on to the next stage of the operation.

"Okay, but on one condition," Shane said.

Fang waited.

Shane said, "Once this is over, I don't want to lose face."

Fang knew what Shane was saying without Shane warning him: *Don't make me retaliate.* But, also, Shane was asking for mutual respect in language that Fang would understand.

"What do you need?" he asked.

"I need to know if this fake business – the business that scammed Charlie – had an actual office. Did they have an address that fronted as a real office?"

Fang nodded.

"What else?"

"My backpack," Shane said. "If you have any leads on who took my backpack…that would be terrific."

Again, Shane knew that Fang had ordered his men to take his backpack, but he couldn't present his theory directly.

"What else?" Fang asked.

"I need money."

Fang raised an eyebrow.

Shane pushed ahead. "Look, I just spent five years in hell. And when I got out, there wasn't much money left. And in order for me to get here, sitting across from you…I'm down to a few bucks. I mean…look at me!" He laughed.

Fang nodded. He pressed a buzzer on his desk, and the security detail who had shown him in stepped into the office to take Shane back downstairs.

Only on his way out did Shane see the wheelchair in the corner of the room, folded and against the wall, like modern art. Shane paused, turning to face Fang.

"About my offer?" Shane asked.

"I'll consider it," Fang said.

"How do I contact you? To follow up?"

"We'll contact *you*," Fang said.

Chapter 51

Shane paid a driver to take a note to Song. He gave detailed directions to the man and then asked him to repeat them to make sure he understood them, but Shane had a bad feeling he was handing over money for a service that would never be rendered. What obligation, other than a moral one, did this stranger have to Shane?

Shane stopped off at a pharmacy before returning to his room. He had a raging headache. He probably hadn't had enough water. Or maybe it was the air pollution, hours spent sucking in more than his daily quota of exhaust fumes.

From outside, the pharmacy looked like the kind of place that might sell party supplies or cheap fireworks. Its sign was gaudy, and the narrow store was packed to capacity. Inside, there was only one man working. Behind him, row after row of boxes, each row stacked to the ceiling, every imaginable medicine.

"I need something for a headache," Shane said. "It's killing me. And it's getting worse."

The pharmacist stared at Shane, smiling, as though diagnosing him by sight alone. He turned and, running his fingers up a row of boxes, found the remedy.

"Paracetamol," the pharmacist said.

Paracetamol was the same as acetaminophen. Tylenol, essentially.

"Anything stronger?" Shane asked.

The pharmacist surveyed Shane's ghastly face. There was, for a brief moment, hope. But then he shook his head.

Shane didn't need morphine, but something stronger than Tylenol would have been appreciated. Apparently, Hong Kong wasn't Cambodia.

"Okay," Shane said, paying. "All right."

"Your change," the pharmacist said, handing over some money.

Shane stepped outside, into a cityscape as unfamiliar as another planet, as disorienting as those days when he'd snort line after line of Oxy, feeling like he was floating through space while uncertain about everything in his life, caring about none of it. He thought about the Walgreens parking lot in Lafayette, the first time Kylie had followed him out to give him the Oxys for his wife, and how she had kissed him to conceal for the surveillance camera that she had just given him drugs. Shane had never bothered to learn Kylie's last name, and he never saw her again after the night in the gas station. He imagined by now she was dead. In that regard, Shane was one of the lucky ones. There weren't many who rose from heroin's ashes.

Shane returned to his room and popped four Paracetamols. He wondered what would happen if he cooked them in a spoon and then mainlined it. A dark thought, but it caused him to laugh – until he thought of Lei.

Shane climbed into bed and pulled the blanket high, up and over his head, curling into himself, like a snail in a shell. Since arriving in Hong Kong, Shane's sleep had brought him to depths he hadn't experienced in years. After his release from the detention center, he feared he would never experience a normal night of sleep ever again. And maybe on a regular basis he wouldn't. But for short stretches –

afternoon naps, or a few hours at night – he'd finally begun to sink into those places in his unconscious mind that had remained off-limits for five years. He always had to stay alert enough to wake up at the slightest sound, ready to defend himself.

Today's afternoon nap left him with a crease across his face and his brain pleasantly anesthetized. But when he looked at his phone and saw the time, he rolled out of bed and quickly changed into fresh clothes.

"Shit, shit, shit," he said, afraid he might be late.

As it turned out, he wasn't late because Song was nowhere to be found.

Shane was at the top of the Ritz Carlton in the Ozone Bar, the highest bar in the world, on the 118th floor.

All the seats were unusual geometric shapes. The floor, possibly marble, featured a geometric pattern. The ceiling had multiple layers of geometric designs. It was like walking inside of a snowflake, surrounded by ordered chaos.

The waitstaff and customers alike watched him as he entered. As with yesterday's adventure, Shane was overwhelmingly underdressed.

Fuck 'em, he thought.

All along the wall were cushioned nooks for large group, each nook equipped with seven or eight pillows. Shane took a seat at the bar. He ordered a drink called Penicillin. It set him back eighteen bucks.

"Do you take Blue Cross?" he asked the bartender, but the joke was lost on him. "I want to run a tab."

"I just need a card," the bartender said, "and I'll give it right back."

Shane hesitated. Then he brought up the Apple card on his phone and handed it over. There was probably enough credit to cover a few drinks…but not much more.

"What's in this?" Shane asked when the bartender returned with his phone.

"Scotch whisky," the bartender said. "Ginger. Honey Syrup. And lemon juice."

"Damn," Shane said. "That's the healthiest thing I've put in my body in years."

He took another sip. He couldn't deny it. It was a damn good drink.

"Sir?" the bartender said, and he motioned toward the entrance.

Shane swiveled and saw Song standing at the end of the bar. She was wearing a dress she must have worn in another time, back when she and Charlie regularly went to places like this, but the dress was wrinkled now and Song looked uneasy.

Shane waved her over.

"You look lovely," Shane said.

Song said nothing. She was holding a purse that had probably been the height of fashion six years ago. Shane wouldn't have known one way or the other, nor would he have cared, but he could see that she was self-conscious by the way she held it in front of her, covering it with her hands. She reached up and fixed her hair, though it didn't need fixing. She couldn't focus on just Shane; she kept looking past him, as though making sure no one was judging her.

The prospect of resurrecting a piece of her old life by coming here had probably appealed to her, but now that she was actually here, among her former peers, the reality of how far she had fallen was starting to sink in.

"I have good news," Shane said. "Just…" He wanted to tell her to relax. He put a hand on her shoulder and said, "Please. I want you to have a good time."

The bartender offered her a menu, but she already knew what she wanted. A glass of white wine. The Chardonnay from Australia. A large glass.

"You've been here before?" Shane asked.

Song nodded.

Shane said, "And here I thought I was doing something special for you. Silly me."

"No," she said. "It's very nice." She looked down, as though ashamed. "I haven't been here in many years."

"Well," Shane said, "it's my first time."

The bartender delivered the Chardonnay.

"Cheers!" Shane said, and they clinked their glasses together.

He remembered the afternoon lunch on Lake Martin, surrounded by gators, the day before he left for the Philippines, he and Corbett drinking in separate canoes. Corbett had played his part to perfection. Not once did he express any hesitation about what he was about to set in motion for Shane, no sorrow for the man whose life he was about to ruin.

"You have good news?"

"Yes I do," Shane said, smiling. "I met with Fang."

Song's entire demeanor changed. She began rubbing her arms, as though the temperature had dropped by thirty degrees. Inside this Fortress of Solitude of a bar, high up in the polar wilds of Hong Kong, it wasn't difficult to imagine it was colder than it actually was.

"Everything will be okay," Shane said.

"No it won't," Song said. "You don't know what you're doing."

"Trust me," Shane said.

Song shook her head. "You have no idea. You trust Fang?" She laughed. The laugh was loud, unhinged. A few people looked over to see what was happening.

Shane was starting to feel anger bubble up. It was the kind of anger that many of his clients would come to talk to him about, how their marriages had soured and the slightest criticisms would send them into a rage. They wanted to burn it all down – their marriages, their domestic life, the American dream. *All of it.* And Shane had always talked them down off the cliff. He was good at it. He was never judgmental; he never raised his voice. He would start asking probing questions that would lead them back to wanting to salvage everything that had gone wrong.

But that Shane – Shane the useful therapist – was dead and buried. That Shane had died two years into his incarceration.

"It's too late now," Shane said, putting an end to the conversation. "I have a stake in this, too, you know. I'm not in Hong Kong on a goddamned peacekeeping mission. I'm here because someone destroyed my life." He lowered his voice and leaned closer. "My *fucking* life. And what are you going to do? Spend your life in a cage? Like an animal? If I was you, I'd rather be dead than accept that *that* was my fate. I know, I know. That's a pretty *privileged* thing to say. Because I don't have to live that way." He reached up and took off his eyepatch. Song flinched at the sight of him. "I spent five years locked up in hell for, what? For trusting my business partner? I lost my eye. I learned how to fight because every week someone came at me. *Every week.* There's shit that happened to me there that I won't even talk about. Shit I'll *never* talk about. So maybe my point of view isn't so privileged after all. Maybe it's *informed.*"

Song said, "Whatever you offered Fang, he'll kill me. And then he'll kill you."

"I'll give it even odds," Shane said.

Song leaned back in her chair and glared at Shane.

When she stood up, she fell to her knees and then pitched forward. She was weak – most certainly malnourished.

Shane joined her on the floor. "Okay, just breathe. There you go. Everything's going to be all right." To the bartender, he said, "Cash me out."

Bar tab paid and Song back on her feet, Shane helped his companion outside.

"I'll get you a cab," he said.

"I can't go back there tonight," she said. "What if he's waiting for me?"

Shane said, "Okay. You can come back to my place."

He expected some resistance, but Song nodded.

"Thank you," she said.

Chapter 52

There was only one bed in Shane's room, so he sat in an overstuffed chair. When there was a knock on his door, Song said, "Be careful."

"It's just the food," Shane said.

Shane opened the door and took the bags. From a diner across the street, Shane had ordered beef brisket noodles, pineapple buns, and milk tea – two of each. His credit card was officially tapped out. If Fang didn't accept his offer, he was screwed.

Song sat up in bed and greedily took her food, as though Shane had ordered prime rib and lobster. She ate fastidiously, leaving not a drop of broth on herself or the bedsheets. There were no crumbs from the pineapple buns, either. The milk tea was absorbed into her system as though intravenously.

Within thirty minutes of finishing everything, she fell asleep on top of the blankets. Shane removed the spare blanket from the closet, unfolded it, and placed it over her.

Since the detention center hadn't returned his laptop, Shane composed a long, detailed handwritten narrative of his arrangement with Fang on hotel stationary. He would send it to his attorney in the morning, explaining that the document should be opened only in the event of his death and only if his death was suspicious. His attorney had handled legal issues relating to his and Corbett's business. His name was Paul Landry, a large man with a thick Cajun accent, and his business was made up of clients he'd met at Red's Gym and golf courses. He had a small office in the Oil Center, with only one employee who answered the phones and scheduled appointments. He would be surprised to find himself as an intermediary between a man he'd probably assumed was deceased and one of the higher-ranking officers of the Hong Kong mafia.

Shane folded the stationary, stuffed them into an envelope with the hotel's logo, and then ate the rest of his brisket noodles, which were cold and bloated now, no longer at their peak.

Chapter 53

When Shane woke up, Song was gone.

Shane stood slowly, his body stiff from a night spent sleeping upright in a chair. His neck hurt. His right shoulder blade hurt. His lower back hurt.

After showering and getting dressed, he headed downstairs for coffee, but the apartment manager called out for him as he passed her office. She was a kind but worried woman, unable to look Shane in the eye, peering down at his tattoos instead.

"Yes?" he asked.

"You receive a message," the manager said.

"And?" Shane asked.

"Yes," the manager said. "The person said…take the 3:10 ferry to Macau."

"That's all?"

"That's all," she said, nodding, shutting her eyes, as though bracing for pain. But then she spied one last look at his arms.

"Thank you." He started to leave but stopped. "Oh! One more question. Do you have six month rentals?"

The look of worry eased from her face. "Yes. One month. Six month. One year. Different prices."

"Perfect," Shane said. "Let's talk after coffee."

"No milk tea? Milk tea is very good."

"Coffee first," Shane said. "Milk tea later."

This news made the manager happy. She smiled and nodded. The day was turning out to be a good one for her.

Shane stepped outside. Across the street was a café, so Shane hustled over, entered, and sat down, only to realize that there was no coffee on the menu.

Shane tried to hide the disappointment on his face as he ordered, but he feared his face only registered disappointment these days.

"Okay," he said. "Milk tea."

Waiting for his order, Shane searched Google for the Walgreens where he had gone to get pain pills the day before his wife died. The pharmacy was open twenty-four hours. It would have been midnight back in Louisiana. The witching hour.

Before he could give it too much thought, he called the number. He worked his way thought the automated system, opting to talk to a pharmacy specialist. During normal business hours, the wait might have taken thirty minutes – if he was lucky. Today, someone picked up on the first ring.

"Walgreens Pharmacy," the voice said – a man, older. There was no noise in the background, only Muzak.

"Hi there," Shane said, adding some pep to his voice. "I have a really odd question."

The man laughed. He said, "Trust me, I've heard everything."

"All right then!" He felt like he was about to step over the lip of a canyon. "Eight years ago, my wife was dying of cancer."

The pharmacist was silent. Maybe he realized he'd made a mistake staying on the line after Shane's warning.

"I had to go to the pharmacy one night for pain pills. A woman who worked there at your pharmacy was particularly helpful. I really wanted to thank her. But I'm not sure anyone still works there from that long ago."

"Well. This is my twentieth year. Do you have a name?"

"Kylie," Shane said.

"Kylie?"

"Mmmhmm."

"Do you mind if I ask how she was helpful?" the pharmacist asked.

"The thing is, I didn't have a prescription," Shane said, "so she sent me packing. But then she came out to my car and gave me some pills."

"Let me guess," the pharmacist said. "OxyContin?"

"I don't want to get anyone in trouble," Shane said.

"Yeah…no. Kylie worked here. I remember her because I was her supervisor. But she had some – how shall I say – legal trouble."

"Legal trouble as in…?"

"As in she was arrested," the pharmacist said.

Shane said, "Oh wow. I hope it wasn't because of what she did for me."

"No, no. She was arrested for selling pills."

The server delivered the tea. Shane smiled up at her and nodded.

"Do you remember her last name?" Shane asked.

"Rouse. You know…like the grocery store chain. That's the only reason I remember it. No relation, though."

There was a long pause as Shane stared down into his tea, trying to make sense of everything.

"I'm sorry…what did you say your name was?" the pharmacist said.

"Shane Doyle." He took a deep breath. He said, "My wife died the next day. I just wanted to thank her for being so compassionate. It was a rough time."

"I'm sorry about your wife," the pharmacist said, "I've probably said too much. It's late here. It's been a long day. Loose lips, you know."

"Gotcha," Shane said.

"Is there anything else I can do for you?"

"Nope. I do appreciate it," Shane said.

"Alrighty then," the pharmacist said. "You have a good night."

"It's morning where I'm at," Shane said. "But I'll certainly try."

He clicked off the call before the pharmacist could ask where he was.

Shane googled *Kylie Rouse*, and the first story that came up was about the arrest.

She was found with OxyContin, Lithium, methadone, and Soma, a muscle relaxant – enough of each for fifty people.

Why was she getting prescriptions filled if she already had so much at her disposal?

He scrolled down, and there she was. Her mugshot. He felt no nostalgia seeing her after so many years. He felt nothing. But his hands began to shake.

Shane's arm swiped the tea off the table. The cup shattered across the floor.

"I'm sorry!" he called out as the server rushed over to see what had happened. "I'm sorry, I'm sorry!"

The man making the milk tea behind a counter stopped what he was doing to see what had happened, but then he went back to work.

Nothing was adding up. It probably would have been smarter to let old ghosts rest. But that wasn't Shane's way.

Chapter 54

Shane stood on the ferry, peering out toward Macau. Most cities lost their mystery in the daylight, but Macau still looked like the cover of an old sci-fi novel with its glass domes, its space-needle structures, and a building that looked like it was going to bloom into another building. The day's haze offered an especially eerie feel, like those early 1970s movies about air pollution on a post-apocalyptic planet.

"You made it." The voice came from behind. Fang was in his wheelchair. His legs, Shane saw now, were as limp as a ragdoll's. The security guard from Fang's penthouse stood behind the chair, his beefy hands gripping the chair's handles.

"Do you have what I need?" Shane asked.

The security guard pulled a manila envelope from his suit jacket. He handed it to Fang who hesitated to hand it over.

"The address," Fang said, "is in Vietnam. Ho Chi Minh City. They sometimes met clients there."

"Were you keeping tabs on Charlie?" Shane asked.

"We followed him there once, yes," Fang said. "We follow everyone, all the time."

Shane snatched the envelope from Fang's fingers and opened it. He pulled out the file and studied it, then returned it, fastened the clasp, and said, "You should know, I wrote a detailed document about our agreement and I filed it with my attorney. Should I go missing or end up dead under mysterious circumstances, I've asked my attorney to give the document to Interpol."

Fang studied Shane. "It's an insult in this part of the world to suggest that someone's lying."

"Every time I've given someone the benefit of the doubt in the past six years," Shane said, "I've gotten fucked over. So let's just say it's a me thing, okay? Even though we know otherwise." He took a deep breath. "The money?"

Again, the security guard reached into his suit jacket.

"I'll be expecting a rabbit the next time," Shane said and smiled, but no one joined him.

The security guard unnecessarily handed it to Fang, who handed it to Shane.

"Ten thousand U.S. in cash," Fang said, "and we wired another ten to your bank account in Lafayette."

"I see what you're doing," Shane said. "Letting me know that you have all my information." He sighed. "Twenty thousand? That's a far cry from two million."

"I saw your bank balance," Fang said. "Twenty thousand is plenty for now. Once you deliver, you'll get the rest. Disperse it as you see fit."

"Smuggling fentanyl and whatever the fuck else you smuggle into Europe and the U.S. – that's a hell of a lot of dead people on your conscience."

"I sleep just fine," Fang said.

"How involved was Charlie's wife?"

Fang smiled. "Let's just say, he couldn't have done it without her."

"The better angels of our nature," Shane said. "I guess that doesn't exist in this love story." When Fang didn't respond, Shane said, "Oh yeah…where's my backpack? Your valet isn't wearing it, and I *know* it's not inside his suit jacket."

Fang said, "It'll be returned to you before you leave Hong Kong."

The security guard pulled from inside his jacket pocket an envelope. He gave it to Shane.

"What's this? A love letter?"

"Plane tickets and a hotel reservation," Fang said.

Shane laughed. "You're better than Expedia. More efficient." Shane tucked the smaller envelope inside the larger envelope. "You do realize," he said, "that I can only hand over to you the people who stole the money. I can't actually *get* you the money."

"That won't be a problem," Fang said. He grinned and asked, "Would you like to be present when we extract that information?"

Would he?

"Let me think on it," Shane said.

"Consult with your better angels?" Fang asked.

The ferry was pulling into the port.

"Don't forget my backpack," Shane said.

"I never forget anything," Fang said, and motioned for his man to push him to the front of the line.

Chapter 55

Back in Hong Kong, Shane returned to the high rise of caged homes and found Song as he had found her that first time: sitting on her bed, trying to block out the world around her. He spoke to her through the locked chain-link door.

"Do you have any suitcases?" Shane asked.

Song looked up. She nodded.

"Where are they?"

Song lifted a thin sheet that covered her bed.

"Under here," she said, motioning to the space under her bed.

"Start packing," Shane said. He handed her an address he'd written on an envelope.

"What's this?"

"It's your apartment for the next six months."

He handed her an envelope. There was five thousand dollars inside.

In a lower voice, so as not to draw attention to Song, Shane said, "This should help until you get the rest of the insurance money."

Shane knew that Song considered everything Shane was doing an act of empathy. But it wasn't. As with Lei, it was a means to an end. He understood now, as he had never understood before, that everything in his life was intertwined: his interest in method acting, his interest in R. D. Laing, his career as a therapist, his career in advertising. They had all been about creating identities, but what he hadn't understood until now was that the creation of identity was transactional and that empathy was the currency. He had spent his life building and breaking down identities, his and others, manipulating identities, crawling inside of identities. When all was said and done, the creation of identity was all about survival. And life was a continuous act of breaking them down and then building them back up. You have a gambling problem? Let's change you. You want to play this role on TV? Dig deeper. You don't want to get raped in a detention center eight thousand six hundred miles from home? Crawl into a different skin.

Shane had already decided on his way to the cage home that he wasn't going to give Song the insurance money. She had ruined too many lives; she sure as hell shouldn't be rewarded for all the evil shit she'd been involved with. Shane's old instincts would have been to feel sorry for her, to blame himself for her current circumstance, but Shane's new instincts were refined, sharper, and he was the one who was going to walk away with the two million dollars, not her. But he needed her to *believe* that he was going to do right thing. He needed her to *believe* that he pitied her when in truth he had to buy enough time for himself. And this was how he could do it. This was the transaction.

From behind him, the man who had given him information about Fang said, "You're still alive."

Even in the cage, the man was so close that Shane could both feel and smell his breath.

"The day is still young," Shane said.

Chapter 56

Shane's backpack was inside his room, on his bed, upon his return.

Shane took this violation of his space as an aggressive message from Fang, letting Shane know who held the power, just as depositing money into Shane's personal account had been Fang's way of showing dominance.

Inside the backpack were photocopies of the retired cop's documents. Fang had kept the original documents for himself.

Shane ripped up the airline ticket to Vietnam and the hotel reservation, tossing them in a trashcan. He pulled out his phone and booked an early morning flight to Ho Chi Minh City and then found a room on AirBnb.

Shane still needed Fang and Fang still needed Shane, but he wasn't going to let Fang steer the ship.

Shane quickly packed his belongings and then took a long nap, waking at two in the morning. He took a cab to a dim sum joint that opened at three a.m.

There was only one other person in the restaurant, an old man. Was he part of Fang's detail? He didn't look like mafia, but what did Hong Kong mafia look like? As was becoming increasingly clear, anyone might have been a Triad member.

Shane was served a tea cup and chopsticks in a bowl filled with tea.

The server, noticing Shane's confusion, said, "Wash."

"I don't understand."

"Wash, wash," the server said before walking away.

The old man said, "It's an old urban legend that dishwashers don't know how to do their job, so you have clean your utensils in tea."

"Really?" Shane said. "That's a wild one."

The old man said, "American or Canadian?"

"American. Your English is good. Did you live there?"

"San Francisco for thirty years," he said. "Simi Valley, actually."

"Ah. Tech guy?"

The old man nodded. He didn't elaborate. Shane swirled his chopsticks through the lukewarm tea.

The server arrived with the tea – this one for drinking. Shane could smell the jasmine. He poured himself a cup.

"Cheers," the old man said, raising his own tea glass toward Shane.

"Cheers."

"And you?" the old man said. "What are you doing in Hong Kong? Work? Pleasure?"

"I don't know how to answer that," Shane said. "I'm going through a transitional period in my life."

"You're in a liminal space," the old man said.

"Yes. A liminal space. I like that."

"Did you just get here, or are you headed somewhere?" He motioned to Shane's backpack.

"Leaving," he said.

"Where next?"

"Thailand," Shane lied.

"Oh. Where in Thailand?"

Shane hesitated a beat too long. "Bangkok?"

"You don't sound sure."

"Actually, I lied," Shane said. "I'm not going to Thailand."

"Oh?"

"I'm going to Vietnam. Ho Chi Minh City."

The man nodded. His eyes wandered down to Shane's backpack and then back up to Shane.

"In Southeast Asia," the man said, "a lot of people are on the run from something."

Shane said, "My life is complicated."

"Everyone's life is complicated," the man said. "Some just have a talent at making it more complicated than it needs to be."

"The thing is," Shane said. "I'm having a hard time knowing who I can trust and who I can't. And I'm afraid that's never going to change now."

When their custard buns arrived, the man said, "Would you like to join me? In a place like this, you shouldn't eat alone."

Every innate instinct told Shane to take the man up on his offer. This is what you do in this world: you accept invitations, you agree to be communal – this was how people endured. It wasn't just a nicety to spend time with people you didn't know; it was necessary for the survival of the species. People weren't programmed to be alone. They needed to interact; they needed the company of strangers.

"Thank you," Shane said. "But I'm good."

The man looked both surprised and hurt, but he turned his attention back to his tea and food, and he said nothing else to Shane for the remainder of their time together.

Chapter 57

The flight from Hong Kong to Ho Chi Minh City was a short one. Shane had barely dozed off when the flight attendant nudged him to bring his chair back into the upright position.

In the airport, Shane found only one ATM that worked. The denominations were ludicrous: 100,000, 200,000, 500,000. Ho Chi Minh adorned every bill with his slick-backed hair and wispy beard. He looked like the benevolent old man who lived quietly next door, fussily tending his garden. No wonder his supporters called him Uncle Ho.

The cab driver didn't speak any English, so Shane showed him the map to his Airbnb on his phone. It took some serious studying on the driver's part, but he eventually committed the route to memory, smiled, and returned the phone.

The traffic was unlike anything Shane had ever seen – far more dense and chaotic than Cambodia, even. And yet there was something soothing about it, like synchronized swimming. Everyone would move to the right and then everyone would move to the left – a vehicular school of fish – though occasionally it was necessary to drive directly into traffic, inching forward until the goal was accomplished. From above, it probably looked like a postmodern Busby Berkeley musical.

Despite the strange tranquility, Shane checked to make sure his seatbelt was secure.

People rode their scooters on the sidewalk, weaving in and out of pedestrians. Or they drove their scooters right up alongside the taxi. They were so close that Shane could see what was on their phones, which they stared at whenever they came to a stop. The physics of what people transported on their scooters didn't seem possible: two-by-fours, upon which they would sit; dozens of boxes piled insanely on the back like something from a video game; entire families of five, no one wearing helmets.

Shane's Airbnb was in an alley so narrow he wasn't sure the cab driver could squeeze his car down it. But he did, pulling up in front of a tucked-away ice cream parlor.

"This is it?" Shane asked.

The man said nothing as he pointed to the ice cream parlor.

Shane tried reading the meter, but the numbers didn't make any sense. He knew, however, how much a ride from the airport to District 1 was supposed to be, so he increased the amount by fifty percent and then rounded up. Whatever the fee was supposed to be, the driver was joyously awoken from his slumber by what he received.

Shane slid himself and his backpack out of the backseat. There were customers in the ice cream shop. As soon as Shane stepped inside, the girl behind the counter – she couldn't have been older than sixteen – stopped what she was doing and handed Shane an envelope. Inside the envelope was a room key and a coupon for ten percent off ice cream while he stayed there. She pointed to the door in the back. As with Lei Leung and the coffee shop in Phnom Penh,

Shane would be staying in a room above an active business. He hoped his fate would fare better.

Chapter 58

Shane's heart was pounding when he woke up. He reached up and touched his eye. He had been crying. It was weird, but he only cried now from the remaining eye. The sewn-up socket no longer produced tears. But he did still feel a pulse in it, and sometimes the pulse fluttered like a bird's nervous heart.

He put on his shoes and went downstairs. The only person in the ice cream shop was the young girl who had given him the envelope. She was wearing earbuds and looking at her phone. The lights were off, probably to cut down overhead costs, but it was inching into late afternoon, and the place was getting overtaken by shadows.

When the girl noticed Shane's shadow, she turned quickly and gasped. She pulled out her earbuds and put her hand on her chest to slow her pounding heart. She smiled, embarrassed, and said, "I'm sorry."

"It's okay. I didn't want to scare you."

"Do you need something?" she asked. "Is your room okay?"

"It's fine," Shane said. "I just want some ice cream." He showed her the coupon.

"Oh!" The girl laughed. She turned and flipped a switch, and the lights blinked on. Shane wished she hadn't. He preferred the shadows.

"Let's see," Shane said. He realized, as he studied the menu, that every ice cream had alcohol in it. Bourbon, apple, and granola. Bailey's and coffee. Kahlua, almond, and dark chocolate.

"The red wine and cherry, I guess?" Shane said.

The girl smiled and got to work.

"One scoop, two scoop, three scoop?"

"Let's start with one," Shane said.

He watched as she lifted the curved glass door and scooped out the red wine and cherry. Her breath steamed the display case, causing her to momentarily disappear. When she emerged from the cooler's depths, she handed over the cup and smiled.

She was a sweet kid, polite and shy. It was times like these when he regretted not having kids of his own. But that ship had sailed; he was the end of the line.

"Thank you," Shane said and paid her. He sat at one of the few tables lined in the narrow walkway. He said, "Has anyone asked about me?"

She looked at Shane, confused.

"Did anybody come by looking for me?"

She shook her head. "No," she said.

Shane nodded. "Good."

As he ate the ice cream, he was aware of the thunderous silence in the room. He wondered why he and Cheryl had not been more ambitious about traveling. She would have loved a place like this. An ice cream shop tucked away in an alley? Hell yeah! He hated that he had no clear memory of her burial or the weeks after. By drowning his grief with Oxy, he had dishonored her.

Had he become a better person since then? He hoped so, but he doubted it. He wasn't sure anyone ever really changed all that much.

A person was who they were. What most people thought was change was just a construct layered on top of the real self. And it didn't take much for that construct to drop to the wayside.

After years as a therapist, after a lifetime of dealing with his own often-self-destructive compulsions, he was convinced that this was true. Maybe it was time to accept who he was and embrace it. Maybe it was time to lean into who he had always been and who he would always be.

Chapter 59

Crossing a street in Ho Chi Minh City required faith in your species, something Shane had long ago lost. The stream of scooters, cars, SUVs, and busses was endless. Shane watched other pedestrians walk directly into traffic, as confident as Jesus walking on water, and frankly no less impressive. The vehicles miraculously weaved around the pedestrians. It was hypnotizing to watch, like magnets repelling each other.

"Shoes?"

A middle-aged Vietnamese man had come upon Shane without him realizing it, and he was bending toward Shane's shoes with shoe polish and a rag. Shane was wearing gym shoes, which did not need polishing.

"No, no," Shane said before the man touched his shoe with the rag, which would have indicated that a transaction was occurring. "I don't need it."

The man looked up and said, "I clean?"

"No," Shane said, shaking his head.

"I have glue," the man said, pulling a bottle of glue from his kit.

"No!" Shane said more harshly. Why would his shoes need glue?

"I glue," the man said, and Shane waved his hand to indicate he didn't need anything and then, in an attempt to escape, stepped into traffic. Better to get struck dead than to be solicited.

Shane had no sooner crossed the street when an older man on a scooter zipped up to him. He came to a stop but twisted his throttle a few times, revving his engine.

"Where are you from?"

Shane kept walking, waving the man away.

The man accelerated just enough to pull ahead of Shane to keep the conversation going.

"How long are you here? Where are you staying? Where are you going?"

Shane finally stopped walking. He knew that, culturally speaking, he wasn't supposed to lose his cool. But *goddamn*…

"I don't need a ride," Shane said. "And you don't need to know where I'm going."

To be fair, Shane didn't know where he was going – not exactly. He knew only the general direction. He needed to plug the address that Fang had given him into Google Maps, but he wasn't going to do it while a stranger hovered over him.

"Do you have a minute?" the man asked. "Let me show you something. Hold on, boss."

Shane didn't know why he continued standing there. He was hot and sweating. The scar tissue under his eye patch was beginning to itch.

The man pulled out a notebook about the size of a paperback book.

"Look, look," he said, opening it and pointing. "Come here. Let me show you."

Christ on a cross. But he stepped closer anyway. The man was short, almost too short for the small scooter, and probably not much younger than Shane. He wore a drab shirt and drab pants. His helmet had green tape on it to give the impression that he worked for Grab, the legitimate ride-sharing app, but it was clear he was working on his own, hustling for business.

"What's this?" Shane asked, giving in, nodding toward the notebook.

"People I give rides to," he said. "Look. 'Mr. Bao…'" He patted his chest. "That's me." He looked back down at the journal, reading the entries. "'Mr. Bao made my trip to Saigon a joy. He was so helpful and kind. I'll have memories for a lifetime!'" He showed the handwritten endorsement to Shane and then he pulled up a photo on his phone. "Very beautiful," he said. "She is from Utah!"

"Is she Mormon?"

Bao laughed. It wasn't clear he knew what a Mormon was.

Bao turned to another page and began reading. Shane noticed that the handwriting on this page was the same as the last page. He hadn't even gone to the effort to enlist different people to write the fake endorsements. And the photos on his phone could have been anyone.

Shane suddenly liked this guy. His con was so unsophisticated that it was heartbreaking.

"Okay," Shane said. "How much to be my private chauffeur for a few days?"

"You tell me," Bao said.

"No, no," Shane said. "You tell *me*."

"You decide," Bao said.

Shane said, "I'm not going to play this game."

"How much you want to pay?" Bao asked.

"Never mind," Shane said and started walking.

Bao yelled out a price.

Shane paused.

"Per day?" he asked.

Bao nodded. "Yes. Per day."

"Okay," Shane said. "Let's do this."

Chapter 60

When the scooter stopped at the opening of an alley, Shane got off and removed the helmet. He handed the helmet to Bao, who held it in front of him like a bomb.

"I don't know how long I'll be," Shane said.

"I wait for you," Bao said.

"Might be a while," Shane said.

"I wait."

Shane nodded.

The driver had taken him to the address for the fraudulent business.

The map on his phone led him into an alley, but once he reached the end of the alley, Google Maps was hopeless. Shane could turn right or left. Each option resulted in a dead-end. There were small businesses on each side as well as homes, where family members sat on tiny plastic chairs, smoking, eyeing Shane.

One family, sitting around a freshly-lit grill on the ground, drank beer while waiting for the flames to calm. They smiled at Shane. Shane smiled in return, though he was clearly lost, eyeing his phone and then looking all around him. Nothing matched the address he'd been given.

He was tempted to send a message to Fang, letting him know he was worthless, but then he saw stairwells leading up to…he didn't know what. More homes? Businesses, perhaps?

Shane took the stairs.

Standing in front of a nondescript door, he saw a tiny plaque of numbers screwed into the wall. The numbers matched the address Fang had given him.

He tried the doorknob, expecting it to be locked, but it wasn't. When he opened the door, he expected the place to be abandoned, but it wasn't.

A young man in a white shirt and black pants greeted him when the door opened. The room was narrow but deep. There were tables near the entrance, a bar beyond the tables, and more tables beyond the bar. A band was playing at the far end of the room. Shane hadn't heard any music before the door had opened. He hadn't heard anything at all. It was like entering a vault, soundproof and secure – hidden.

The young man showed Shane to a seat at the bar, motioning for him to sit. He handed Shane a leather-bound menu. There was no food, only drinks. Hundreds of drinks. High-end cocktails. It felt like stepping into a mirage, equal parts surreal and alluring.

Clearly, the bogus business had moved out and the new business had moved in.

Using a blank wall as its canvas, a slide projector illuminated vacation photos from the 1950s. The slides were all of the U.S., too. The Grand Canyon. The giant sequoias of Kings Canyon National Park. The famous geysers of Yellowstone National Park. The photos had the rich hyper-realism of Kodachrome film, a pallet of warm, inviting colors Shane wished he could live inside. Even as a child, photos that had been shot in Kodachrome made him nostalgic for an era he'd never experienced.

Shane heard a clicking noise and turned to see a Super 8 projector running. He followed the spray of light to a home movie on the wall above the entrance – a boy, aged ten, jerkily skating on a gym shoe, courtesy of amateurish stop-motion effects. Though it looked like the 1970s, the stop-and-go motions reminded Shane of old Charlie Chaplin comedies.

The walls were covered with framed vacation photos, but unlike the Kodachrome slides or the movie, these appeared newer.

The young man with the white shirt returned, laughing when he saw Shane watching the movie. He didn't speak English, so Shane pointed to the drink he wanted.

"No English?" Shane asked.

"No, no," he said, giggling as he rounded the bar to give Shane's order to the bartender.

Shane drank three Ramos Gin Fizzes without speaking to anyone. He watched the bartenders work their magic: shaving fruit rind into dust, inserting blocks of sculpted ice into glasses that were barely larger, hot-boxing specialty drinks under a dome that looked more like an eighth-grade science project than an alcoholic beverage.

Shane went to the restroom to break the seal.

As he stood at the urinal, he studied a framed photo of a foggy bluff overlooking lesser bluffs and a body of water. He was drunk enough to disappear inside the photo, just as he had been disappearing into the family vacation slides and the weird eight-millimeter movies.

He flushed and zipped, pumped soap onto his hands and rubbed them together as painstakingly as a fly would.

Back at the bar, another man (also wearing a white shirt and black pants) approached Shane and said, "Your boy had to leave. I'll take your orders. I like your tattoos. They're very cute."

"Cute?"

Shane's tattoos were anything but cute. In another country, Shane might have thought the man was hitting on him, but this man looked earnest.

"What do Americans say? Pretty?" he asked.

"I don't think so," Shane said. To change the subject, he offered his hand and said, "Shane."

"Tom," Tom said.

"American name?"

He said, "My grandfather was an American soldier. His name was Tom."

"Oh."

"You're American?" he asked.

"Yes." Shane wanted him to trust him. He said, "Do you have any tattoos?"

"My father would kill me," he said. "But I have one."

"Oh yeah?"

Tom pulled down his lower lip. Inside, on the soft meat of his lip, was the outline of a dragon.

"Holy shit," Shane said, and Tom laughed.

"I almost cried," he said. He shrugged.

"Oh, I definitely would have cried. No question."

Tom laughed again. He seemed fascinated by Shane.

"What happened to your eye?"

"You're the first person to ask me."

"Really?"

"Really. You sure want to hear?"

Tom nodded.

"Four men held me down while a fifth man took a spoon and dug it out."

Tom smiled but didn't laugh. He wasn't sure if Shane was fucking with him.

"Is that true?"

"That is one hundred percent true."

"Why?"

"How late are you open? It's a long story."

"Are you a gangster? There are a lot of gangsters in America, aren't there?"

"Nope, not a gangster," Shane said, "and this happened in the Philippines."

Tom said, "I'm not going to the Philippines!" He finally laughed, but he still looked uncertain if his reaction was the right one.

"Can I see?"

"What?"

Tom pointed to the eyepatch.

"Why not," Shane said. He reached up and lowered the patch. Tom didn't flinch.

"My grandfather lost his eye in the American War."

It took Shane a moment to realize he was talking about the Vietnam War. Funny how that went. Everything was point of view. Shane assumed his grandfather hadn't lost an eye to an American. He'd probably lost it fighting the Vietcong. There was still tension between the north and the south.

Shane replaced the patch over the knot of scar tissue.

"The war of northern aggression," Shane said. When Tom looked confused, he said, "It's a joke. That's what the Confederates called the Civil War. Only it's different here." He shook his head. "Bad joke."

"Did you fight in the war?"

"Jesus. How old do I look?" Shane laughed. "No, I didn't. No wars, in fact. I got lucky." He sipped the last of his Ramos Gin Fizz out with the straw. He liked the kind of buzz it gave him – a euphoric weightlessness, unlike whiskey, which had always made him want to punch the loudest person in a bar in the mouth.

"So tell me," Shane said. "How long's this joint been open?"

"Joint?"

"The bar."

"Oh. Three years."

"Before it was a bar, what was it?"

Tom shrugged. "Empty, I think."

Shane looked around. "Who owns it now?"

"He does," Tom said, pointing to a man sitting in a back corner. He wasn't Vietnamese. Swedish, perhaps? Dutch?

"He owns the building, too?"

"No, no," Tom said. "Woman owns the building. She comes by sometimes. He just rents the space for the bar."

Shane nodded. He said, "I'm starting to sober up. I should probably order another drink. What do you think?"

"I think so," Tom said.

"Let me see that tattoo again," Shane said.

Tom pulled down his lower lip for another peek.

"Why a dragon?" Shane asked.

"I like dragons," Tom said.

Was it really that simple? There was no deeper meaning. No symbolism. No personal connection. For so much pain and risk, he ended up choosing something only because he liked it. Shane wished everyone's motives were so straightforward.

"I like it," Shane said. "It's cute," he added, teasing him.

Tom smiled and blushed, accepting it for the compliment it was.

Chapter 61

Shane waited for the man in the corner to get up to take a piss. When he finally headed for the restroom, Shane followed, sidling up at the urinal next to him. As Shane stared at the same photo he had stared at earlier, he said, "I hear you own this place."

The man's slicked-back hair was silver, not blond. He was older than Shane had realized. At the sound of Shane's voice, the man's stream of urine paused. He likely had prostate issues.

"I do," he said.

After a few beats, his stream started up again.

Shane said, "I know the woman who owns the building. Hanh."

The stream stopped again – this time for good. He zipped up.

"Hanh? No. Her name is Kim."

"Kim?"

"Kim Tran."

Shane felt himself two places at once: inside the photo, wherever the photo had been taken, and inside the restroom, trying to keep this man from leaving.

"Maybe she bought it from Hanh," Shane said.

"No," the man said. He washed his hands and then combed his hair, slicking it back. The hair was thick and enviable.

"Well, damn. Maybe I'm in the wrong building!" Shane said, laughing. He flushed the urinal and said, "I'm all mixed up now."

"Government owned building before Kim. Took it away from previous owner."

"Really? Who was the previous owner?"

"Kim Tran."

"Kim Tran? The woman who owns it now?"

He nodded and dried his hands.

"Strange world," he said.

"Strange world indeed."

"She runs a hostess bar in Japan Town. Lucky Lady."

"Does she?"

The bar's owner nodded before leaving the restroom.

Nothing made sense.

Back at the bar, Shane settled his tab.

What Shane hadn't told Tom – what he hadn't told anyone – was that his tattoos were memories of every movie he had seen with Cheryl, beginning with everything they had seen together in their film art class at LSU. The chess pieces were from Bergman's *The Seventh Seal*; the globe hoisted by fingertips was from Charlie Chaplin's *The Great Dictator*; the eye with a razor held up to it, Luis Buñuel's *Un Chien Andalou*. There were so many movie memories indelibly inked across him, images from *Metropolis*, *Stagecoach*, *Breathless*, 8 ½, *The Birds*, *Scorpio Rising*, *Dr. Strangelove*, *Bicycle Thieves*, *Stranger than Paradise, In the Mood for Love*. Every time he would remember another movie, he would go to the resident tattoo artist for the Sigue Sigue Sputnik gang. Shane made it to seventy-five movies during his time in detention, but there were so many more. It had given Shane some comfort to look down at his arms and summon a memory of him and Cheryl in the student union watching the latest Jim Jarmusch or David Lynch film together. The tattoo might trigger other details from that particular day – what perfume she was wearing, the way her car sounded when she pulled into the parking space of their apartment complex, what her kisses tasted like. The memory of their time together was like Braille in that he experienced it laterally, through whatever senses still retained its essence. The tattoos were the medium through which he could access those memories.

To Tom, he said, "You said your father would kill if he knew about your tattoo. But what would he really do?"

Tom's expression grew somber. He said, "He'd disown me. Never talk to me again."

"That serious," Shane said.

"Yes. That serious."

Shane cupped Tom's shoulder in his palm and said, "I'm sorry to hear that. Because you're a good kid."

Tom smiled then ducked his head, proud.

Chapter 62

By the time Shane stumbled out of the alley, Bao was asleep on his scooter.

A young security guard in a blue uniform sat on an upside-down plastic bucket and smoked a cigarette. An old woman sliced up cucumbers at her bánh mì cart.

Shane ordered two bánh mì. Squinting, he watched as the woman smeared liver pâté inside the baguette and then mayonnaise, picking out various unidentifiable processed meats to stuff inside, along with cucumbers, cilantro, and a few other things Shane didn't recognize.

He paid her and walked over to the scooter, nudging Bao.

"I got you a snack," he said and handed over one of the sandwiches.

Together, they ate their respective bánh mì. It might have been the best goddamn sandwich Shane had ever eaten. He was just drunk enough for the food to induce a kind of tunnel vision whereupon he began thinking that this moment, of all the moments in his life, was among the most poignant he'd ever experienced. Here he was breaking bread with a stranger in a country he didn't know, in a city whose history would forever be intertwined with his own country's history – and how unimaginable it would have been when he was a child of five or six, watching the war unfold on his parents' black-

and-white TV, to imagine himself standing here enjoying this sandwich.

"You okay?" Bao asked.

"Hunh?"

Shane had dozed off. At some point he had sat down on the curb to finish his sandwich and fallen sound asleep.

"Shit," Shane said. "The past few weeks are catching up to me, I guess."

"You drink too much," Bao said and laughed.

"Yes," Shane said. "I drink too much."

The woman and her bánh mì cart were already gone for the night. There was a different security guard sitting on the bucket.

"I should probably call it a night," he said.

Shane got onto the back of the scooter. When Bao handed him his helmet, Shane declined.

"No helmet," he said. "I want to feel the air."

Honestly, the idea of a helmet surrounding his head made him want to puke.

"Ready?" Bao asked.

"As ready as I'll ever be," Shane said, and Bao pulled in front of a moving car, nearly killing the two of them. But this was Vietnam, Shane told himself. Nothing bad had ever happened here.

Shane laughed at his own dark joke.

Fifteen minutes later, as they pulled into the alley with the ice cream shop, Shane saw two men standing not far from the shop's door. It was late enough that the alley was otherwise dark and empty.

"Stop," Shane said to Bao. "Turn around."

"This is where you told me," Bao said.

"No, let's go. Hurry."

Bao turned the scooter around and zipped out of the alley.

The two men, Shane suspected, were Fang's goons. Once Fang had realized that Shane didn't check into his complimentary hotel room, he surely tracked him down.

"Where?" Bao asked.

"I don't know. Hotel," Shane said.

"Yes, boss," Bao said, and deftly zipped around the few cars still on the street. In no time, Bao pulled up to a five-star hotel.

"You overestimate my worth," Shane said.

"Nice hotel," Bao said.

"Too nice."

Shane didn't have a choice, really. He got off the scooter.

"Tomorrow night," Shane said. "Meet me here? Six o'clock?"

"Sure thing, boss."

"And quit calling me boss, okay?"

Bao saluted Shane and drove away.

Shane walked into the hotel without any luggage, still visibly drunk but cognizant enough at least to realize that anyone looking at him could see that he'd been drinking. He worried that they would deny him a room, but when he walked up to the front desk, the woman behind the computer smiled.

"Checking in?" she asked.

"I don't have a reservation," Shane said. "Do you have an available room?" He showed her his passport.

"Let's see," she said and began typing. "Yes!" she said. She typed some more, but the more she typed, the more confused she looked. "You already have room," she said.

"No, I..." Shane began, but then he said, "What hotel is this?"

"Rex Hotel," she said.

Fuck.

"Yes, I do have a reservation," he said. Rex was the hotel that Fang had reserved for him. "I forgot," Shane said.

The woman smiled again. All confusion washed away.

She swiped a room key and pointed toward the elevators. Bao was compromised. He had likely been enlisted by Fang's goons. How much would it cost to hire a motorbike taxi driver to follow and solicit business from a foreigner? Next to nothing.

"Thank you," the woman said.

"Trust no one," Shane said, saying aloud what he meant to keep inside his head.

The woman looked confused.

Shane shook his head. "I meant…thank you."

Chapter 63

Shane didn't want to sleep, knowing that Fang had won this round, trapping Shane like a spider in a web, but what Shane desired and what his physical being craved weren't the same, and his body eventually won.

Shane slept hard, waking eight hours later in the same position, a crease across his face from the seam of the pillow. The room was as dark as a cave, but when he jerked open the curtains, light blared in.

The streets were already full of motorists, the sidewalks alive with pedestrians.

Shane showered and then put back on his dirty clothes. Few things in life were sadder than pulling on yesterday's underwear.

When Shane left the hotel, Bao was already across the street on his motorbike, even though it was hours earlier than Shane had asked to meet up with him.

As Shane walked past, he looked Bao in the eyes and said, "Fuck off."

He knew it was against everything one was taught about Southeast Asia, that he was making Bao lose face. Several people slowed down walking to see what was going to happen.

"Mr. Shane!" Bao called out. He was off his bike and trying to catch up to Shane on foot. "Mr. Shane! Why are you mad?"

Shane stopped walking and spun around. Bao almost slammed into him.

"Because you fucking set me up with those two Chinese motherfuckers," Shane said. "How much did they pay you?"

Bao shook his head. "I don't know what you're talking about."

"The hell you don't," Shane said. "You were hired to follow me, right? Even better if I hired you to take me around Saigon. Which I did." Shane laughed, wagging his head. It was the laugh of someone who was barely controlling his desire to punch another person.

Bao said nothing.

An old Vietnamese woman making sugarcane juice at a street stall was the only person still watching them. The juice was green, and she was placing each cup into a snug plastic bag with handles. She said something to someone hidden in the shade of the storefront, her voice strangely familiar from all those years Shane had watched footage of Vietnam on the news. Was there a word for a deep familiarity with something that you had only experienced from another medium? An old man joined the woman to watch. He was shirtless. He was old enough to have fought in the war.

The old man said something in Vietnamese to Bao, and Bao answered, holding up his hands and shaking them to indicate that everything was okay.

"What was that all about?"

"He wants to know if I need his help."

Shane looked over at the old man. The old man stared impassively back. He couldn't have weighed more than a hundred pounds. But never underestimate someone who had survived as long as he had survived, under the conditions that he had survived. In eighty long years, nothing had brought him down. And this was his turf, not Shane's.

"No," Shane said, lowering his voice. "You won't need his help."

Shane turned and kept walking. When he looked over his shoulder, he saw Bao making a phone call, his eyes on Shane.

Shane decided to make it easy. He paused in front of a shop that sold egg coffee. He pointed to the sign for Bao's benefit. Then he walked inside.

He climbed four flights to reach the coffee house, passing other businesses and residences along the way, until he reached an old woman sweeping the landing outside the coffee house door.

"Xin chào!" she said, stepping aside with her broom and motioning for Shane to enter.

"Thank you," Shane said.

There were only a few people inside. The room was high-ceilinged with different-sized photos framed and running all the way up one wall. Christmas lights were draped from the ceiling even though Christmas was months away.

A woman who might have been the daughter of the woman sweeping the landing offered him a menu, but Shane waved it away. "Just egg coffee."

"Hot or cold?" she asked.

"Hot."

Shane had never heard of egg coffee until he met a Vietnamese man in the detention center in Manila. The man was from Hanoi and spoke about it the way other men might speak of a woman they desired. He had a faraway look whenever he described it. Two weeks later, he was found dead in one of the cells – hung from a wooden beam.

When Shane's coffee arrived, yellow and bubbling, he thought, *this is for you, friend,* and spooned out some of the creamy goo and sipped it from the spoon. His old cellmate wasn't wrong. It reminded Shane of something from his childhood – custard? meringue? – but there was a bitterness, too, from the coffee that rested below the whisked egg, and sweetness from the condensed milk. It was coffee that needed to be excavated. With each taste, Shane performed a kind of stratigraphy on the drink, studying each layer and its relationship with what came before it. It was like drinking liquid tiramisu – but not quite. Whatever it was or wasn't like, the experience put Shane in a deep, contemplative state. The taste transported him to a place he had never been: Vietnam of the past, a hotel in Hanoi in the 1940s, the early years of the first Indochina War.

Shane was lost in this reverie when Fang's two men entered the coffee house, walked directly to Shane, and sat down across from him. Shane recognized them. The heavyweight and the bantam. The bantam was holding a briefcase and a shopping bag. Both wore light-colored suits.

Shane carefully scooped out another spoonful of egg coffee and held it to his mouth. He blew gently on it and then inserted the spoon in his mouth. He shut his eyes and made a sound of satisfaction.

"Have you had egg coffee?" Shane asked. "It's kind of…otherworldly."

The heavyweight said, "You're being a pain in the ass." His English was impeccable. There was barely an accent to be found.

"Where did you grow up?" Shane asked.

"New Jersey, numbnuts."

"Oh."

"That's right. *Oh.*"

"Does your friend think I'm a pain in the ass?"

"He grew up in Guangzhou. You'll have to ask him in Mandarin."

"What's your name?" Shane asked.

The heavyweight hesitated. Then he said, "Joe."

Shane nodded. He brought another spoonful of egg coffee to his mouth. He tried not letting the presence of others diminish his pleasure.

Joe said, "That looks disgusting." He motioned to the egg coffee.

Shane said, "I can see where a man from New Jersey might think that."

"What Fang doesn't understand," Joe said, "is why you're being so goddamned difficult. I tried explaining what you Irish fucks are like, how your whole purpose in life is to bust someone else's balls, but his exposure to leprechauns is limited."

"Let's see. First, his lackeys steal my backpack, which was full of research that my dead friend Luke spent the last years of his life putting together. And when I ask for it back, it's full of photocopies. And I'm supposed to be, what, pliable? Happy go lucky? Put on my green cellophane hat and dance a jig? Is that it? Nah. Fuck that."

Joe took a deep breath. He motioned to his associate, who set the briefcase on the table, opened it, and pulled out a thick three-ring binder. He handed it to Shane.

Shane started flipping through it. All the evidence that had been inside the backpack had been laminated and scrupulously annotated. Shane flipped to the annotations that had been compiled at the back – page after page of information that had been fleshed out from receipts, notes, phone records, addresses. The dossier included photos and blueprints. It was both impressive and daunting.

"We were busy collating it at Kinko's," Joe said.

"You've got a sense of humor. I like that."

"Turn to page 342," he said.

Shane turned to page 342.

There were long, detailed bios for several people – all men.

"What's this?" Shane asked.

"Those are the people who invested in your friend's business. You know – the ones who killed themselves. Or disappeared."

"I think you can safely stop referring to Corbett as my friend."

"Whatever. Your former business partner then."

"Business partner," Shane said. "Not much better." His laugh was as bitter as the coffee.

Shane skimmed through a few of the lengthy profiles. These men included a weapons researcher, an owner of a factory farm that mistreated animals, and a CEO of an electronic components company with harsh factory conditions for his workers. None of these men were saints.

"This is pretty damned impressive. Who compiled it?"

Joe said nothing, just stared at Shane.

"You did this?" Shane asked.

"I have a PhD in Comparative Literature from SUNY Binghamton," Joe said. "I put my research skills to good use."

"Fuck. Why aren't you a professor at a nice little liberal arts college somewhere?"

"Do you know how much those nice little liberal arts colleges pay?" Joe said. He shook his head. "Besides, my father was a Triad. His father was a Triad. It's in the blood." He motioned to the server.

"Two of those," he said, pointing to Shane's coffee. "I'll try that shit," he said to Shane. "When in Rome, right?"

Shane flipped to the back of the dossier. There, he found a profile of himself.

"I guess you know everything about me," Shane said.

"How are the demons?" Joe asked. "Still chasing the dragon?"

"Demons are in the basement," Shane said. "And I'm too old to play with dragons."

"Those were dark times," Joe said. "I'm sorry about your loss."

Shane nodded. He didn't want to talk about his wife with a stranger, especially a Chinese gangster from New Jersey.

When Shane flipped to the end of his own biography, he landed on a photo of Kylie. Her mugshot.

"She good in the sack?" Joe asked.

"I wouldn't remember," Shane said.

"Oh yeah, that's right. The dark times."

Shane nodded.

"I've been reading some R. D. Laing," Joe said. "I saw you wrote a thesis on him, so… Interesting, I guess, but kind of dated. Hippy dippy shit."

Shane shut the dossier.

"You're thorough," Shane said.

"Long layovers."

"So, what's not in here? What don't you know yet?"

The coffee arrived.

Joe started to stir it, but his associate waved his hand and said something in Mandarin. Joe stopped stirring, watched as his buddy demonstrated how to drink it, and then Joe said something in Mandarin. He spooned the gooey egg up to his mouth and tried it.

"What do you think?" Shane asked.

"Too sweet," he said. "I'm not a big dessert guy."

"Back to my question," Shane asked. "What *don't* you know? It wasn't rhetorical."

"Yeah, so…we don't know where the money is. We don't know where your old partner is. But that's your job. We don't know who all is involved except for the people you've told us were involved."

"The three Vietnamese," Shane said.

"We don't know if you were involved."

"Are you shitting me?"

"Not shitting you," Joe said. "Hey, look…they could still have set you up as a fall guy while cutting you out."

"I don't even want the fucking money," Shane said.

"Maybe, maybe not," Joe said. "That's yet to be seen."

"Unfuckingbelievable."

Joe shrugged. He spooned up more coffee.

"It's growing on me," Joe said. He tapped the side of the cup with his spoon and sighed. "Here's what doesn't make sense. The people your business partner conned? They're all horrible people. Like genuinely rotten. But you? By all accounts, you're not. Unless…"

"Unless?"

"Unless you were in on the con."

"Well, I wasn't. Tell Fang to go fuck himself."

"Actually," Joe said, "Fang doesn't think you were. *I'm* the one who floated that theory to him."

"Then fuck you."

There was silence. They could have been three old friends who met in a coffeehouse once a week to enjoy each other's company.

Joe said, "How're you liking Vietnam?"

Shane didn't answer.

Joe said, "We're thinking about checking out the War Remnants Museum, Independence Palace, maybe go to where the monk set himself on fire to protest the war."

Shane said, "It wasn't the war he was protesting."

"No?"

It was a protest against the government's persecution of Buddhists. It was a Catholic versus Buddhist kind of thing."

Joe said, "Really? Shit. You learn something every day." He turned to his partner and spoke in Mandarin. The partner lifted the shopping bag and handed it over the table to Shane.

"What's this? A gift?"

"Actually, it is."

Shane opened it and peered inside. It was a pair of nice pants and a dress shirt. Also, a packet of new underwear, socks, and shoes.

"I suppose you keyed into my room to check the tags on my clothes for their sizes."

Joe shrugged.

"Okay," Shane said. He placed the dossier inside the bag and stood. "You'll pick up the tab?" he asked, motioning to the coffee.

"My treat," Joe said. "Why not." As Shane passed, Joe said, "And Shane?"

"Yes?"

"We're working together, okay? There's no need to hide from us."

Shane smiled. "I couldn't if I wanted to," he said.

Chapter 64

Sitting on a park bench, Shane poured over the dossier, occasionally looking up to watch the endless stream of scooters go by. It was hypnotic. He saw a woman ride by with a tie-dyed skirt and a flannel shirt; she wore fashionable sunglasses, like Audrey Hepburn in *Breakfast at Tiffany's*. He saw men and women both dressed in their retail work clothes – red polo shirts with plastic nametags. He saw a man with two cell phones, one in each shirt pocket. He saw people wearing fully insulated bodysuits with the hood pulled up and the helmet over the hood. Almost everyone wore a mask.

Shane returned to the dossier. He flipped through its pages until he came to section on Charlie Leung.

In it was information that Shane already knew from Lei. What he didn't know was that most of Charlie's investment earnings had come from companies that manufactured weapons to be used in war. Biological war, cyberwar, conventional war. According to the dossier, he closely monitored war activities around the world and then backed the winning team, regardless of moral implications. A profit was a profit, apparently.

It wasn't enough to smuggle chemicals for illegal drugs into North America and Europe. You had to game out a good return on other people's misery. You made investments in pain and death. A portfolio wasn't complete without investments in torture.

Damn. That was some cynical shit.

But how much of this dossier was legit? How much was manufactured to manipulate Shane into despising everyone in it, including himself?

The same man who had wanted to shine Shane's shoes approached him again, crouching with a rag.

"No!" Shane said, louder than he meant.

"I have glue!" the man said, reaching for a squeeze bottle of glue.

"Please don't!" Shane said. "Go!"

"Let me…," the man began, the tip of the glue bottle almost touching Shane's shoe.

"I don't need any fucking glue!" Shane yelled, and the man stopped. He looked up at Shane, as though Shane had hurt his feelings. He stood from the ground, wiping his knees, and then picked up his bulky old shoeshine kit and walked away.

"Jesus Christ!" Shane said to no one.

His hands were shaking. He felt so close to what he was looking for and also no closer than he had been back in the Philippines. How was that possible?

He watched an old woman wearing a conical hat made of bamboo sweep leaves off the sidewalk in the park. The mere sight of her relaxed Shane. Despite the heat, a breeze continued blowing leaves onto the sidewalk; her job, like Sisyphus's, had no end. After some time, she sat on a bench across from Shane, pulled a wrapped sandwich from a pocket, and began eating her meal.

Shane gathered his crap and headed back to the Rex Hotel. As he walked through the park, he saw Bao in the distance keeping pace with him on his scooter. It was hard not to pity the guy. He'd have made a terrible detective. An even worse spy.

Shane waved at him.

Bao looked away, pretending he hadn't seen Shane.

Shane walked over to him, got on the back of the scooter, and said, "The Rex, please."

"Yes, boss," Bao said, pulling into traffic. "Rex Hotel."

Chapter 65

Shane was so tired. He curled into a ball, bringing his knees to his chest, and fell asleep. He dreamed about trying to buy Oxy from Duchamp's clinic, except that the clinic was staffed with Vietnamese, and no one could understand Shane. They kept showing him drugs that weren't what he wanted or needed. *No, not that, I need Oxy, do you know what Oxy is, doesn't anyone here understand me?* But the staff *didn't* understand as they smiled and showed him medicated shampoos and sprays for foot fungus and herbal teas. As for Duchamp, with his stupid soul patch, he was nowhere to be found.

Shane woke up shivering. He had slept on top of the bed sheets with the AC on high.

It wasn't uncommon for people with addictive personalities to dream about old addictions. From his patients he had heard about their compulsive shopping dreams, their binge-eating dreams, their video-game playing dreams. They dreamed about exercise, work, and watching pornography. They dreamed about cutting themselves, seeking out pain, and smoking.

Smoking dreams were the hardest to shake. Former smokers continued to smoke as their dream selves. It was as though the subconscious was taunting the conscious, trying to pass a lit cigarette from one state of awareness to another. *Go on…take it.* Shane would send his addicts across town to make an appointment with a hypnotist, who could methodically bring them to their center of radiant energy, the eye of the storm, and begin the delicate work of rewiring their brains, as though defusing a bomb with a timer that ticked and ticked and ticked.

Shane rubbed his face, trying to wake up, but the dream still haunted him. He hadn't thought about Duchamp in years. It was after the man had folded his Oxy tent and taken his pill mill circus to another town that Shane had spiraled into the abyss. Was Duchamp even a doctor? Whose lives was he destroying these days?

Shane showered, dressed, and headed out for breakfast.

Bao was waiting for Shane outside Hotel Rex, half-asleep and reclining atop his scooter in what would have been an impossible position for Shane. Shane wondered if Bao ever went home.

When Bao saw Shane, he sat up and started his bike.

"Very nice!" Bao said.

"What?"

Bao indicated the new clothes.

"Oh yeah. Nice," Shane said flatly.

"High roller!"

"Hardly," Shane said.

"Where go? Casino?"

"Japan Town," Shane said.

Bao's eyes lit up. "You find a nice girl tonight?"

"What do you mean?"

"You get a massage with a happy ending?"

"Oh. Okay. No, no. It's nothing like that."

"Sure thing," Bao said. "Whatever you say, boss." He playfully saluted Shane.

Shane got onto the back of the bike. He put on the spare helmet.

Bao pulled into traffic and then zipped between cars and other motorbikes, dodging and weaving. It was like a well-rehearsed fight sequence, alternating between offense and defense while fending off the occasional surprise attack from unexpected directions.

It was a short drive to Japan Town, which had its own entrance and security guard.

"Look," Shane said. "Why don't you go home and get some sleep. Please. I'm not going to have any fun if I know you're out here lurking."

"I'm good," Bao said.

"No, I mean it," Shane said. "I want you to go home."

Bao stared at Shane, resolute.

Shane pulled out his wallet and removed two million five hundred thousand in Vietnamese dong, the equivalent of one hundred dollars.

Bao took the money and, without a word, drove away.

Was that all it took?

For the first time since arriving at the airport, Shane felt a weight lifted from him. He hadn't realized how much Bao had been stifling him, but now that he was gone, Shane felt rejuvenated, like a man who'd finally escaped a bad marriage. He walked over the threshold and nodded at the guard, who regarded Shane before looking back down at his phone.

Japan Town was city within a city – a labyrinth.

With its narrow streets, it was planned for pedestrians, but motorbikes still weaved through the crowd, and an occasional car would enter before its driver realized his foolish mistake. Dozens of Chinese lanterns, strung from one side of the narrow street to the other, illuminated the businesses. Neon signs turned the air purple or red or pink, and you could reach into an open window and take hold of somebody's beer or grilled meat skewer or Japanese cheesecake, if you were so inclined. It was like waking up inside of a hive, each street honeycombed with bars and restaurants and pharmacies and coffee shops.

A swarm of young women, possibly Japanese, stood outside a massage parlor. They wore flowing white dresses and held large laminated menus. One of them approached Shane with one such menu. She pointed at its offerings while another woman took hold of Shane's arm, trying to steer him into their den.

"No, no," Shane said.

The women silently retreated back to their sisters in arms.

The hostess bars, according to his research, weren't the same as bargirl bars in Cambodia. Women flirted and asked for high-priced drinks, but they didn't have sex with you. For that, you had to visit the women with the flowing white dresses, or any of the other, less discreet massage parlors in Japan Town. Or find a freelancer on the street. There were options. But the hostess bar wasn't one of them. And Japan Town was overrun with hostess bars.

From overhead, Japan Town looked like a maze, which made finding the bar he was looking for a chore.

Just when he was ready to give up, it appeared before him in a neon haze. Lucky Lady. A doorman stood out front, but he wasn't giving anyone the hard sell.

Shane approached, wondering if the man had photos of people who weren't allowed inside, but he just opened the door for Shane and nodded for him to enter. No hackles raised at the sight of him. In fact, no reaction at all.

Fortunately, Shane was dressed the part. Even his eye-patch looked perversely stylish with his new clothes. It was like how changing the musical score on a TV show could turn the exact same scene from comedy into horror.

The bar was divided into two halves: front and back. A slightly parted gold lame curtain separated the two. From what Shane could see, there were several people in the back half, where music thumped and lights swirled, but in the front half…nobody was there except for the bartenders. They were two women, Vietnamese not Japanese, named Chau and Hang. They were the hostesses. When Hang, the younger of the two, realized that Shane wasn't going to buy her a drink, she wandered away and stared into her phone. With Hang out of the picture, Shane bought Chau a drink.

Chau was twenty-nine. She had a scar from where her cleft lip had been repaired. She wasn't self-conscious about it and seemed genuinely interested in Shane's eye-patch, focusing on it from time to time.

"It's cute," she said, pointing to it.

The Vietnamese, Shane was learning, thought a lot of things were cute. Even if they weren't.

"What happened?" she asked after her third drink. "Your eye."

Shane considered telling her the truth, but instead he said, "Cancer." This was a lie, but it was close enough to the truth to be credible.

"Is that a tumor?" she asked, pointing to the exposed lump.

Shane adjusted his eyepatch, trying to hide the lump.

He nodded. "I need to get back with my dermatologist," he said. "But I've been busy."

"What do you do?"

"Travel writer," Shane said, blurting out the first thing that popped into his head.

"Oh, you write?" Chau said. "I always wanted to be a writer."

"Really? What kind?"

"I love fantasy," Chau said. To Hang, she said, "We have a famous writer here."

Hang looked up from her phone, uninterested, and then back down, scrolling.

Chau rolled her eyes.

"Another drink?" Shane asked, wanting to change the subject.

Chau smiled and made herself another.

"I heard that a woman owns this bar?" Shane asked. "Kim Tran?"

Chau shrugged. "My boss is a man. He's in there." She pointed toward the back half of the bar.

"Oh yeah? If he comes out here, could you point him out? But just nod at me. I can't write an honest review of this place if your boss starts buying me drinks." He smiled.

Chau laughed. Her eyes were glassy. The alcohol was starting to hit her.

Three drinks later, and her boss still hadn't come out.

"I should probably take a look back there," Shane said, but when he stood, he lost his footing. "Whoa!" he said, regaining his balance. The drinks had packed a punch. "Fuck," he muttered as he walked unsteadily toward the lamé curtain. One of his feet, asleep, tingled. He hoped nobody made a move at him. He was in no condition to fight.

That's when he remembered that he hadn't eaten in hours. He vaguely remembered drinking egg coffee, the thought of which now made him queasy.

When he stepped into the other room, he was momentarily blinded by a swirling light that swiped across his face. He blinked and steadied himself. His vision faded from white. There were only a dozen people in the room, most of them employees. A few women danced while an older expat sat slumped in a chair, watching. There was a DJ with two women rubbing against him, one on either side. The DJ had bleached hair and painted nails. He was wearing a Tom Ford t-shirt, the same Tom Ford t-shirt Kenny had worn during the commercial shoot in Abbeville. Shane stepped deeper into the room, the curtain shutting behind him. He squinted. It *was* Kenny.

Someone touched his arm, and Shane swung around, ready to fight, but it was another Vietnamese man, probably in his thirties but looking much older, his face bloated and prematurely aged.

"Would you like a seat? I'll send a girl over to take your order," he said.

The man was Tam. He'd put on at least fifty pounds. He was soft and puffy now. His smile was the same, but sadder – and there were deep creases at the corners of his mouth. His eyes were haunted. Tam had been the more sensitive of the two, and whatever bargain he had struck was clearly weighing on him.

He didn't recognize Shane.

Keep it together, Shane told himself.

"Nah, I'm good. I'm drinking at the bar," he said, unblinking. "I just wanted to see what's back here."

Tam patted Shane's arm, as though they were two old friends. He said, "I hope you're having a good time."

"Helluva place you've got here," Shane said. "Are you the owner?"

In his younger days, Tam might have blushed, but there were probably circulation issues with his blood now. The stress, the guilt – it was all going to kill him. Shane guessed he had another ten years. Fifteen tops. "My mother's the owner."

Mother?

Shane tamped down any surprise. Instead, he made a show of looking around in admiration. "I'd love to meet your mother," he said.

"If she comes, I'll introduce you." He bowed, half-heartedly, before walking away.

Shane returned to the bar.

"Another round," Shane said. "And let's bring your friend Hang over, too."

Chau spoke to Hang in Vietnamese, and like a switch flipping from off to on, Hang's entire demeanor changed as she tucked her phone into a purse and joined Chau and a man who was fantasizing about how he could murder at least two people presently in the bar.

"To life!" Shane said.

"*Một, Hai, Ba, Dzô!*" Chau said, bringing the shot glass to her lips.

"Exactly," Shane said.

Chapter 66

Several drinks later Tam approached Shane at the bar.

"She's outside," Tam said.

"Who?"

"My mother. You said you'd like to meet her."

"Yes, of course!"

Shane couldn't remember the last time he'd been this drunk. He made his way to the exit. He felt propelled forward as he pushed open the door and stepped outside, as though someone had pushed him – but no one was behind him.

Outside, he almost slammed into a woman, but the doorman, laughing, caught Shane.

"Excuse me! Sorry, sorry!" Shane said.

When Shane looked up, he recognized Hanh, confirming every suspicion he'd had. Hanh from Manila. Hanh of the lost passport. Hanh who had lured Shane to the airport with the promise of trip to Hong Kong. Here was the woman who had set fire to his life.

But there was no recognition in her eyes.

"Are you okay?" she asked.

Shane nodded.

He cocked his head and said, "Kim Tran?"

She hesitated before answering. "Yes?"

"I was just talking about you."

She looked suspicious now, glancing over at her doorman, who stepped closer.

"I was at another bar last night. District 1. The bar with the old home movies playing."

"Oh, yes." Upon hearing about the District 1 bar, she relaxed – but not by much.

Shane imagined reaching out and choking her right there in Japan Town. He imagined pressing his thumbs into her windpipe, waiting for the trachea to collapse under the pressure. He imagined gouging out her eyes. He wanted so badly to slam her head repeatedly against the concrete and watch life drain from her eyes the way he had been forced to see life drain from so many others' eyes. He wanted to kill her, and he believed in that moment that no one could have stopped him. Not the doorman. Not any of the pedestrians. Neither Kenny nor Tam, if they came running outside to help. He could taste adrenaline at the back of his throat. He swallowed. Took a breath.

"Great place," Shane said. "And your kids? Here? They run this place? Kenny and Tam, right?" The puzzle pieces were snapping into place, but there was still so much he couldn't see.

Hanh stared at him. Shane could see her suspicion kicking back in. She didn't know who he was, but she sensed something wasn't right.

"You've had a lot to drink," she said. "You should go back to your room now."

The smugness in her voice. The fact that she didn't recognize a man whose life she had destroyed.

"Indeed I have," he said. "Drank a lot." He adjusted his eyepatch. "All of it here, too. Adding to your coffers." He smiled. "Isn't that a strange word? *Coffers.*"

"Be careful," Hanh said – a warning. She said something in Vietnamese to the doorman before making her way around Shane to enter her bar.

And that was that. She was done with him.

If Shane had acted on his darkest desires, if he had done the thing he had dreamed so often of doing, he'd have set off a tripwire and sent Corbett into hiding. Shane understood how federal prosecutors felt as they worked their way up the ladder of a massive conspiracy case. Delaying punishment for lower-level criminals in service to the greater good. Or worse: letting evil people walk free due to an agreement. Information in exchange for freedom. Now, *that* must have been a kick in the balls.

But it took greater discipline and focus to do the thing that was necessary. In this case, the necessary thing was to find his old partner, Phil Corbett, and rip the man's fucking heart out with his bare hands.

In the meantime, Shane needed to push down what would have given him satisfaction. He needed to walk away, unfulfilled. That was, sad to say, the only smart move.

Chapter 67

Shane decided to walk back to the Rex Hotel. He stepped around the young men trying to lure him into their restaurants. He declined invitations by doormen to enter hostess bars. He ignored the barber who offered him a VIP massage room.

When he found his way out of the labyrinth of Japan Town, he felt a pressure released from his chest. He could breathe better. His heart wasn't pounding quite as hard.

Bao was nowhere to be seen. Thank God.

Shane found the nearest bar, walked in, and ordered a drink. It wasn't a hostess bar, but the bartender, a young Vietnamese woman wearing a Beverly Hills Polo Lounge T-shirt, chatted him up.

Shane was polite and answered the bartender's questions, but he couldn't remember anything they'd talked about when he left five mixed drinks and four shots later.

Strangely, what had bothered him most was how negligible he was to Hanh. The fact that the sight of him had jarred no recognition whatsoever – that was some cold sociopathic shit.

Shane weaved down the sidewalk, looking for another bar. A young woman standing under an awning of a long-vacant business said, "You need girlfriend?"

Shane paused. He tried to see her, but she was standing in the shadows.

"I absolutely do not," he said, laughing.

"Let me be your girlfriend," she said.

Shane stepped closer. She was older than he had first thought. She was still pretty, but no hostess bar would have hired her. She was on her own out here.

"How much?" Shane asked.

He was feeling those old reckless impulses bubbling back up. The compulsions. The adrenaline spreading through him like a leak in a gas tank, waiting for the tossed match.

"We go back to my place," she said. On her phone, she opened the calculator app and typed "400,000." She tapped it. "Vietnam," she said unnecessarily. Then she multiplied it and showed him a new number: 16.91. "American," she said.

"Seventeen dollars?" he asked.

Before he could make a decision, she took him by the hand and led him two blocks and then down an alley. The alley branched off into a street that was probably a market of some kind in the day but not much at night, except for a few kids selling fruit and an old woman selling cigarettes.

Shane felt like a child being pulled through a store by an angry mother. He wasn't sure how old she was. She could have been thirty-five or fifty-five.

As she led him into a building and up two flights of stairs, he said, "I don't have a condom."

"I have," she said.

His breathing was labored as he climbed the stairs. He couldn't remember the last time he was this drunk. He was dizzy and out of breath by the time they reached her door.

This is a mistake, he thought. But like so many other times in his past when he'd had the same thought, he kept going.

Before walking inside her room, she touched his face and said, "Handsome man."

"Thank you," he said, "but no. Not anymore."

"Handsome," she said again, touching his face.

"Please. Don't." He was afraid he might hurt her if she said the lie again.

She led him inside, and he drunk-collapsed onto the bed, sighing loudly. The mattress was thin; the springs poked through. He flicked off his shoes using his feet. He fell all the way back onto some pillows, simultaneously sitting and reclining.

He was relieved not to be standing.

The woman unbuttoned his shirt and rubbed her hands across his chest and belly.

The wall next to him came alive, the ancient paint swirling, but then he saw the nearly microscopic ants, the tiniest ants he'd ever seen, thousands of them. Some were heading up the wall, some were heading down. The ones coming down made contact with the ones going up, buzzing each time they touched, like tiny electric shocks, making sure they were from the same colony, sharing food they carried, warning of any trouble ahead.

Shane shut his eyes.

He told himself to stay awake, but he started drifting off.

He imagined the old monk sitting down in the middle of a Saigon intersection. Two younger monks had poured the gasoline over him, and the monk on the ground lit a match and set it on his own lap. And then the flames overtook him.

Feeling the pressure of the prostitute's hands as she unbuckled his belt, Shane floated back up to the surface of consciousness. She tugged down his pants. He tried imagining what it felt like to set yourself on fire, to *burn to death*. The monk did not scream out. He did not gesticulate. He had remained in one position until the fire melted his face, and then he fell sideways.

Jesus, he thought. *Jesus Christ.*

Was he crying?

He thought he heard something and opened his eyes. The woman had him in her mouth. But against the wall behind her, he saw a shadow that belonged to neither of them.

The woman's eyes locked on his.

Shane tried sitting up, but she was pressing him down with her palm on his chest.

She said something in Vietnamese and then tried putting him back in her mouth, but Shane pushed her head away.

A man crawled out from under the bed. He was holding Shane's wallet. He looked back at Shane and the woman, and then he ran toward the door.

"Fuck!" Shane yelled, and he forced the woman away. She scrambled back to him, trying to hold him down, but he kicked her in the chest this time, using both feet since his pants were around his ankles. The kick knocked her halfway across the room.

Shane quickly pulled up his pants and, without his shoes, ran out the door.

The wallet had his ATM card, his credit cards, his cash.

Shane ran as fast as he could down two flights of stairs, sliding on his socks as he rounded the corner, almost falling. The man had just about cleared the door when Shane grabbed onto the back of his collar and pulled him inside. The man was using his arms to keep from getting pulled all the way in, but Shane leaned forward and bit the man's ear.

The man howled in pain.

The prostitute had made it down stairs now. She was pulling on Shane, trying to break him free from her accomplice.

Shane bit down harder this time, tasting cartilage, and the man let go of the doorframe, sending all three of them tumbling backward, falling to the ground.

Shane elbowed the woman underneath him several times until he felt something snap. A rib or two. She was coughing now, trying to get out from under Shane.

Shane put the thief in a chokehold and squeezed. When the man didn't turn over Shane's wallet, Shane tightened his grip on the man's neck, jerking the man's head, trying to snap it.

The man tossed aside the wallet, and Shane let go. He pushed the man aside, and together the thief and the prostitute coughed and heaved. Shane checked his wallet. Everything was still inside it. He didn't want to go back upstairs for his shoes and risk the two of them plotting against him. He didn't know if they had weapons. He didn't know if any weapons were hidden somewhere on the first-floor landing.

Shane stepped outside in his socks.

He retraced his steps until he reached a major street, and he looked for a hotel. In front of a hotel, he would find a taxi. And then he would find a way back home.

Chapter 68

Someone was nudging Shane. At first he thought he was dreaming. When he realized he wasn't, he opened his eyes and tried scrambling to his feet but lost his balance and landed on his knees.

He wasn't in his room, where he should have been. He was in front of the ice cream shop. He had fallen asleep outside last night, too drunk to punch in the code to unlock the front door. He was lucky one of the trucks that backed down the alley to deliver goods to the stores hadn't run over him.

Staring down at him was the girl who worked in the ice cream shop. She had backed up, frightened by his flailing.

"I'm sorry," Shane said, raising his hands, palms out. "I'm sorry, I'm sorry. You scared me."

He smiled at her, and she smiled back – a cautious smile.

Shane stood and stepped away from the front door, giving her a wide berth but still bracing himself against the storefront to keep from falling.

She punched in the code and opened the door. She held it open for Shane to go inside.

"Thank you," Shane said.

As he passed, he felt her hand on his arm.

"You okay?" she asked.

Shane said, “Yes, thank you. I’m okay.”

“Where are your shoes?”

“I don’t know.”

After he climbed the stairs and keyed into his room, he took a long piss and then caught sight of himself in the bathroom mirror. His face was swollen. His eye was bloodshot. His cheek had been scraped with sharp fingernails. His clothes were filthy.

One thing was clear. He had lied to the young ice cream attendant. By any reasonable definition, he most definitely wasn’t okay.

Chapter 69

Shane couldn't remember the last time he'd eaten. He needed coffee. And water. He needed something for his headache, too.

By the time he made it back downstairs, the ice cream shop was full of noontime customers. He and the girl exchanged a quick glance as she scooped out ice cream into a cup. He nodded at her, letting her know that he was fine now.

Bao was waiting outside. For all Bao knew, he had dropped Shane off at Japan Town's entrance for a night of hedonism. He grinned as Shane approached until he saw Shane's face.

"I'm okay," Shane said. "I don't want to talk about it."

Bao nodded.

"I need shoes," Shane said. "And then I need something to eat. Anything."

Bao took Shane to a large indoor market, where they found both shoes and food. They ate pho together. Shane made Bao promise that he wouldn't talk.

"My head," Shane said.

Bao understood.

They ate in silence, and then Bao took Shane to the War Remnants Museum.

"Am I meeting someone here?" Shane asked.

Bao looked confused.

"The Chinese gangsters? You know...your new friends? Are they here for an update?"

"No, boss. No Chinese gangsters. Just tourists."

"Oh." He looked around. "I'm confused. Did I mention that I wanted to go here?"

"No, boss. You're American. I take many Americans here."

Shane nodded, but he remained skeptical.

Was it possible Bao was actually fulfilling his role as tour guide?

Shane bought a ticket and entered the museum, but before he went inside, he studied all the displays outside. There was an M.41 tank, a Chinook helicopter, a flamethrower, an A-1 Skyraider attack bomber, an A-37 Dragonfly attack bomber, and a jeep. Shane had grown up watching the war play out on TV. It had seemed like something happening on another planet, except that his parents always paid close attention to it, shaking their heads and wondering aloud if it would ever end. Shane was surprised at how small everything was in real life, so much smaller than he'd imagined.

Shane entered the museum and studied the anti-war posters and newspaper headlines from around the world, including ones from the U.S. He walked into the exhibit for Agent Orange. Another exhibit reproduced the notorious tiger cages, originally built by the French, where political prisoners were held during the Vietnam War.

This had to have been one of the top-ten worst places to go with a hangover. Way to go, Bao!

But as Shane walked from display to display, his head throbbing and mouth parched, an obvious fact gained critical mass – namely, that there was only one perspective in the museum, the perspective of the North Vietnamese. And from this perspective, one side was right and one side was wrong.

Shane didn't believe in polemics. He believed in the gray space in between. The older Shane became, the less he believed that such a thing as objective truth existed. A pacifist his entire life, an advocate for gun control, Shane was prepared to kill someone now. Maybe more than one person. There it was: the gray space in between.

Morality was a moveable feast. One man's line in the sand was another man's breakfast.

For five years, he had fixated on Hanh setting him up and abandoning him at the Manila airport. Shane had waited for the moment that he would stand in front of her again; he had craved the look of recognition when she realized it was him. But when the moment came, she didn't recognize him at all. He was nobody to her.

As he stared at a display case of defused mortar shells, Shane crawled inside Hanh's head, trying to imagine himself in such a circumstance. He burrowed in, trying to imagine feeling nothing at the sight of him. And then it came to him, the obvious answer: Shane wasn't memorable because he wasn't the only person she had set up. There must have been other bogus companies, more victims of their crimes, and Shane had been only one of several. But how many? And if Shane's theory proved true, how much money were they sitting on? Tens of millions? *Hundreds* of millions?

Shane started laughing because it was all so obvious now. Shane was just one mark. He wasn't anyone special. The scam was larger than him; it was larger than Charlie Leung and the others who'd taken their lives.

"Oh, man!" Shane said aloud, almost relieved, as tourists from around the world avoided the maniacally laughing man with the eyepatch.

A guard shushed Shane, but this only made Shane laugh harder.

Chapter 70

Shane saw Bao across the street talking to a man holding a long pole with buckets on either side. The two men smiled and nodded, they shook hands, and then Bao returned to Shane, faithful driver that he was.

"Friend of yours?" Shane asked.

Bao nodded. He said, "He look for tourists like you."

"Oh yeah?"

"He go to tourist spots, look for Americans."

"What for?"

Bao said, "He give you coconut, tell you it's free. He have you hold the pole and wear the hat, and he take photo of you. Then he wants money for the photo. He cheat people."

"Well," Shane said. "He's not alone, brother."

Chapter 71

Back in his room, Shane looked for evidence to support his theory. He couldn't find any, but he knew in his gut he was right.

Shane lay across his bed, licking ice cream from a cone that was melting faster than he could consume it.

"Son of a bitch," he said when ice cream dripped onto a stack of papers. The ice cream was called White Russian, and it tasted like coffee liqueur and vodka, a drink his mother might have made for herself on Christmas Eve while his father poured himself a whiskey, neat. What would his parents have thought of the mess Shane had found himself in? Jesus. He was glad they weren't alive to witness it. How bad did your life have to get before you were glad your parents were dead?

Shane finished the ice cream.

According to the charges against Shane, in his capacity as CEO of a fictitious investment firm, he had advertised shares for a product called "Pre Funded Reversed Pension Plan" in which he lured investors to purchase shares for $215 per share in exchange for a payout, down the road, of $75,000 in the form of gold. These shares were purchased with virtual currencies. The victims who were targeted were high-value assets, all involved in illegal conduct of their own, such as money laundering, and all beholden to people with more power and influence, often in criminal organizations, which made someone like Charlie Leung an ideal candidate.

The deep fake commercial wasn't made to lure investors. That had already been done by Hanh and, likely, others. The point of the commercial was to put a name to the business, a person who could hang for their crimes.

Until his trip to the War Remnants Museum, Shane thought he'd been looking at the full picture when in reality he'd been looking only at the tail of a dog. What he was failing to see was the rest of the dog, the dozens of people having a picnic, the woman with the parasol, the water surrounding an island, and the boats on the water. He was looking at a small cluster of dots up close instead of standing back to see the entire canvas.

Corbett and company hadn't scammed just the folks that Shane had been accused of scamming, and Shane wasn't the only fall guy. He was a single dot. The Pre Funded Reversed Pension Plan, or whatever the fuck it was called, wasn't their only scam. There were likely dozens of other grifts. Possibly hundreds. And there were likely dozens of Shanes rotting in prisons around the world. In Africa. In Eastern Europe. In countries Shane had never heard of.

The fact that Corbett's betrayal wasn't personal allowed Shane to get past the last hurdle: emotional attachment. He and Corbett were never brothers. This wasn't Cain killing Abel. Corbett was the shark and Shane was the prey, and now that Shane understood their roles without ambiguity, there was only one thing left to do. Close the deal.

Chapter 72

That night, Shane returned to the hidden bar.

Tom was working. Shane thought of the kid's hidden tattooed inner lip, inside a hidden bar that had once been a sham operation hiding its true intentions, operated by people who weren't who they said they were. The layers of deception was like a set of Russian nesting dolls, where you twist open one deceit only to find another.

"Shane!" Tom said. "Welcome!"

The lights were dimmer, highlighting the slide show and eight-millimeter movie to greater effect. There were different slides tonight (New York, late 1950s) and a different movie (a child playing with an Evel Knievel toy motorcycle). Two timelines clashing together. There was also a kaleidoscope of cellophane colors slowly rotating past a bulb, changing the room's hue from green to red to blue. The effect of it all was like dropping acid at a party, like the scene in *Midnight Cowboy* where Joe Buck, wearing cowboy hat and boots, finds himself among hippies. This was the sort of movie reference that would have delighted Cheryl.

"Same?" Tom asked now, smiling.

"Same," Shane confirmed.

Tom yelled out the drink order.

When he turned his attention back to Shane, he noticed the injuries to Shane's face.

"Are you okay?" Tom asked.

"A little roughed up, is all."

"Someone attack you?" Tom asked, suddenly worried.

"It was my fault," Shane said. "I was someplace I shouldn't have been."

Tom nodded but changed the subject.

"How do you like our food?"

"I like it," Shane said. He noted, from the corner of his eye, that the tall Nordic boss was sitting where he had sat last time. "Very tasty," Shane added. "Not too spicy."

"What have you seen so far?" Tom asked.

Shane wanted to tell him that he had gone to Japan Town and saw the two men and the woman who had set him up. He wanted to tell him that he saw a side of himself that he hadn't known existed as he broke a prostitute's ribs and almost choked a thief to death.

"I went to the War Remnants Museum this morning," Shane said. "Have you been?"

"They take us there for field trip. And Independence Palace."

Shane's drink arrived. The gin milkshake.

The boss got up and made his way to the restroom.

"Don't let anyone take my drink?" Shane said to Tom.

Tom knocked on the wooden bar, as though to say, *you got it.*

Shane entered the restroom. The boss was standing at Shane's old urinal; Shane, creature of habit, begrudgingly took the next one over.

"We meet again!" Shane said, unzipping.

The boss peeked over. "Yes. Welcome. You must like this place."

"I do!" Shane said.

He wanted to grill the boss about Hanh, but he was distracted by the photo in front of him. It was the same photo as the one in front of the other urinal. The one of the bluffs.

"Who took these?" Shane asked. "The photos?"

The boss jiggled out the last few drops and zipped up. He walked to the sink and washed his hands.

"They were already here when we moved in," he said.

"Do you know where this is?" Shane asked.

"Not Saigon," he said and laughed. "Enjoy your night." He left the restroom.

As Shane zipped up, he noticed that there was a subtle but not insignificant difference between the two photos. In the photo in front of him stood a man. In relation to everything else in the photo, Shane could barely make the guy out. His features were blurry. And yet there was something about the way he was standing that was familiar.

Shane absently washed his hands, excessively soaping and then running them under too-hot water. "Shit!" he said when he burned himself. He returned to the urinal and took a photo of the photo and then tried zooming in, but he still couldn't make out the man's features. In the distance in both photos, however, was a mountain with distinctive features. It looked eerily like a mountain giving birth to another mountain. Shane had never seen anything quite like it.

Using Google Lens, he searched the photo of the photo.

There were hundreds of matches for a place called Reine Village.

When Shane googled "Reine Village," a Google Map came up for it. It was in Norway.

Shane pinched his fingers and zoomed out, revealing an archipelago named Lofoten. And when he zoomed out even further, he saw that it was in northern Norway, jutting out into the Norwegian Sea.

"Fuck me," Shane said.

He remembered Hanh's passport stamps for Norway – the first hint of her deception.

Shane started to leave but stopped and turned back around, facing the stall. He walked toward it and knocked to make sure no one was inside. Then he pushed the door open.

Nothing.

He exited the men's room and, without knocking, walked into the women's room.

On the wall above the tissue dispenser was a massive drawing of a shark, the kind of drawing you'd find in a nineteenth-century seafaring book. It was too large for a frame in a place as precarious as the restroom stall, but a sheet of Plexiglass, which had been drilled into the wall, covered the poster.

Shane stepped closer and read the caption at the bottom.

Greenland Shark.

The first time he had ever heard of the Greenland Shark was in a canoe on Lake Martin.

What had Corbett told him? That the Greenland Shark lived to be at least two hundred and fifty years old? Possibly more than five hundred years?

Go to the Norwegian Sea, he had said, *and check it out for yourself.*

Well now. Maybe he would.

Chapter 73

Back at the bar, Shane motioned Tom over.

"The woman who owns this building?" Shane said. "She have a husband?"

Tom nodded.

"American?"

Tom nodded again.

Shane pulled up a photo of Corbett on his phone. "Is this him?"

"Yes," Tom said. "But he's never here. I've only seen him once."

"They have kids? Two boys?"

"Yes. Two boys." Tom smiled, remembering something, and pulled his phone from his pocket. He scrolled through his photos. "Christmas," he said. "Last year. Big party." He showed the photo to Shane.

There it was: Corbett and Hanh and Kenny and Tam. One big happy family.

Shane felt his heart squeeze, as though it were a balloon between two hands. Shane pulled from his wallet the equivalent of one hundred dollars for Tom.

"This is for you," Shane said. "And just you."

Tom took the tip before any of his coworkers could see it.

"I was never here, okay?" Shane said.

Understanding the import, Tom solemnly nodded.

Shane reached for Tom's hand, but the pain in his chest returned, this time at the thought of Cheryl seeing him the way he looked now and knowing what he was going to do next. Her heart would have broken for the man she loved.

"You okay?" Tom asked.

"Forget you ever knew me," he said.

Without missing a beat, Tom walked away, treating Shane as though he were already gone.

And, like that, he was.

Chapter 74

Shane gathered his stuff at the Rex Hotel and brought it all back to the apartment at the ice cream shop. He found a red-eye to Oslo and booked it. He could get some sleep on the plane, if need be.

When he tried leaving the ice cream shop with his backpack and duffel, he spotted Bao outside looking at his phone. Shane had managed to lose him for a while, but he was back on round-the-clock duty, no doubt updating the Chinese gangsters.

Shane made his way back through the ice cream shop toward the stairs that led up to his apartment. He shined his iPhone's flashlight around until he found an unmarked door. Carefully, he tried the knob. It wasn't locked.

Thank God.

He stepped out into an alley of sorts. It was difficult to discern in Vietnam the difference between an alley and a street. The ice cream shop was already in an alley, so what was this? An alley behind an alley?

Shane walked toward where he thought he could emerge onto a main street, far enough away to avoid Bao, but after a few minutes of walking, he lost all sense of direction. Where he thought he was heading, he wasn't.

"Goddamn it," he muttered.

He was soaked in his own gin-tinged sweat. He saw four men crouched in the alley, drinking beer. When he got close, he saw that they had circled a rat and a scorpion, and that the two were fighting it out. One of the men kept pushing the scorpion toward the rat with a stick. When Shane passed, the man with the stick looked up at Shane and watched him. Shane anticipated trouble. But then the other three men let out a series of whoops and laughs. Either the rat or the scorpion must have come out victorious. Shane turned back to see if the man with the stick was still watching him. He wasn't.

Shane weaved between buildings, ending up on other, less-promising alleys. He was afraid he was going to miss his flight. Getting a taxi at this time of the night was worrisome enough. But now he was at least twenty minutes behind schedule. Sweat continued to drip from his face. He felt the old panic settling in. Just as he was considering retracing his step, he emerged onto Đ. Lê Lai, one of the busier streets during the day. It was dead tonight, however – dead except for one motorbike heading toward him.

The motorbike slowed down at the sight of Shane.

Shane tried waving him away – he had too much luggage for a motorbike – but the driver stopped anyway.

It was Bao.

"I prefer a car," Shane said. "This backpack's so heavy, I'll probably fall backwards off the bike."

Bao moved as close to the handlebars as possible, motioned for Shane to put the backpack behind him, and then motioned for Shane to sit behind the backpack. Shane knew that people traveled with entire families and sometimes packed dozens of boxes onto the backs of scooters, but he could see only one outcome: dying on a Vietnam highway.

Bao handed Shane a helmet.

"Where go?" Bao asked.

"Where do you think?"

"Airport," Bao said.

"Bingo."

Bao accelerated as he always did, with little caution, only this time, in a city of over nine million people, theirs were the only two heartbeats on the road.

PART FOUR

Chapter 75

There were no quick flights to Oslo. Twenty-one hours with a layover in Istanbul was the best he could manage on such short notice.

Shane tried sleeping on the first leg but couldn't. He was still trying to wrap his head around what he had learned last night. Corbett and Hanh, husband and wife, and their two children, Tam and Kenny?

Given the larger-than-usual Vietnamese population in Southern Louisiana, it was possible – likely, even – that Corbett had met Hanh there. Maybe even in Abbeville, where Shane had gone to meet Tam and Kenny. Ah, what a sweet little family! Instead of playing Monopoly or Clue, they created phony companies and stole millions of dollars. And they were damn good at it.

"On your way home?" the man sitting in his row asked him.

Shane had a window seat; the other passenger, an aisle. An empty seat remained mercifully open between them.

The lights had been dimmed on the plane, but Shane could see enough that the man was in his forties with shock-white hair. His accent sounded German.

"Nope," Shane said. "You?"

The man nodded. "Berlin," he said.

"Corbett," Shane said, reaching out to shake the man's hand.

"Anders."

"What brought you to Vietnam, Anders?" Shane asked.

"I produce movies," Anders said.

"Oh really? What kind of movies?"

"Very European," Anders said. "You know…*cinema*." He laughed. He leaned closer. "Twenty-minute shots of two horses mating." He raised his eyebrows, waiting for Shane's response, but Shane didn't give him the response he wanted.

"Horse-fucking is big in Vietnam, is it?" Shane asked.

Anders looked shocked by the reply.

"No, no. God no. I have a big action movie script, so I'm looking for funding. Two weeks ago, I was in Singapore. Last week, China. This week, Vietnam."

"What's the budget?"

"One hundred million. Very expensive for Germany."

Shane knew it was a cliché, but he said it anyway. "When I was in college, I was a huge Fritz Lang fan. I met my future wife in a film arts class. We fell in love watching movies like *M*."

"Is that so?" Anders said. "You're married then," he said.

"No. She died. It's been a while now."

"Ah, I'm sorry. She must have been young."

Shane nodded. He knew he was the one who had opened that door, but he didn't want to talk about it.

"What about you? Married?"

Anders shook his head. "Too busy, I guess," he said.

"I hear you."

"You don't look Norwegian," Anders said. "On holiday?"

"Business trip."

Anders nodded. "I'm sorry if I'm prying," he said, smiling.

"No, it's just…complicated."

"I see."

"How did your trip go?" Shane asked. "Did you get funding for the movie?"

"Possibly. The funny thing is, the movie could easily be made for five million. Or less. At a certain point, it's all about who stars in it. I could find a perfectly fine German actor to play the lead, or I could try to get Robert Downey, Jr. One movie is five million, the other is a hundred million."

"I hadn't thought of it that way."

"The irony? It's easier to get a hundred million dollars with Robert Downey Jr. attached than it is getting five million with the very fine German actor."

"Let me guess," Shane said. "The German actor was in the movie with the two randy horses."

"Exactly!" Anders said, laughing. He pointed out the window. "China. That's where the money is."

"I would imagine so."

"Mafia money…but it's still money." He shrugged, like, *Eh, what are you gonna do?*

Shane said nothing. He felt a cold sweat break out on the back of his neck.

Anders said, "I had a meeting with a man named Fang Zhong. You ever heard of him, Shane?"

Shane could hear his own heart beating. Fang's reach was impressive. The son of a bitch couldn't let Shane out of his sight.

"Anyway," Anders said, "he was willing to put up two-thirds of the money. Seventy-five million! Imagine that. He said he's expecting a big payday soon."

"What's this movie about?" Shane asked.

Anders leaned across the empty seat. He said, "It's about a guy whose business partner betrayed him, and he ends up in a Manila prison for five years."

If they weren't on an airplane, Shane would have grabbed Anders by the ears and slammed his face onto the armrest, breaking his nose. Instead, he said, "Let me guess. You're not a producer, are you?"

"And your name's not Corbett. See how that goes?"

"I guess it goes without saying you've never seen *M*."

Anders said, "You really should have given more notice. Do you have any idea how close I came to missing this flight?"

"Funny," Shane said. "You don't look Chinese to me."

Anders said, "You've seen Goodfellas, I'm sure. You remember why Robert DeNiro couldn't become a made man?"

"Because he was Irish, not Italian."

"You *do* know your movies," Anders said.

"Things didn't end up well for him, though."

Anders shrugged. "We'll see."

"When we separate in Istanbul and you head to Berlin…can I expect a new babysitter?"

"Yes."

"Why you? Why not my old buddies Cheech and Chong?"

"I was closer to the airport." He looked beyond Shane, out the plane's porthole window. "Everyone thinks of the Triads like an octopus. Tentacles reaching out in every direction. But it's more like water during Noah's Flood. We're everywhere all at once."

"You realize I was going to send for the boys once I reached Oslo," Shane said. "I hope everyone at the home office realizes I wasn't trying to escape."

"Oh, I'm sure your intentions are good," Anders said without any irony. "Fang gets nervous, is all. You know how he is."

"Not really, no," Shane said.

Shane reclined in his chair and shut his eyes.

He said, "Let me guess. You're not even German."

Anders, whose name probably wasn't Anders, said, "Estonian." He dropped the German accent.

Shane laughed. He shifted in his seat, trying to get comfortable, but after a few minutes of twisting his torso one way and then the other, he gave up. Comfort wasn't in the cards.

Chapter 76

No one sat in his row on the second leg of the flight to Oslo.

This time Shane did sleep, albeit in fits and starts. He had the obsessive and recurring dream that kept picking back up where it had left off each time he woke up and then fell back to sleep. It was a dream about his father's hoarding, and how, in the dream, Shane had to wade through soggy boxes, empty and open tuna cans, paper towel rolls, bubble wrap, sheets of Styrofoam…but in the dream, all of this crap was weighing down the plane, and his father was in the last row, near the restrooms. The pilot kept telling everyone to return to their seats and fasten their seatbelts, but Shane couldn't reach his seat because of all of his father's useless shit. He'd trip and fall to his knees, all while the flight attendants, already strapped into their seats, angrily gestured for him to sit down.

When he woke up with a start, he nudged the guy across the aisle.

The man opened his eyes; he may have been asleep.

Shane said, "Tell Joe I'm staying at the Radisson Blu."

The man rubbed his eyes, squinting at Shane. He turned and looked at the seatmate next to him, in case Shane was actually addressing someone else instead, but the seatmate was sound asleep.

"I'm sorry?" he said.

His heart still pounding from the dream of his hoarding father, Shane said, "Cut the bullshit, buddy. Tell those two Chinese gangster assholes I'll be at the Radisson Blu."

This time, the man's eyes searched the cabin for a flight attendant.

Then a hand reached from the seat behind Shane and patted his arm.

A voice: "The Radisson Blue, you say?"

Shane leaned into the aisle and tried craning his neck, but he couldn't see who was sitting behind him.

"Yeah," he said. "Radisson Blu." To the man across the aisle, he said, "Hey, sorry. I thought you were…" He shook his head to say never mind. "Have a good trip, mate."

Chapter 77

In the airport, Shane boarded the train to Oslo and then watched as the man who had been sitting behind him also boarded. The aisle was full of travelers and their suitcases, children, even a dog in a crate. Shane snaked his way through the train car, pretended to drop something, and then crawled out another door, exiting the train altogether.

A few minutes later, the train departed with the man who had been following Shane. He'd had one job to do, and he'd failed. Fang wasn't going to be happy.

Shane headed back to the ticket counter and booked a flight to Lofoten.

He sent his gangster buddies a message on Signal: If you want the money, quit having lackeys follow me. I'll let you know where I'm going when I need you. Just hang tight in Oslo.

A few minutes later, as Shane approached his gate, a message from Joe: We're just trying to help.

Shane wrote: Fuck you. Wait in Oslo.

Shane took a seat and waited for his flight.

Chapter 78

The plane to Lofoten was so small that even Shane's carry-ons had to be checked as luggage. When the plane landed, the dozen or so passengers waited in what looked like a garage for the luggage to appear. There was no carousel. Shane had seen nicer bus terminals. On the plus side, there was no waiting. It took only a few minutes to send everyone on their merry way.

Shane's rental was the only car parked at the far corner of the rental car lot. Other than the passengers on the plane, who quickly scattered to their rides, and the few people who worked unloading luggage and the sole receptionist at the rental car office, the airport was dead.

Shane drove a few miles to his Airbnb and checked in. It was a cozy cabin in a scenic expanse of eight red cabins. Out back sat a hot tub, though no one else seemed to be staying there. The hot tub was Shane's alone. There were mountains in the distance. After the past few weeks in countries famous for their noise pollution, Lofoten was eerily quiet.

Now what?

It was possible Corbett wasn't here. After all, Shane had followed a hunch based on photos on a restroom wall in Vietnam. This leap of faith seemed preposterous now. But if he was here, how hard would it be to find him?

Lofoten was the name of the archipelago. Its entire population was 24,500.

The photo on the wall in the restroom was taken in the municipality of Moskenes, population 982.

Reine was the fishing village where the mountains in the photo were located. Its population was 314.

If Corbett was here, Shane was going to find the son of a bitch, even if it took going door to door.

But not today. Jet lag had taken root.

He took a nap first, his sleep Norwegian-Sea deep, all the way down to where the Greenland shark resides, gray and implacable. When Shane finally floated back up to the surface of consciousness, back into the sunlight, six hours had passed and he felt renewed.

He showered, changed into clothes that needed washing, and ventured out.

His drive across the archipelago was post-apocalyptic. His was the only car on the road. He zipped into several businesses – a gas station, a grocery store – but everything was closed. Was it a holiday?

He checked his phone and saw that Joe had left a dozen messages.

Where the hell are you?

And: *You better not be playing us, fool.*

It was four o'clock.

Parked at the side of the road, he studied his phone, trying to understand what was happening. That's when he saw that it wasn't, as he had assumed, four p.m. It was four a.m. The sun was still out. He hadn't slept six hours. He was in a part of the world, at a time of the year, when the sun never set. He had slept twelve hours. It was the middle of the night.

"Oh shit."

Shane turned his car around and headed back to the condo, where he waited not for the sun to rise but for his body to synch up with the only reality he had ever known: that light meant day.

It wasn't right that darkness would never come. It wasn't the natural order of how things worked. In Shane's world, darkness always came.

Chapter 79

Shane's sense of time was upside-down here.

He stayed awake and watched the sun, which remained visible all night, rise slightly. At long last, after hours of doing nothing, it was morning. The difference between night and day was virtually nonexistent.

On his way to get something to eat, Shane passed sheep and fields of purple heather, and orange-beaked puffins. He drove in and out of fog. The weather changed three times. It was like driving from one postcard to another.

Shane pulled over at a market and bought a grocery sack of munitions, mostly produce. The woman working the cash register was neither friendly nor unfriendly. She had probably spent her life dealing with tourists who couldn't speak the language or understand the currency.

Outside, he pulled one of the baskets of raspberries from his sack and ate a few. They were the plumpest, sweetest raspberries Shane had ever eaten. The air was the freshest he had breathed in years. It was the opposite of the air in Ho Chi Minh City. His surroundings deserved better than to be hanging in front of a urinal in Vietnam. It was, perhaps, the most beautiful place he'd ever been.

Shane didn't have a clear plan for finding Corbett. There were so few people in town that he could easily start showing Corbett's photo to strangers, but Corbett would likely catch wind of it. To Shane's advantage, Corbett probably assumed Shane was still rotting away in Manila. All Corbett needed, though, was the faintest whiff that Shane *wasn't* still locked up for him to disappear, possibly forever.

Shane sent Joe a message on Signal: Come to Lofoten.

Joe responded: You better not be setting us up.

Shane wrote: Fuck you. Come to Lofoten.

Joe replied: K, Bitch.

Shane knew he should stop eating the raspberries – his stomach would pay for his sins – but he told himself *just two more.*

As he brought a raspberry to his mouth, he heard a noise. A moan. Sitting on the ground was a man leaning up against the market wall, passed out. Drugs or alcohol, Shane couldn't tell. The man had a birthmark on his cheek. It was large enough that you couldn't pretend it wasn't there. A few customers glanced over at him on their way in or out of the market, but no one stopped to see if he was okay.

Shane looked away. He got into his rental and drove back to his place.

His plan was to pan fry a reindeer steak. He'd bought a one-pound slab at the market, but once he spread all the food on the counter, he lost his appetite and put it all away for later.

"Where the fuck are you, Corbett?" he asked the empty room.

What would it be like to lay eyes on the bastard again after all these years?

Even if Shane found him, he didn't have a plan. He needed to wait for his Chinese gang compatriots to arrive. Corbett was too smart for Shane to approach him without a strategy.

Shane tried to sleep, but the ever-present sunlight wasn't going to let him. He remained on the couch for several hours, in the same position, expecting to hear from Joe, but he heard nothing.

Ever since he'd gotten released, he'd put off two tasks, pushing them from his consciousness. The first was to see what had become of his cat Larry. He assumed his old boy was dead. He assumed the house had been confiscated for some bullshit reason having to do with his legal issues in the Philippines. He assumed his cat sitter had given up waiting for him and walked away from it all, possibly having to drop Larry off at the Humane Society herself.

The other thing Shane had put off was googling Cole Mast. Cole had been his client with the long red beard, thick red eyebrows, and seed cap. He was the man Shane had driven to Lake Charles for a night of gambling, only for it to end in an abandoned gas station, the two of them shooting heroin together. Even after Shane had rebuilt his own life, he couldn't bring himself to find out what had happened to Cole.

Fuck it, he thought and googled him now.

The internet was painfully slow.

"Come on," Shane said. "Come on."

The screen seemed to freeze.

Shane was about to give up when the search results appeared. And there it was, the first one, the result he feared: Cole's obituary.

"Goddamn it," Shane said. "Mother*fuck!*"

He'd died two years after their night together. No cause of death was given. It may or may not have been Shane's fault, but Shane certainly hadn't helped. He had to assume that a line could be drawn from the abandoned gas station to the funeral home, a downward trajectory that could have been averted with a different therapist.

Shane clutched his phone so hard, he risked breaking it.

He got up and, locking the door behind him, headed back to the market. He had no idea what time it was, if anything was open or closed. He didn't care.

Chapter 80

The man with the birthmark was still sitting out front, still passed out.

Shane walked tentatively toward him, the way you'd approach a raccoon or an opossum.

"Hey, buddy," Shane said.

Once close enough, Shane crouched next to the man.

"Hey. You still with us?"

The parking lot was empty. No one was walking into or out of the market. The sun was still out, of course, but it was probably evening, possibly after midnight.

The man's eyes began to open, but there was no focus left in them, no light.

Shane looked around to see if anyone could give him a hand, but no one else was out.

"It's just us," Shane said. "Hold tight."

Shane drove his rental closer and opened the passenger-side door. The man wasn't overweight, but he was tall and big-boned. He looked like someone who'd spent his life working on a ship or chopping wood.

"You're gonna have to help me," Shane said to the man, who seemed to have some vague understanding now of what was going on. He'd slung his arm around Shane's neck and put some effort into rising to his feet, but he remained unstable all the way to the car. Once the man found the car's seat, he fell ass-first inside.

"Good enough," Shane said. "That'll work."

Shane lifted the man's legs, situating his feet on the floorboard. He didn't bother buckling him in. He shut the door and then, from the driver's side, lifted the man into a version of a sitting position, the way you might manipulate a corpse to pass as a living thing.

On the way back to his place, Shane said, "No promises except that you'll at least sleep on a couch instead of the ground."

The man said something, but Shane couldn't make it out.

"One requirement," Shane said. "Don't die on me. Okay?"

Silent, the man committed to nothing.

Chapter 81

Shane couldn't sleep. An unholy combination of jet lag, confusion, and sunlight plagued him. Meanwhile, the messages from Joe had piled up by the time Shane finally checked Signal.

We're here. Where the fuck are you?

Hello? You gonna answer me or what?

Look, asshole, we're eating reindeer for the second time today. I better hear from you in the next ten minutes.

The last message had come in over two hours ago.

The man with the birthmark stirred on the couch. Shane sat in a chair across from him. He still hadn't slept, couldn't remember the last time he'd slept, and still wasn't sure if it was morning or night.

Shane typed: Hang tight, numb nuts.

To the man on his couch, Shane said, "Everything's cool. You're all right. I didn't want you to die out there."

The man blinked a few times then pushed himself upright. He looked around. He seemed only mildly surprised to be inside instead of outdoors.

When he spoke, the language wasn't recognizable.

"Do you know any English?" Shane asked.

He nodded.

"Okay, good. So here's what's going to happen. I'm going to get you some help. You've been asleep for hours. You hungry?"

He shook his head.

"What's your name?"

"Egil."

"Great. So, listen, Egil. Like I said, you've been asleep for hours, so I've been doing some research. Google. I found a place called 400 Years Club. Don't ask. I don't why it's called 400 Years Club. Dumb name. But it's like AA. I'm taking you there. Is that all right?"

Egil said nothing. He wiped his mouth. He looked around again.

"Where am I?" he asked.

"You're in the apartment of a man who's going to save your life, whether you want it or not."

Egil nodded. "Oh," he said.

Shane pulled his chair closer to the couch and held out his hand.

"Shane," he said. "I used to be a therapist."

Egil studied Shane's hand a moment before reaching out his own.

"Egil," he said. "I used to be a husband and a father."

Shane didn't ask as the two men shook hands.

Chapter 82

When morning finally came, Shane took a soak in the outdoor hot tub and then drove to a store to buy clothes for Egil. Norway wasn't a cheap country, and Shane felt bad that he bought some of the cheapest clothes he could find. But this wasn't Cambodia, and beggars couldn't be choosers.

Shane had agreed to meet the Chinese gangsters for brunch. The restaurant had tall windows with a view of mountains and ships bobbing in the bluest water Shane had ever seen. Forgoing the buffet, Shane ordered a reindeer sandwich. It arrived on an artisanal bun with white cheese and slices of grilled red pepper.

"You sure you don't want anything?" Shane asked.

Joe shook his head.

"What's your buddy's name? We never got into that in Vietnam."

"It's not important," Joe said.

Shane stopped mid-bite. His eyes cut toward Joe's partner, as if to say, *Are you listening to this shit? He just said your name isn't important!*

"I'll be happy if I never eat reindeer again," Joe said.

"Have you had the sandwich? It's like roast beef," Shane said. "But gamey."

Joe stared at the sandwich with disapproval.

Shane said, "You shouldn't be so goddamned judgmental. You grew up in Jersey, for fuck's sake. And what the hell kind of Chinese gangster name is Joe?"

Joe, ignoring the jabs, said, "Why do you keep going rogue on us?"

"That's the thing," Shane said. "I'm *not* going rogue. I just don't want someone riding my ass twenty-four/seven."

"You could at least give us a heads-up," Joe said.

"Why? You've had someone following me pretty much every step of the way."

"True," Joe said. "But it makes Fang uneasy, the way you just leave."

"It's called the Irish Goodbye. It's in my blood." Shane sighed. "Look, Fang could justifiably feel uneasy if he had actually paid back all the money he stole from Song. But he has jack-shit at stake. So he can get his panties out of a wad and just relax."

Joe said, "Don't use that kind of language when you talk about Fang."

Shane took another bite of his sandwich.

Joe wagged his head. "You're a real piece of work," he said. "I'm starting to see why your business partner had you locked up thousands of miles away from him."

"I used to be nice," Shane said.

"And what?" Joe said. "You're just an asshole now?"

"Pretty much," Shane said.

"Okay, so what's the plan?"

Until now, Shane's plan was to lead them to Corbett, but now that they were this close, Shane didn't want to give Corbett up so easily.

"The plan," Shane said, "is that I take you to the people who have the money."

"What the hell are we waiting for? Why are we just sitting here while you eat some nasty-ass reindeer?"

"Because I don't know where any of those people are. But I'm close. I feel it in my bones. This is the center of their operations. And I don't want you fucking it up. You don't know Corbett. He didn't get this far to let it all go."

"But he *is* here, right?" Joe said. "Corbett"

"I don't know," Shane said. "Maybe."

"Maybe? Are you shitting me?"

"Maybe's better than nothing," Shane said.

A vein on Joe's head was starting to bulge. His partner said nothing, just stared at Shane, unblinking. A true sociopath.

Joe said, "Okay. Do you think we can at least pick up some speed? I don't want to spend the rest of my life in this Godforsaken place."

Shane picked up a single French fry and bit it in half. He chewed slowly, deliberately.

"Jesus Christ," Joe said.

Shane finished the French fry and picked up another.

When Joe realized that he wasn't going to be able to rush Shane, he picked up a handful of Shane's fries and shoved them into his mouth.

Joe's associate reached over and collected the remainder of Shane's reindeer sandwich. Instead of taking a bite, he made a fist, crushing the sandwich in his palm.

"So he does speak English?" Shane asked Joe. To the associate, he said, "You *do* speak English, don't you?"

Joe said, "No, he reads body language. And he can tell you're being a prick."

The associate said nothing. He wiped his hand across the linen tablecloth.

Shane settled his bill, and together the three men gathered around Joe's rental. Joe popped the trunk. Inside was their luggage. Tucked between the two suitcases was a paper bag from Starbucks, the kind with a straw handle. Joe looked around the parking lot before reaching into the bag and pulling a .38 into view.

"There's a silencer in there. And two boxes of bullets," Joe said. "But I don't want you using any of this, hear? We need Corbett alive. This is just for self-protection. You kill him, and we're all fucked. We'll never find that money. It's as good as gone."

"They let you on the plane with that?" Shane asked.

Joe looked confused. "What? No! We picked this up from our contact in Oslo."

"Wait a minute. You drove up from Oslo?"

Joe nodded.

"That's, like, *twenty hours*."

"Not with lead foot here," Joe said, motioning toward his silent partner.

Shane took the Starbucks bag.

"So…," Joe said. "What now?"

"Go back to your room and rest."

"And what are you going to do? Consult a psychic?" Joe shook his head. "Nah, we'll follow you."

"If you follow me," Shane said, "you'll be disappointed."

"You're putting us in a bind," Joe said.

"Is that so?"

"You're putting *me* in a bind," Joe said. "With Fang," he added.

Shane headed for his car. Without turning around, he called out, "Patience!"

"This is bullshit and you know it," Joe said.

Shane raised the Starbucks bag into the air, as though thanking them for a caramel latte and a scone. He pressed the key fob and the trunk hissed open. He tucked the bag inside the trunk, beneath the mat and inside the wheel well, and then he shut the trunk.

"Talk to you soon!" Shane called out without looking back.

Chapter 83

Shane returned to his apartment with the new clothes. He could hear the shower running.

He knocked on the bathroom door and said, "I'm back. I put a bag of clothes for you on the bed in the spare room."

He went downstairs and made coffee. He'd left the gun in the trunk of the rental. It reminded him of the bomb in the trunk of the car in opening scene of *Touch of Evil* – a continuous shot that ends with the car exploding. Cheryl had missed class the day they watched *Touch of Evil*, and the anxiety of the bomb in the trunk only heightened Shane's personal anxiety that maybe she had dropped the class and he'd never see her again. That was the first time he realized he wanted to spend time with her, more than the silent time they had spent sitting near each other in a darkened classroom.

Shane heard footsteps and turned. Egil was unsteadily making his way down the stairs.

"You need help? Hold on."

"No, I'm okay," he said.

The new clothes had done wonders for him, but he was clearly struggling.

"Dress for success!" Shane said, a bit too enthusiastically.

The reference was lost on Egil.

"It was a popular book in the U.S.," Shane added.

Still nothing.

Shane poured him a cup of coffee.

"Milk? Sugar?"

"Black," Egil said and sat down on the couch. His hands were shaking. He tried picking up the cup of coffee but couldn't.

Shane sat next to him. He picked up Egil's coffee cup and held it to his mouth, and Egil sipped. He nodded to indicate that he was good. Shane set the cup down and then squeezed Egil's shoulder before moving back to his own chair.

"I should say upfront," Shane said, "that I've been where you're at now. Worse, in fact."

Egil looked up at Shane; he wiped his face with his right hand. The span of his hand was impressive. He would have made a great receiver in the NFL.

"Did you lose your job?" Shane asked. "I lost my job. I lost everything."

"I rent boats," Egil said. "Small shop. I'm the owner." He reached down and picked up his coffee cup. His hands were steadier this time. "I haven't been there in four months."

When Shane was a therapist, he would get someone to open up by asking about their interests. Eventually, he would see the light in their eyes. He would hear their voices speed up with excitement. Sometimes it was a subtle shift. Often, he could see it in the body language, a gradual openness, like a blooming flower.

"What kinds of boats do you rent?" Shane asked.

Egil shrugged. "Small utility boat," he said. "Aluminum fishing boats. I've got one cabin cruiser. The weather here is unpredictable."

"I noticed," Shane said. He smiled, waiting for him to let his guard down, but he didn't. He decided to change the subject. "If I thought you needed medical help detoxing, I'd take you to a facility. But I don't think you're there yet. You okay going with me to this 400 Years Club place?"

Egil nodded. Shane recognized his expression as that of a man who didn't have the will to have conviction one way or the other.

When Shane had reached that point, he wanted help and wanted it desperately…but he couldn't muster the emotions necessary to seek it out or to express appreciation when it came his way.

"Good," Shane said. "This place we're going? Stupid slogan. *A place to sit. A place to start again.* If we get there and it seems like a crock of bullshit, just give me a look and we'll go. Okay?"

Egil nodded again. He looked down into his cup of coffee, as though looking into his own murky future.

Chapter 84

The meeting was in an old smokehouse – a red wooden structure, like nearly every other structure on Lofoten from what Shane could tell. The building stood alone. A river rolled behind the building. The sun was still out, of course, but it was evening, and the sky was gray. It was significantly colder now.

A few men stood outside, smoking.

Shane and Egil walked to the front door. The door was adorned with a silver knocker in the shape of a shark.

"What's that?" Shane asked.

"Greenland shark," Egil said. "Lives to be 400 years old. Maybe older."

"Ah ha! The 400 Years Club!" Shane said. "I get it now. My brain's not working. It's the sun. It's making me crazy."

Egil said nothing as Shane opened the door, motioning Egil in first.

Inside stood five more men milling about. They all looked like fishermen. They all looked haunted.

The room was grim, seemingly abandoned except for these meetings: the wood ceilings and beams blackened from decades of smoke, the plank floors splintered and stained. There was no insulation, so it was no warmer inside than outside. A dozen metal folding chairs were set up in a circle. Against one of the walls: a folding table with a percolator for coffee. A few men nodded at Egil, and he nodded back.

Shane picked up the flyer from the chair before sitting.

It read, *We meet weekly at the smokehouse. For those who've been under too long. We listen harder than we talk. If you've tried everything else, or if you haven't tried anything yet, we'll be there. Look for the shark on the door.*

It was signed *Russell Duchamp.*

Shane looked up, and there he stood: the pill mill doctor of Lafayette, with his soul patch and acne scars. He had just walked into the smokehouse, smiling, shaking hands. He saw Shane and Egil, and he offered a friendly wave. There was no recognition, no fear.

Shane nodded in return to the wave – a cautious acknowledgment.

He tried not to show any emotion, but he could feel the artery in his neck thump, his heartbeat grinding from first to third gear.

When he looked back down, he saw that he had murdered the flyer. It was a ball in his right hand.

"They stored cod here," Egil said, "during World War Two. The Nazis needed cod liver oil for their explosives."

The room smelled like nothing Shane had ever smelled in his life, probably from nearly a hundred years of storing fish.

"Norway helped the Nazis?" Shane asked.

Egil said, "The people in charge? What's the word? Puppet?"

"A puppet government?" Shane asked. "Makes sense."

Egil nodded.

Shane kept his eyes on Duchamp, who had poured himself a cup of coffee from the percolator. As he walked toward the boarded-up fireplace, he motioned for everyone to come and sit.

"Welcome," Duchamp said to Egil and Shane. "You speak English?"

Shane and Egil both nodded.

"Good," Duchamp said. "I speak a little Norwegian, but not much."

"Not from here?" Shane asked.

"Not even close!" Duchamp said. "Louisiana." He squinted at Shane. "American?"

"Yes, sir. Chicago."

"Chicago! What brings you here?"

"Here? This place? Just helping my friend out."

"No. Here. *Norway.*"

"Oh. Vacation. Met this fella outside a market. I…" Shane tipped his head toward Egil. How much more should he say? "I've been where he's at. I couldn't *not* help him."

"God, no," Duchamp said. By now, everyone had taken a seat. "Are we all here?" Duchamp asked the gathering.

Shane heard the door open; someone else had stepped inside. He knew it was going to be Corbett, he felt it in his bones, but when he turned around, he saw a woman carrying another percolator to replenish the coffee. Her hair was long and red. Dyed. She was wearing a cashmere cardigan and blue jeans with a pair of white Converse Chuck Taylors.

Shane's heart had sped up. The unconscious mind knew what the conscious mind was slow to realize. As she looked around the room, he saw it now, he *felt* it, the brain catching up to the heart: the woman was Kylie.

She saw him watching her and smiled.

Like Duchamp, Kylie didn't recognize him, either. Why would she? How long had it been now since the last time either of them had seen each other? Seven years and change? So much had happened to him. It wasn't just the tattoos or the missing eye or the tumor. The darkness in his heart had physically altered him.

Were she and Duchamp business partners? Lovers? Husband and wife?

For all the rage inside him, Shane had yet to kill anyone. Tam, Kenny, Hanh, Duchamp, Kylie. They were all still living, breathing. Not only that, but they were continuing on with their lives as though nothing was different.

Egil nudged Shane and then motioned to Shane's hands. They were shaking.

Shane rubbed his hands across his thighs a few times to settle his nerves.

"It's the cold," he whispered, but Egil didn't look convinced.

Shane opened Signal. He sent Joe a pinned map of the smokehouse.

He wrote: You need to be here. Right now!

Duchamp motioned with his hands for everyone to stop talking. He said, "Good to see so many friends here. I hope the friends we don't see tonight are doing well. I hope they're not here for reasons other than the reasons that brought them here in the first place." He nodded thoughtfully. "As all of you know, I'm not from here. I grew up not far from the Mississippi River. My daddy used to say, 'You don't rush the river. You don't fight the tide. You just keep paddlin'. Little by little, you find your way back.'"

The room of fishermen nodded.

Duchamp said, "If you want to talk tonight, we'll listen. If you don't, that's okay, too. There's always next week." He looked over at Shane and Egil. "We've got two new friends here tonight. Care to introduce yourselves?"

"Egil," Egil said.

"You want to tell us a little something about yourself?"

Egil said, "I killed my wife and child."

Everyone sat up. A few people muttered something to the person next to them.

Shane had already been feeling on edge, but he recognized the shift of the mood in the room, the danger it brought. He'd felt it so many times before in Manila, and he became so good at detecting it that he could taste it first. It tasted like a nickel resting on the back of his tongue.

"I'd been drinking," Egil said. "We were going from Sørvågen to Tind, and I got confused, I couldn't see the road. The fog was thick. It was mørketid. The time of darkness. I hadn't slept in a week. That's why I was drinking that day. We weren't supposed to drive. All I wanted was to sleep. But something came up. My daughter Ada, she was invited to a party. I couldn't see the road." He began crying.

Shane put his arm around Egil's shoulders as Egil leaned forward. He was crying – his shoulders were shaking – but he wasn't making any noise. And then he let out a gasp – the sound a dying man makes taking a last breath – and then his breathing resumed.

Duchamp said, "There's no judgment here. We all come here wounded, some worse than others. The whole point of this club is to have a place where we can tell our stories, especially those stories we can't tell anyone else."

Shane turned and looked back at Kylie, but she was fixated on Egil. What Shane couldn't see so many years ago he saw with perfect clarity now: Kylie was looking for their next mark. That was the whole purpose of the 400 Years Club. That had been the whole purpose of the pill mill. They recruited; they groomed; they brought men who had lost everything even further down, stripping them of everything; and once they'd accomplished that, once the mark was ready, they handed the operation over to Corbett, the impresario, who was lying in wait. This was why Shane had never seen Kylie actually take any pills. What the bearded man had shot into Kylie's arm that night in the abandoned gas station was probably just sugar. The real stuff was waiting for Shane's return. And, as it turned out, his client's. Cole Mast. Rest in peace. Their scheme was elaborate and painstaking, including years of grooming Shane, but the payout was massive.

"Do you want to say more?" Duchamp asked, and Egil shook his head. He had straightened up now, but he was still emotional.

The door opened again, and this time Joe and his associate entered into the room. They couldn't have stood out more if they'd tried: two Chinese men among a room of Norwegian fishermen in a smokehouse on an archipelago north of the Arctic Circle. Joe was holding a cattle prod. There was no blending in, no assimilation. Sometimes, the truth was plain as day: they didn't belong here. Even so, they remained by the door.

Duchamp, looking uneasy, turned his attention away from the men. To Shane, he said, "And you, stranger?"

It was as though he knew now that Shane's presence was of more import than Shane had let on. Duchamp had pressed down on *stranger* for emphasis.

"Well, let's see. My story begins seven years ago," Shane began. "My wife was dying, and a young woman offered me OxyContin to give her some relief from the excruciating pain. My wife died the next day, so I started taking Oxy to get me through it. Just one pill. Then two. Then whatever I could get my hands on. That's when I was introduced to a doctor."

Duchamp took a seat now, staring at Shane as he talked, strategizing, glancing up occasionally at the Chinese men in the room, trying to formulate a plan. Kylie had circumnavigated the room to get a better look at Shane.

"Anyway… It's a long story. The upshot of it was that I ended up in a Philippine detention center for five years. I lost my eye. Terrible things happened to me there. Things I'll never talk about. Certainly not here. The only things that kept me alive were my tattoos. They're memories of my wife Cheryl. I met her in college, in a film arts class." Shane shook his head. It was the first time he'd spoken to anyone about Cheryl in years. Even the man who had tattooed him in Manila didn't know the story. Shane looked around at the other men in the room. "I think maybe this meeting is over?"

Duchamp said, "Regrettably, he's right."

Confused, the men were slow to stand, but as Duchamp and Kylie shook hands and whispered goodbye, the men reluctantly shuffled out until the only ones remaining were Duchamp, Kylie, Egil, Shane, and Fang's two men.

"Shane?" Kylie said, still unsure.

"Hey, doll. It's been a while," Shane said, "hasn't it?"

"Jesus," Kylie said, "I'm so glad you're still alive. I heard rumors."

"Did you? Rumors?"

She walked closer to hug him.

"No, don't," Shane said, holding up his hands. "Just…stay right there."

Joe readjusted his grip on the cattle prod. His associate removed a gun from inside his coat.

"Where's Corbett?" Shane asked.

"Who?" Duchamp asked.

Shane laughed. To give up Corbett would mean the end of their entire enterprise. They were foolish enough to think they were going to live through the night.

"It's okay," Shane said. "I'll find him. I found you, after all, and I wasn't even looking for you."

Egil said, "I don't understand."

"These are bad people," Shane said, motioning to Duchamp and Kylie. "They ruined my life. They've ruined a lot of people's lives."

"Why?"

Shane shrugged. "The money's good?"

"What now?" Duchamp asked. He had dropped the nurturing father-figure act. He had returned to who he really was, the charlatan from the swamp. A Cajun confidence man from Acadiana. A born grifter. For someone like him, redemption wasn't on the table.

To Joe, Shane said, "Is Fang going to pay me? My understanding is that I'd get paid in tiers. On signing. Upon delivery. And upon retrieving the money."

Joe pulled from a pocket inside his jacket a single folded sheet of printer paper. He opened it up and pointed to the top of the page.

"That's the offshore account," Joe said. "Here's your account number."

His finger moved down the page.

"And here," Joe said, "is the deposit. The rest you'll receive upon recovery."

"Two million?" Shane said, taking the sheet of paper, folding it several times, tucking it away. "Not bad."

"You want my advice?" Joe asked.

"Sure."

"Download the app, boomer. It makes the transactions easier." His smile said, *Eat shit.*

"If this is about money," Duchamp said. "I'm sure we can figure something out."

Kylie, standing next to Duchamp, looked scared but hopeful.

Shane removed his eyepatch. Even Joe winced.

"Do you have the ability to surgically implant an eye that I could see out of?"

Duchamp shook his head. "Of course not."

"Then it's not about the money." Shane put the eyepatch back on.

"What's going to happen to us?" Kylie asked.

"You're going to have to ask these gentlemen. Your fates are no longer within my purview."

Duchamp snorted. "Purview, my ass. This whole *deal* has been within your purview."

"There it is!" Shane said. "That Cajun spunk!"

Duchamp started to make a move toward Joe, but Joe raised the prod, flipped it on, and touched it to Duchamp's arm, causing him to fall to the ground and thrash around. When Kylie screamed, he touched her as well, as though anointing her, provoking the same results.

Shane watched with detachment. He was tempted to ask if Joe could repeat the action so that he could watch it again. It was the first time he felt he'd stepped inside the skin of a sociopath. Shane *wasn't* a sociopath, but he understood now the quiet interest in another person's pain. He thought he might actually be able to watch dispassionately whatever torture was in store for them – the dismantling of their skeletons, the periodic searing of flesh, the removal of teeth with pliers and a ball-peen hammer.

But when Shane looked over at Egil and saw the look of terror on his face, he felt humanity return to his being, and he knew he needed to leave before the delivery of true pain and suffering began.

With his associate momentarily away, likely retrieving from their trunk a variety of tools and devices, Joe said, "Are you sure they have the money?"

"Not all of it, no," Shane said. "But they have more than I first thought. Pretty sure I played a very small role in a much bigger operation."

"What are you going to do to them?" Egil asked. He fumbled with a pack of cigarettes, trying to free a smoke.

"We'll start," Joe said, "by tying one end of a rope on his ankle and the other end on hers, and then we'll hang them from the rafter like fish tied by their tails. That's all I know for certain. Torture is like jazz. I might want to head one way, but Tao may want to go in another direction, so I'll adjust. Or maybe he'll adjust. We have to read each other's emotions. Jazz is all about tension and release."

For the first time, Shane saw why Joe did what he did, and he instantly regretted all the times he'd flipped him shit, treated him like a lackey, or pretended they weren't so different. There was a depth of sociopathy that Shane hadn't seen until now. Unlike Shane, who convinced himself for a moment that he could watch these two being tortured, Joe was actually going to do it…and he was going to enjoy it. It filled a dark hole in his life. It gave him purpose.

Egil had given up retrieving his cigarette.

"We good?" Shane asked, and Joe nodded.

Shane and Egil passed the elusive Tao on their way out. Tao nodded goodbye, as though they were passing each other in a park, but he was holding a blowtorch in one hand and a toolbox in the other.

It was hard to imagine someone like Tao sleeping in a womb, incubating in amniotic fluid, and dreaming of his own mother's heartbeat – but he must surely have, as they all had: the only bond between monsters and men.

Chapter 85

Egil had finally lit his cigarette. He didn't bother to roll down the passenger-side window. The rental filled with smoke.

Shane looked in the rearview mirror. No one was following them

He remembered Corbett calling him the night before he was arrested. He had asked Shane if he ever thought he'd get married again, and Shane admitted that something had died inside him. And then Shane asked Corbett the same question.

I'm still hopeful, Corbett said. *I still see a wife in my future. A wife and two children. Boys.*

Shane had said, *That's where you and me are different, Corb. I'm not hopeful. Don't get me wrong. I'm grateful I'm still here. I'm grateful I'm still alive. But I'm not hopeful.*

That's what I was afraid of, Corbett said.

That was likely the moment Shane's fate had been sealed. He imagined now that Corbett had called Hanh to give her the go-ahead to turn him in at the airport.

He shivered now thinking of his own sealed fate.

The drive was the prettiest Shane had ever taken. Mountains and bodies of unpolluted water and clusters of purple flowers bending toward the car as a gentle wind blew. It was after eleven at night, but the sun told a different story.

"My place," Egil said, pointing to a small wooden structure.

"Your home?"

"No," Egil said. "Boat rentals."

Shane eased the car into the lot.

"Can I see it?" Shane asked.

Egil eyed him with suspicion. Anything was possible given all the turns and twists, the night's convoluted syntax.

A sign jutting out from the wall read, EGIL'S BOAT RENTALS.

Nothing clever. Nothing vague.

"You smell that?" Shane asked.

Egil made a sound of affirmation.

Gasoline.

A bell rang overhead when Egil opened the door and they stepped inside.

There wasn't much inside the place. A pad of receipts. An old cash register. A counter for taking orders. A few chairs, probably for customers to relax while Egil got their boat ready. Only the necessities.

On the wall, above a display of spearguns, was a banner that read: SPEARFISHING HEAVEN! And next to the banner was a photo of two men, each holding an enormous fish.

"What day is it?" Shane asked.

"The seventh?" Egil said.

"No, the day of the week."

"Tuesday." He thought about it. "No. Wednesday."

Shane checked his watch. It was after midnight.

Shane removed one of the spearguns and examined it. Between the two of them, Corbett had been the man's man – fishing, kayaking, watching football all weekend: college ball on Saturdays,

NFL on Sundays. Shane was – and had always been – the sensitive type. The empath. He liked foreign films. He read the classics. He teared up when he heard certain songs from high school.

Shane motioned to another set of hooks on the wall.

"What went here?" Shane asked.

"Speargun," Egil said.

"You sell a lot of these, do you?"

"Not sell. Rent. But that one…"

"What?"

"Someone didn't return it."

"Really?"

As Shane put the speargun he was holding back onto the hooks, he looked out the only window in the room. What he saw was a mountain giving birth to another mountain.

"Where are we?"

Egil dropped the cigarette butt on the wooden floor and, with the tip of his boot, snuffed it out.

"Reine," he said.

Those mountains were the same mountains from the poster on the wall of the men's room in Saigon.

Reine was where mountains birthed mountains, where people lived in wooden houses painted brick-red, and where Shane knew he would find Corbett.

His vision of Corbett wasn't a dream or a trance or a religious ecstasy. It was knowing the man's habits: every Wednesday, from noon until one-thirty, Corbett could be found in a boat on a body of water.

It was Wednesday. It wasn't noon, but it was midnight.

"Why would it smell like gasoline outside?" Shane asked.

"Boat," Egil said.

"Exactly." Shane walked to the wall of keys and said, "May I?"

Egil clearly didn't like where any of this was going; he was a man whose face gave up the game each and every time. He'd have been terrible at poker. But he was also a man who didn't get in the way of another man's bad decisions.

He reached up and handed Shane a key.

When he started walking to the door, either to show Shane the boat or to go with him, Shane shook his head.

"Just tell me which one it is," Shane said.

"Third one," Egil said. "The Askeladden."

"Fancy," Shane said and smiled. "Don't worry. No harm will come to it."

Outside, Shane popped his trunk and pulled out the Starbucks bag.

Shane walked over to the Askeladden and climbed down into it. It bobbed under him. The engine wouldn't turn over the first time he twisted the key, but after letting it rest a few seconds, he tried again and it started right up.

Shane removed the gun and the silencer from the bag. He screwed the silencer into the barrel, and then he loaded the gun.

It was downright chilly as the sun hid behind a gathering of clouds. This would mark the third time Shane had ever been inside a boat, but something about being in Norway, here in a fishing village, surrounded by wooden structures and boats that looked like every old dime-store painting he'd seen for sale at Goodwill – it made Shane feel, unlike the two times on Lake Martin, as though he'd been doing this his entire life.

He accelerated and steered the boat out from the dock as fog rolled in. The mist felt good against his face. He reached up and adjusted his eyepatch. He wiped the dampness from his face with the crook of his arm.

Was the weather like this the night Egil crashed his car with his wife and child inside it?

Were Kylie and Duchamp still alive?

It had been a few hours since they'd left the smokehouse.

Probably not.

He felt something in the pit of his stomach…but it may have been hunger.

Shane squinted. He saw another boat in the distance. It wasn't a rowboat, but it wasn't very large. It had an outboard motor. Despite its size, a name had been written along the side of it. The script was small, and Shane couldn't make it out until he was within fifteen yards from it.

The Kingfisher.

A joke, no doubt. The Kingfisher was the nickname for Huey Long, governor of Louisiana long before either of them had been born. A populist. A divisive figure.

"You realize that Huey Long was assassinated, don't you?" Shane called out.

The figure in the boat turned. He had a long, full beard and piercing eyes. It wasn't Corbett. It was the man from the gas station. Where Kylie and Duchamp had jumpstarted Shane's descent, the bearded man had guaranteed it.

Fog rolled between them.

When the bearded man appeared again, he didn't recognize Shane, but why would he? They'd met only once, many years ago.

"You know your Louisiana history," the man said. "But the assassin was shot at least sixty times."

"Dead is dead," Shane said.

"I can't argue that," the man said. "Name's Corbett."

Corbett?

"Shane," Shane said. "Shane Doyle."

More fog. Shane lifted the gun with the silencer.

"Don't do that," Shane said when he saw Corbett reaching for the spear gun.

Corbett sat up.

Shane squinted at Corbett. He could see now that it was him. He was like that optical illusion where you saw either a beautiful woman or an old hag. Until now, he had seen only one or the other. He finally saw both.

"Jesus. That was you in the gas station that night," Shane said. "You destroyed my life."

"And then I resurrected you," Corbett said.

"That's what you call it? Resurrected?" Shane laughed. "Kylie's looking good. The arctic air works wonders. Even old Duchamp seems rejuvenated."

"You saw them then?"

"I did. But I had to go. They had company. Two men I met in Hong Kong paid them a visit. Or was it Macau? These last few weeks have blurred together. I'm having a hard time keeping it all straight. Hey. Aren't you going to tell me I'm looking good?"

"It's good to see you," Corbett said, smiling. It was the old smile that Shane had fallen for the night they met in the basement bar and Corbett had invited Shane into his life. That was Corbett's most dangerous weapon. His smile alone could make you think you were his best friend.

Shane said nothing.

"How much do you want?" Corbett asked.

"How much? For what? For five years of my life? Or to keep me from killing your wife and kids?"

Corbett stiffened. He swallowed hard. So there *was* something he cared about.

"Oh, I saw them in Saigon," Shane said. "Like you…like everyone, really…they didn't recognize me. My feelings were hurt, but I got over it."

"Are you going to kill me?" Corbett asked.

"I had no idea Duchamp and Kylie were… What are they? Are they married?"

Corbett nodded.

"Were they married when I met them?"

"Yes, they were married."

"Ah, all right. That explains a few things. But…when Kylie got arrested…"

"Gotta hand it to you. You've really done your research."

"I had an assist. An ex-cop. If it wasn't for him, I'd still be in that detention center in Manila. He was a variable you hadn't counted on."

"I see."

"What were we talking about? Oh yeah. The arrest."

Corbett said, "A county sheriff wanted a cut of our business. The Oxy business. He didn't know about the rest. But we couldn't have that. Duchamp paid off the district attorney to drop the charges. You gotta love Louisiana. The grift is real. There's always someone to pay off, to make things right."

"Until there's not," Shane said.

"I have to disagree with you there, old friend. Everyone has a price."

Shane thought about the last time they were on the water together, the day before Corbett had sent Shane to his fate in Manila. It hadn't been a spontaneous decision on Corbett's part. In fact, nothing about his actions had been spontaneous.

Shane said, "I'm assuming you still haven't been to therapy?"

"Are you serious? This is the conversation we're having?"

"We could have a session right now," Shane said. "Free of charge."

Corbett laughed, shook his head.

Shane extended his arm with the gun for a better shot.

"We're having a session," Shane said. "I think it'll do you good."

Corbett leaned back, resting his arms on the bench's padded backrest. He looked perturbed but strangely relaxed. Shane had to assume this wasn't the first time Corbett's life had been threatened.

"What brings you here today?" Shane asked.

"Stop," Corbett said. "Let's just cut to the chase. How much do you want?"

"What brings you here today?" Shane asked again.

Corbett shook his head. "I'm a creature of habit. You already know that. It's just…the time change. I never adjusted to it. Some people don't. Especially with the seasons up here."

"How have you been sleeping?" Shane asked.

Corbett squinted at Shane, cocked his head.

"Sleep," Shane said. "How've you been sleeping?"

"I just told you."

"Okay," Shane said. "Not well. How do you define yourself?"

"I'm an entrepreneur," Corbett said.

"I was expecting you to say, I don't know…*decent.* Or *goodhearted.* But entrepreneur? Sure. Let's go with that." Shane stepped closer to the edge of the boat. "How would you like this to end?"

"That's enough. I'm done. I'm going to head back now," Corbett said. "I just need to start the engine." He raised his hands to show that he wasn't going to reach for the speargun.

"Do you have any idea what it meant to me to have a friend? At that time in my life. Someone I could trust! To finally have someone in my life I considered a friend."

Corbett reached for the engine.

"I thought I owed my life to you," Shane said. "I honestly believed you had saved me, and you know what? I'd have walked in front of a fucking train for you."

"But you did walk in front of a train for me," Corbett said. "You made the ultimate sacrifice. And I'm grateful for that. Truly."

A thick billow of fog rolled toward them.

Shane shot Corbett in the head. The silencer muffled the noise.

Corbett pitched sideways. His chin slammed against a handrail and he slid awkwardly onto the deck.

Shane pulled up next to Corbett's boat and tied the two boats together. Then he climbed over into Corbett's boat. He took out his phone and took a photo of Corbett's ruptured head and then put his phone away.

There was rope for mooring, one end tied to an eyehook. Shane tied the other end – the end used for tying to a dock or a pier – around Corbett's ankle.

He climbed back into his own boat and untied the two boats. As the fog enveloped them, Shane fired his gun into the water, toward the hull of Corbett's boat, four times. The fog kept coming, but in the thinner mist Shane could see that the boat was sinking.

Shane dropped his gun with the silencer overboard, into the water. He emptied the Starbucks bag with its boxes of bullets.

By the time the fog cleared again, there was only one boat in the water. From a distance, it would have looked like a great illusion.

Shane drove his boat back to shore. Once off the boat, he stuffed the Starbucks bag into a public trashcan near the boat rental office.

He poked his head inside the boat rental shop, tossed the boat keys toward Egil, and said, "Ready whenever you are."

A few minutes later, Egil joined him inside the rental car.

No words were spoken yet both men seemed to understand each other perfectly. It was honest and primordial, the way Shane imagined men communicated hundreds of thousands of years ago, before language became the most powerful weapon in their arsenal, the tool of betrayal.

Shane drove them back to his cabin, gathered together his backpack, and booked his next flight.

Chapter 86

Instead of flying back to Oslo, Shane flew further north to Tromsø.

Tromsø was an island with a significantly larger population than the entirety of Lofoten. Furthermore, it had a university, a downtown, a transit system, tourist attractions, large hotels with rooftop bars, and pubs. It was a good place to disappear for a few days.

Shane stayed in a tiny room in a nice hotel that overlooked the Tromsøysundet Strait. At midnight, the sun still up, Shane walked around downtown. Noise came from bars, but the streets were otherwise empty, businesses closed.

A young woman appeared from around a corner, swaying and stumbling as she walked by Shane, not seeming to notice him. When he turned to see if she was okay, she leaned against a wall and vomited onto the sidewalk. It was startling to see someone so drunk in the daylight even though it wasn't day. It was like last call in a bar when the bartender flips on the lights, causing everyone to wince and moan, their collective flaws pulsing in the spotlight – the acne and yellow teeth and filth beneath the nails.

Shane went back to his room and slept.

The next morning, he found a business office with a color printer. He emailed himself the photo he had taken of Corbett's corpse, pulled it up on the business center's computer, and printed it. As the photo slowly inched its way out of the printer, Shane looked around at the other customers and employees. No one cared that a murderer was printing up a photo of the man he had killed.

Shane chose an envelope from the business center, paid up, and addressed it to the hostess bar in Japan Town, in care of Hanh, Tam, and Kenny. No note. Just a piss-poor copy of a photo of their dead husband and father.

At the Tromsø post office, he mailed it.

Shane didn't hear anything from Joe or Fang or any of the Triads, but when he downloaded the app for the offshore account and checked the balance, he saw that enough money had been deposited to last him multiple lifetimes.

"Holy shit," Shane whispered as he stood next to the Arctic Cathedral, an imposing church that looked like the world's largest triangle.

If Shane's theory was correct – that there had been multiple fake companies and many more victims than just the ones he knew about in Southeast Asia – there would have been more than enough to satisfy even the insatiable cravings of a man like Fang.

As for Song getting her money? Shane had given her all that he was going to give her. That was more than enough. She wasn't some innocent bystander. The rest, Shane would keep.

Another reason Shane had chosen Tromsø for his housekeeping was because he saw online that the university was hosting an Ingmar Bergman Festival. Today they would be showing, back to back, the famous Bergman trilogy: *Through a Glass Darkly*, *Winter Light*, and *The Silence.*

The festival was held in a small theater on campus. When Shane entered to watch the first film, he thought maybe he'd shown up at the wrong time, but as show time neared, a dozen more cineastes arrived, mostly alone, leaving plenty of seats between themselves and the next patron.

The lights lowered on time, and the movie started playing.

Shane had a difficult time staying awake. His head kept dropping, and over and over he'd twitch back awake and try to concentrate. Midway through the film, he looked over at the seats to his right, expecting to see Cheryl, but no one was there.

Shane's favorite memories of Cheryl were from those first weeks of the semester, before they were even friends, when they would instinctively seek each other out in the lecture hall and then sit with one seat between them, and how Shane was always aware of her presence in the dark, so close he could hear her breathe: his pulse quickening at the anticipation of what could be. Her presence made the movies they watched all that more intense. They had seen *Battleship Potemkin* together, and *The Grand Illusion*, and, of course, *Persona.* The class started each Tuesday at one p.m., but the darkness of the screening room, along with the phantasmagoria of being lost in a movie, always caused disorientation when the movie ended and they stumbled together out of the building, blinking into the light, having forgotten that it wasn't yet nighttime and that the sun was still up.

One day, after watching a John Ford movie in class, Shane asked Cheryl out on a date.

"Jesus," she said. "I was starting to think you'd never ask me!"

And so it began – the dating, the deciding whether or not to keep dating, the mapping out of plans for graduate school, the marriage, the miscarriage, the jobs, the careers, the birthdays, the parents' funerals, his parents first and then hers, the good days and the bad though mostly good, all the years adding up slowly at first and then flying by, the illness, the remission, the illness again, and then…

How was it that Cheryl no longer existed in this world? It was a cruel lack of imagination on his part in that he didn't believe either of them would ever die. Everyone else would…but *them?* They would live forever. And no one would ever tell him otherwise.

When the Bergman movie ended and the lights came up, Shane rose from his chair and left the theater. He had treated the event like a séance when in reality the dead weren't ever coming back, and Shane would have to learn to live with that. But not today. Today there was still hope.

Lafayette, Louisiana

Shane knocked on his own front door.

It was obvious someone was living in his house, but who? Had it been sold by tax collectors for failure to pay property tax?

Shane rang the bell this time and then knocked harder.

A woman opened the door, leaving the glass door locked between them.

Shane stood before her with his backpack by his side, silent.

The woman was in her twenties. She was wearing prescription glasses and holding a pen in one hand and a cell phone in the other.

Before Shane could introduce himself, an ancient black cat walked arthritically to the door. The cat was blind, both eyes opaque, but it appeared to have had no trouble navigating the room.

"Larry?" Shane asked, addressing the cat.

"Oh my God," the woman said. "Mr. Doyle? Is that you?"

Shane looked more closely at the woman.

"Alyssa?"

Alyssa bent down and scooped up Larry. Then she unlocked and opened the door, letting Shane inside.

Shane pulled the luggage in behind him and shut the door.

"He's still alive," Shane said.

Alyssa handed Larry to Shane. The cat was seventeen – worse for wear, sure, but still kicking.

"I'm so sorry," Alyssa said. "This is really embarrassing. When you didn't come back, I didn't know what to do about Larry. I took him back to my place for a while, but when I got accepted to the PhD program here, I…"

"It's fine," Shane said. "You have no idea how happy this makes me."

"I can probably find someplace to go tonight. A hotel or something. If you don't mind my stuff being here for a week or two…"

The house had two bedrooms. Shane's room and a guest room he'd never used.

"Stay," Shane said. "I want you to stay."

"Are you sure?"

Shane, holding Larry up against him, listening to the old man's purr, nodded.

That night, Shane sat in the reading chair in his sunroom. The vertical blinds were shut. The lights were off. Alyssa was in the guest bedroom, listening to something on her computer. He had told her she could stay as long as she wanted. Every few minutes, she laughed at something she was watching. For a fraction of a second, Shane would think it was his wife Cheryl in the other room laughing.

It wasn't.

Larry crawled onto Shane's lap and curled up – ever loyal. There was no need to get inside Larry's head, to understand what made him tick. His actions were his bond. The cat's only betrayal was that one day he, too, would die. It was a betrayal by the universe, one of many, and perhaps the harshest. But at least Larry had waited for Shane to return.

Would someone ever come looking for Shane? The gangsters from Hong Kong? A family of thieves from Vietnam? The authorities in Norway?

Maybe. But for his part, all scores had been settled. All loops had been closed. There was nothing more he needed. He was just an old man with an eyepatch, petting his old, blind cat. The cat's purr, louder than it had ever been, sustained him. It was all he needed. It was enough.

If you enjoyed Dark Empath,

Read Johnny Mack's The Pinned Butterfly

"**THE PINNED BUTTERFLY** is noir of a higher order. Taut, fast-moving, emotional, and filled with surprises. Johnny Mack is a modern-day Robert Stone and this novel is an essential piece of crime fiction."

—New York Times bestseller Tod Goldberg,

author of ONLY WAY OUT

www.ingramcontent.com/pod-product-compliance
Lightning Source LLC
LaVergne TN
LVHW100508110826
845146LV00002B/553

* 9 7 9 8 9 9 5 2 9 2 2 0 3 *